THE COMPASS ISLAND INCIDENT
NOVEMBER 1963

WADE FOWLER

MILFORD HOUSE

an imprint of Sunbury Press, Inc.
Mechanicsburg, PA USA

MILFORD
HOUSE

an imprint of Sunbury Press, Inc.
Mechanicsburg, PA USA

For information about special discounts for bulk purchases, please contact Sunbury Press Orders Dept. at (855) 338-8359 or orders@sunburypress.com.

To request one of our authors for speaking engagements or book signings, please contact Sunbury Press Publicity Dept. at publicity@sunburypress.com.

ISBN: 978-1-62006-006-3 (Trade paperback)
ISBN: 978-1-62006-016-2 (Mobipocket)

Library of Congress Control Number: 2017958191

FIRST MILFRED HOUSE PRESS EDITION: October 2017

Product of the United States of America
0 1 1 2 3 5 8 13 21 34 55

Set in Bookman Old Style
Designed by Crystal Devine
Cover by Lawrence Knorr
Edited by Lawrence Knorr

Continue the Enlightenment!

PROLOGUE

TUESDAY, OCTOBER 14, 1969

FALLS CHURCH, VIRGINIA — "Is this world for real or for pretend?"

The words were skywriting above the shoreline of her subconscious. The little girl reached up to touch them and they lost their form. Their dust settled on her skin, sticky and white hot. The psychic napalm ignited a familiar nightmare that burned off the outer layers of her soul, exposing a mad man named John hidden therein. Through his eyes she saw things better left unseen.

John had one knee on the bed. A woman cowered below him. He clenched the collar of her nightgown in his left fist, stretching the fabric tight over her breasts. The sight of her nipples beneath the thin fabric aroused him.

The little girl dreaming in her bed wondered at the strange tumescence building in her groin.

"You never got over Jacob did you? You sleazy slut! The guys at Union Hall are laughing at me. I'll teach you!"

"No John, please! It's not true," the woman wailed. "I wouldn't cheat on you. Ever. It's the beer that's talking."

He backhanded her across her face. His ring bit into her cheek. His knuckles flattened her nose. Blood spurted. The woman screamed.

John sensed the bedroom door opening behind him. He looked over his shoulder as a tall, slender boy of about seven stepped into the room.

"Mom, Dad? What's wrong?" the boy asked.

John rose from the bed and shook his right fist at the boy, who recoiled to the doorway.

"God damn it Mikey. This is none of your business," John said. "Your mother made a mistake and now she's paid for it.

If there's one thing this life has taught me, it's that you have to pay for your mistakes."

The nightmare lurched forward.

She was buried face down under something . . . what was it?

A bale of straw? It was as dark as a photographer's lair. Excruciating pain skewered her with each breath. Was she inhaling fire or air? Gasping and cursing, she struggled onto her back, kicking at whatever it was that held her down. She fumbled about in her pocket for a flashlight. She flipped it on. A dead man lay on top of her. The dead man's eyes bulged; his tongue lolled; blood oozed from a horrible wound on his throat.

She screamed in her sleep, even though part of her knew that this world was for real and her dream was for pretend. She was safe in her bed while her parents, Hiram and Maggie Johnston, slept in the next room.

Or was she?

Her knees banged into the wall as John struggled with a dead man in the dark.

A noise interrupted her dream.

The little girl opened her eyes. Her father stood at the foot of her bed.

"What's the matter, sweetheart?" he asked.

He sat down on the edge of her bed and swept her up in his arms.

Six-year-old Gale Johnston clung to her father like a baby possum.

"Oh daddy, daddy," she sobbed.

"Is this world for real, or for pretend?

1

FORT EUSTIS, VIRGINIA — Dark clouds hunkered down and glowered like bull seals staring down a polar bear. A cold wind hurtled along the James River near historic Williamsburg. The former USS *Compass Island* stirred in her long sleep in a nest of ships forsaken in the purgatory of the James River Reserve Fleet.

At about 2 a.m., an 18-foot fiberglass canoe, painted a dark forest green and propelled by an electric motor, silently approached the fantail of the old ship. After a dangerous passage through choppy water, the canoe's lone occupant was relieved to have arrived at his destination.

Slight and olive-skinned with a smooth countenance suggestive of a man in his mid-40s, Emilio Sanchez was, in fact, 60. He was clad in a wet suit, Neoprene diving socks and a black GORE-TEX windbreaker. A Navy watch cap, pulled over his ears, gave him a gnome-like appearance. A silenced 9 mm Beretta rode in a holster on his utility belt. A commando knife lurked in a snap-down sheath on his right calf.

Sanchez was a dangerous gnome.

He tied the stern of the canoe to the *Compass Island*'s aft mooring line. Walking forward in a crouch along the keel, he stepped over the yoke and forward thwart, steadying the canoe by sliding his left hand along the mooring line. He slid his gloved hands through loops on either end of a short piece of rope. This would be his safety line if he lost his grip. He took a precarious seat on the bow of the canoe facing forward. The stern rose up behind him like the opposing end of a seesaw until it had consumed all of the slack in the tethering rope.

Sanchez grabbed the mooring line with both hands and pushed away from the canoe immersing himself to his waist. The frigid water assaulted his senses. He clenched his teeth, biting off a gasp, pulled his knees to his chest and kicked his feet up, locking his ankles around the mooring line. Supporting his weight with first his legs and then his arms, he wormed his way upward.

He paused about two feet from the lip of the bulwark where the heavy hawser disappeared through its chock. Locking his ankles around the mooring line, he slipped his right wrist free and grabbed a coil of rope from his utility belt. The rope was attached to a small grappling hook, whose metal claws were sheathed in rubber.

He tossed the grappling hook over the bulwark and tugged until it caught tight. Pulling himself to a sitting position, he bumped forward on his butt until he could drop his legs over the bulwark. When his balance was secure, he pushed forward and dropped onto the deck of the old ship.

Sanchez crouched along the rail and listened for several moments for any sign his arrival had been observed, although by whom he couldn't fathom. After more than forty years of CIA wet work, Sanchez was still alive because he was a careful gnome.

The *Compass Island* was berthed with her bow pointing to the north in a tight cluster of derelict auxiliaries whose utility to the United States Navy had long ago expired. Slumbering in front of her, with her bow pointed south, was the former USS *Caloosahatchee*, a fleet oiler. To starboard lay the refrigerated store ship once known as the USS *Rigel*, and to port was the former USS *Sylvania*, a retired combat store ship.

The local press called these old derelicts stockpiled in the James River "The Ghost Fleet," and warned of an impending environmental disaster should rust-thin storage tanks ever breach, spilling thousands of gallons of residual fuel oil into an already fragile ecosystem. Events in his personal life and a recent story in the Virginia Pilot had persuaded Sanchez that the time had come to retrieve a package he had hidden aboard the old ship forty years earlier.

The Pilot's story, bylined Gale Johnston, noted that the *Compass Island* was to be towed across the Atlantic Ocean that fall to be demolished by Able Ltd. of Hartlepool, England, which had won a multimillion dollar Maritime Administration contract to recycle five of the oldest ships in the Ghost Fleet.

The old spy moved forward in a crouch, skirting the helio deck just forward of the fantail.

Leaning over the starboard bridge wing three stories above, Chief Petty Officer Cloyd Murphy caught a glimpse of movement in his night vision goggles. Sanchez hadn't read Gale Johnston's story about how the Navy's elite strike force, the SEALs, often used the ships of the Ghost Fleet as a training ground to test their response to maritime crises.

Murphy keyed the microphone Velcroed about his throat.

"Command, recon," he whispered. "I got a glimpse of movement on the main deck starboard side."

The voice of the mission commander, Lt. Frank Paulson hissed from the bud secured in Murphy's left ear.

"You're recon. Go check it out."

Murphy keyed his mike to acknowledge the order. As the SEAL made his way down the exterior stairs from the bridge wing to the main deck, Sanchez continued along the starboard side of the ship, his passage obscured from Murphy's view by the overhang of the superstructure.

Sanchez had reached the starboard side ladder leading to the ship's forecastle deck by the time Murphy arrived on the main deck. Skirting the ladder, Sanchez flipped on a red-lens flashlight and trained the beam on the door leading to the compartments beneath the forecastle. It was a standard six-dog door just as he remembered it. All six dogs were activated by a single lever, which was snugged in the closed position. Sanchez flipped off the light and took a small spray can of WD-40 from a pouch on his utility belt. He gave the handle and each of the dogs a good shot of the lubricant.

Meanwhile, Murphy had two choices upon coming down the stairs from the bridge wing. He could turn to his left and look aft or turn to his right and look forward. He chose the former and thereby missed the brief beam of subdued light from Sanchez's flashlight which would have bloomed in his night vision goggles had he been looking that way. By the time Murphy turned his attention forward, the stairs leading to the forecastle deck hid Sanchez.

Sanchez moved the handle back and forth, working the WD-40 into the spaces between the metal surfaces of the dogs and the doorframe. He strained hard against the handle and the dogs released their grip with a screech that put Murphy on full alert.

Sanchez sensed movement behind him and darted through the door, not bothering to close it. He heard footfalls whispering on the deck behind him as Murphy charged forward.

Murphy's pulse pounded in his ears as he ran. He was puffing like a two-pack-a-day guy. He decided not to report in with

Lieutenant Paulson because he didn't want his superior to know he was so out of breath, so out of shape. He'd been riding a desk too long. He needed this ops tune-up.

Murphy unholstered his sidearm, a silenced stainless steel Sig Sauer 226. His pistol was loaded with blanks for this training mission, but he chambered a round because that was the protocol. As he neared the threshold, Sanchez exploded through the door. His Beretta was unholstered and unsafetied.

Both men were pros, but Murphy was younger and quicker. He fired first.

Sanchez didn't waste any time wondering how his adversary could have missed at pointblank range. He returned fire, loosing three shots, which took the special ops sailor in the middle of his chest. Murphy died, wondering why his training mission had gone so far off the rails.

Sanchez wasted no time on reflection or recrimination. His reaction was ordained by his training, experience and by a predilection to violence that even his comrades in the secret service had found disconcerting. He picked up Murphy's sidearm and secured it in a zippered pouch on his own belt.

He ripped the microphone from around Murphy's throat and dug the ear bud from his ear. He Velcroed the microphone around his own throat and secured the ear bud in his right ear, just as Lieutenant Paulson checked in.

"Recon. You OK? Murph?"

Sanchez keyed the microphone, but didn't speak, invoking the almost universal signal that communications were OK and there was nothing to report. He dragged Murphy's body well inside the forecastle, retrieved the flashlight from his utility belt and switched it on.

He made his way to the port side, passing by the fan room, sail locker and brig to a small wedge-shaped compartment. The original plans for the ship, which Sanchez consulted before embarking on his mission, identified the compartment as "Bosun's Stores," but aboard the *Compass Island* this had been the emergency radio room.

It was here forty years earlier that Sanchez had secured what he now thought of as his retirement package.

As he inspected the door in the eerie red light cast by his flashlight, he received a rude shock. The door was welded shut, but why? Shit! This mission was a cluster fuck from the get-go. Sanchez pounded the door with the palm of his hand in frustration.

The ear bud hissed.

"God damn it Murph! Report in."

Sanchez's anger and frustration dissipated. He faced an adversary of unknown numbers. The time had come for flight, not fight. He departed the *Compass Island* as silently as he had arrived.

2

FRIDAY, SEPTEMBER 19, 2003

FAIRVIEW, NEW JERSEY — "Care for a nip?"

Jacob Manley couldn't resist the temptation. His eyebrow twitched and he waggled an imaginary cigar. "Of what?"

Sylvia Hanrahan had heard much worse as a barmaid at the Pink Cat, Fairview's once notorious watering hole that recently had been converted into a day care center in an ongoing burst of civic revitalization.

"Of whatever you'd like, Groucho," she said.

"Thanks, but I'd better be getting home."

"You just want to count your money," Hanrahan said.

"Nope. Already did that while I was waiting for you to pee."

"So how much did you win?"

"Three hundred and forty two dollars just like what's his name, the bingo caller said."

"His name is Frank Cox. You know that as well as I do. You just don't like him because he's a flirt."

"There's nothing worse than an old flirt," Manley opined. "Unless it's an old fart. Come on in for a nightcap Jacob. I'm feeling frisky!"

Manley kissed Sylvia on the lips and squeezed her bottom. "Me, too, old girl, but I've got this uneasy feeling right between my shoulder blades. Someone was watching me tonight while we were playing bingo. I'm sure of it. It's best I get on home."

"Of course you were being watched. You won the Super Bingo for God's sake. Father Flynn said it was the biggest pot in four months!"

"No. It was more than that. Someone had me in their cross-hairs all night. I just couldn't tell who," Manley said.

Hanrahan sighed.

"You're playing cops and robbers again, aren't you?"

"You may laugh Sylvia, but if anything happens to me you know what to do."

"Nothing's going to happen to you, unless you've forgotten how to handle that pistol you've been carrying ever since you blackmailed Senator Patterson."

"I may be 82 but I can still hit what I aim at," Manley said.

"To bad you aren't aiming to hit on me." Hanrahan smiled at her own wit.

"And blackmail is a harsh word. I'd call it quid pro quo. He saved our ass; I saved his," Manley said.

Hanrahan nodded, but with consent or condescension? Manley couldn't tell.

"Oh go on with you, old man. You've done your duty. You've walked the little old lady to her door."

Manley kissed her again, foregoing a second bottom squeeze with some regret. Best not to start something he wasn't going to finish. He waited patiently while she fumbled through her purse and found her keys. She opened the door, stepped inside and turned to face him one more time.

"Last chance," she said.

"Hold that thought."

"I will, but remember. If I get frustrated enough, I just might end up with Frank Cox."

"Just make sure you don't end up with Frank's cox," Jacob Manley muttered to himself as she closed the door.

He waited until he heard the dead bolt click before he stepped off her stoop and began the short walk to his place on Tuckahoe Road.

His doorway was dark when he arrived home. Manley was puzzled because he'd left the front light on. Must have burned out. When he stepped onto the porch, his feet crunched on broken glass. The light bulb.

Damn those potheads on Yorkship Square! They were messing with him because he'd sicced the police on them, again. His house key was snapped to a retractable chain clipped to his belt. He inserted the key in the lock without too much trouble even in the dark and turned the deadbolt. He snaked an arm inside and flipped on the foyer light, which worked just fine. He relaxed and stepped inside.

Manley took off his coat and hooked it on the rack on the landing just inside his front door. He turned on the table light next to the television set in the living room. He made his way through the dining room to the back of the house and pushed his way through the swinging door into the kitchen, figuring he'd have a beer before he went to bed. He'd worked up a thirst rubbing elbows with those sanctimonious pissants in the church social hall.

When he flipped on the light, a ski-masked intruder materialized like a marionette dropped from above by an evil puppet master. The intruder pointed a handgun at the middle of Manley's chest.

"No sudden movements old man and maybe we'll both live through this."

The intruder spoke in a raspy whisper concealing his identity.

Manley was startled, but he wasn't prone to panic. He had, after all, won a Silver Star on Omaha Beach and returned home after the war to earn his living as a Camden city cop.

"I don't have very much money, but what I have is right here in my wallet," Manley said.

He reached for the .38 caliber police special he wore in a holster secured in the small of his back.

"I don't want your money. I want the tape and the photographs. Where are they?" the intruder rasped.

Manley yanked the revolver from its holster and loosed a shot that went wide right in his haste. The bullet nicked the intruder in the right arm, before lodging in the kitchen doorframe.

The intruder gasped. He didn't want to kill Manley, at least not yet. But the old man forced his hand. He squeezed off two quick rounds. Both bullets hit their mark.

Manley staggered back three steps, stumbled into the kitchen counter next to the stove and fell on his right side. He pumped his legs, writhing like a dog struck by a car.

The intruder kicked Manley's gun out of reach and stood for a moment observing the old man's death throes with a psychopath's detachment. Then, moving with deliberate purpose, as if he hadn't a care in the world, the intruder, took off the ski mask, opened Jacob Manley's back door and strolled to the passenger's side of a white Ford Crown Victoria parked along Tuckahoe Road with its engine idling.

Jacob Manley's last thoughts were of regret. He didn't want to go to his grave with an unclean soul and there was one task remaining before he embarked on his final voyage.

He explored the wounds on his chest with his fingers and then spelled out a final confession in his own blood on the white Linoleum of the kitchen floor:

"I KILLED JFK."

3

TUESDAY, SEPTEMBER 23, 2003

FAIRVIEW, NEW JERSEY — Sylvia Hanrahan grabbed Mike Kincaid's arm as he lumbered down the center aisle of St. Joan of Arc Catholic Church.

"Your stepfather was a pillar of this community," she said.

It took Kincaid a moment to place her. Then he smiled and bent to embrace the mother of his best friend in high school, the late Chester Hanrahan, killed in Vietnam in 1968.

"So you stuck it out here, too, did you Mrs. Hanrahan? Good for you. Good for you."

His words were insincere. Kincaid felt no loyalty to the crime-ridden shambles hard times had made of the once vibrant working class neighborhood that had nurtured him as a child and as a young man.

He had begged his stepfather to leave Fairview, to come live with him in New Bloomfield, Pennsylvania, where Kincaid had built a comfortable life as publisher of the local weekly newspaper, the Perry County Times. God knows there was plenty of room in his three-bedroom ranch, with Alice dead for two years now.

But Jacob Manley refused to leave Fairview and now Fairview had killed him.

For that matter, Fairview hadn't been particularly solicitous of Sylvia Hanrahan, either.

After she lost her husband in a traffic accident in 1952, Fairview had reduced the new widow to parlaying meager shots of whiskey and generous shots of cleavage into tips as a bar maid at the Pink Cat.

"Heartbreak," Kincaid said. "This town is full of it."

"What?"

Kincaid was embarrassed that he had thought out loud. "Nothing."

As he turned to continue down the aisle, Hanrahan clutched at his arm once again.

"There's something I have to tell you. Please come see me after the service," she said.

She saw the reluctance in his eyes.

"Your stepfather left something with me. He told me to give it to you . . . if anything happened to him."

Kincaid was intrigued. "OK," he whispered. "You still live on Kansas Road?"

Hanrahan smiled. "You know me, Mikey. Old habits die hard."

Mike Kincaid made his way to the front pew and took his place next to his half brother, Monsignor Francis Manley, who had decided upon some reflection to let the parish priest, the Reverend Jon Flynn, officiate at Jacob's funeral.

As Kincaid sat down, Francis arose in a half crouch and wrestled a handkerchief out of his back pocket. The diminutive Father Francis collapsed on the pew with a thump. He blew his nose and smiled up at Kincaid through his tears. Kincaid affirmed Francis' grief with a quick squeeze of his shoulder, but couldn't bring himself to express his own sorrow.

Unlike his older half brother, Kincaid had avoided the wake held the night before. He told Francis that his job kept him away, but the reality was that he didn't want to confront his memories of this place and of its people. Even now, he was afraid his remorse would drive him to seek out one of the bottles of Old Forester bourbon buried in his suitcase.

He glanced over his shoulder, his eyes falling on familiar faces recognizable despite the wrinkles, bags and sags time had etched on mortal flesh. Deja vu rose up like acid in his throat and he was grateful when the service began and he could lose himself in the familiar trappings of Catholicism.

Kincaid was startled when the parish priest, the Rev. Jon Flynn, arose to offer his funeral homily.

"Ladies and gentlemen we are gathered here to bury a hero for all seasons," Flynn said. "Jacob Manley took out a tank single handedly in the hedgerows, fought his way through France and was wounded and presumed dead in September of 1944 in Germany. But Jacob wasn't dead and we should all be grateful because nearly 60 years later, he brokered a deal with U.S. Senator Wiley Patterson that has provided the funding we need to begin the process of reclaiming this little village we all love from the drug dealers and addicts. Four nights ago, those who oppose the revitalization of Fairview murdered Jacob in his own home but they have not erased the enduring mark he left upon Fairview."

The priest slammed his hand down on the lectern, startling the congregants, and his voice rose in a steady crescendo:

"No longer will we countenance crime in our community! We are united in this resolve because of Jacob's sacrifice."

Father Flynn studied the congregants over half-glasses.

His voice was quiet, little more than a whisper, as he continued his homily.

"Jacob's fiancée, Kathleen Jablonski, was inconsolable when she received a telegram from the War Department in October of 1944, informing her that he had been killed in the Hurtgen Forest. She had lost not only the love of her life but also the father of her firstborn son, my colleague Monsignor Francis Manley."

Father Flynn paused as Kincaid's half brother acknowledged the tribute with a brave smile and a wave.

"John Franklin Kincaid was her salvation in those dark days. Unlike most men his age, he was at home and available because he had not been called to arms. His civilian job as an angle smith at the shipyard was considered to be essential to the war effort. Physically, John Kincaid was the antithesis of Jacob Manley. He was tall, blond-haired, blue-eyed and good-looking. But his most distinguishing attribute was his willingness to marry Kathleen and to take on the care of another man's son."

Mike Kincaid scrunched in his pew. Flynn was being far too kind to the memory of his father. Mike was just six years old when John Kincaid abandoned them never to be heard from again, but he remembered the noisy fights in the night and his mother's weepy eyes and bruises the next morning.

"Four months after Kathleen Jablonski wed John Kincaid, came the news from the War Department that Jacob Manley was still alive," Father Flynn said. "By then Kathleen was pregnant with her second son, Mike Kincaid, a newspaperman who now lives in Pennsylvania."

Flynn acknowledged Mike with a sweep of his hand. "Then, one day in August of 1953 John Kincaid punched out at the end of his shift at New York Ship and was never seen or heard from again. The disappearance of Big John Kincaid is Fairview's most enduring mystery."

Mike Kincaid glanced at Francis, who shrugged and grabbed his wrist. Both men appreciated Father Flynn's discretion. The truth of it was that most folk didn't find Big John's disappearance mysterious at all. He was nothing more than a thief, a lout and a wife abuser who had stolen ten thousand dollars belonging to the Industrial Union of Marine and Shipworkers of America and run away from his responsibilities as a husband and as a father. It was as simple as that.

Father Flynn took a sip of water and resumed his homily.

"Jacob Manley was Kathleen's anchor in the bleak days, weeks, months and years following John Kincaid's disappearance. He took on the responsibilities of a husband and father with none of its privileges. He assumed John Kincaid's debts. He paid the mortgage, electric and heat on Kathleen's house on Tuckahoe Road as well as the rent on his apartment on the square for three long years. Talk about your peacetime heroes.

"Kathleen won a divorce and an annulment on grounds of abandonment and finally on June 15, 1956, she and Jacob were married right here in this sanctuary. They loved each other and they loved watching their sons grow into fine young men full of life and full of promise. They had six wonderful years together as husband and wife before Kathleen was taken from us in a cruel twist of fate."

Mike Kincaid's heart pounded. His mother's death was his most painful memory. He dreaded what Father Flynn might say next, and he was certain that he would take no solace in his words. Nothing could make the pain go away. Nothing could alleviate his own guilt. He could have saved her, but he failed her.

Father Flynn continued: "Kathleen died in 1962 after a botched appendectomy and Jacob never remarried. I am told that he brought flowers to her gravesite every Thursday. Flowers every Thursday. Ladies and gentlemen, that is love."

Sylvia Hanrahan sobbed five rows back. Francis Manley blew his nose.

Guilt strangled Mike Kincaid's tears.

4

TUESDAY, SEPTEMBER 23, 2003

CHEWS LANDING, NEW JERSEY — Mike Kincaid trudged back to his car through a dismal drizzle. The skies above St. Joseph Cemetery were weeping for Jacob Manley. Mother Nature had taken on the job because Kincaid refused to do it himself.

Damn it! He didn't cry when Alice died two years ago and he wasn't going to cry now. The grief churned in his guts like a jalapeño on steroids.

Francis Manley had lingered at the graveside with Father Flynn to talk with mourners who had joined the motorcade from St. Joan of Arc Church to the cemetery. His brother was staying in the church rectory where he had found some solace among the trappings of his faith. Kincaid had no such refuge. Moreover, he didn't seek one. The torturous cancer death of his wife had revealed the world to him in all of its unadorned indifference.

"Life consumes life. It's as simple as that," Kincaid said aloud.

Rainwater, feigning tears, dripped from his cheeks.

There was no salve for his soul resident in the wisdom of the ages as dispensed by his earnest priest at St. Bernard's Catholic Church in New Bloomfield. Father Neely had tried his best, but he could not persuade Mike that Alice's death fit into any grand scheme or facilitated any divine purpose.

"Shit happens. It happened to Alice and now it's happened to Jacob," he thought.

Unwilling to countenance any more of the insincere pabulum mourners were still ladling out at the gravesite, Kincaid had decided to keep his own company at the local Motel 6 where he was staying because police had quarantined Jacob's house as a crime scene. That was fine with Kincaid who didn't want to live with the ghosts of his childhood, which abided still in the old house on Tuckahoe Road. They'd sell the place now. And good riddance.

Kincaid raised his head and was surprised to see two men standing, almost at attention, near the hood of his car. There was nothing remarkable about the men. One was tall, although not nearly as tall as Kincaid, and the other was short and sagged like a high school wrestler gone to seed.

As Kincaid drew near, and the difference in their sizes became apparent, the taller of the two strangers straightened and took two steps toward Kincaid.

He extended his right hand. "Mike Kincaid?" he asked.

Kincaid ignored the handshake because he was in no mood for social amenities and was pretty certain nothing good could come from a first meeting in a graveyard. "That's right. And you are?"

The man dropped his hand and narrowed his eyes. "Fronk. Detective Charles Fronk, Camden PD. This is my partner Tom Harriott."

He waggled a thumb over his right shoulder.

"You find out who killed Jacob?" Kincaid asked.

"We got an anonymous tip that maybe you did," Fronk said. Kincaid was stunned. He didn't know how to react. So he laughed. Resident in his laughter was an edge of hysteria. "Right, my motive was I wanted my share of the old man's house. That ought to be good for what, $30,000 or so? That'll buy me a cushy retirement."

"Mr. Manley carried $250,000 worth of life insurance. You and your brother are the beneficiaries. That's a little cushier, don't you think?" Fronk asked.

"Are you this offensive naturally? Or did they send you to school?"

Fronk ducked the jab. "Whadda ya have in the car?"

Kincaid slipped the non sequitur and counterpunched. "Three seats, a steering wheel, glove box, an audio system, two sun visors, a bottle of Geritol and a Frank Sinatra CD."

Fronk crinkled his eyes. "Funny guy. We heard maybe there's more than that."

Kincaid motioned toward his car. "See for yourself. It's unlocked."

Harriott stepped forward. He held a miniature tape recorder in one hand and clicked it to record. "Do you mind stating your name and acknowledging your consent to our searching your vehicle?"

Kincaid puffed out his cheeks. He thought about changing his mind, now that his bluff had been called. He thought about insisting on a warrant—just to piss them off. Then, he concluded that a foul mood and foul weather were clouding his judgment. He had, after all, nothing to hide, although he was uneasy about the .45 Colt automatic in the tire well of his trunk. What the hell. He had a Pennsylvania permit.

"Mike Kincaid, 421 Apple Street, New Bloomfield, Pennsylvania. Officers Fronk and Harriott of the Camden police have my permission to search my car. Now get on with it. I'm tired of standing in the rain. While you're at it, why don't you see if you can find my nail clippers? They fell between the seats two weeks ago."

Fronk opened the driver's side door and popped the trunk release on the floor next to the driver's seat. "You should lock your car. Or, is everyone so trusting where you come from?"

Kincaid decided the question was rhetorical.

"Keep an eye on big boy, while I stick my head in the trunk," Fronk said to his partner.

Harriott took several steps and stood next to Kincaid, who was a good eight inches taller.

"You play basketball?

Harriott broadcast the subliminal unease of a small man confronted by a much larger man.

"Tight end."

Kincaid tried without success to establish eye contact with the Camden cop. "Whadda you guys know that I don't?"

Harriott shrugged. "This is my partner's play. I'm just along for the ride."

Fronk opened the cover to the spare tire well and exclaimed: "Son of a bitch! It's here, right where the snitch said it would be."

Stepping back from the trunk, he pulled a small digital camera from the side pocket of his suit coat and snapped off three pictures. The automatic flash outlined his body against the backdrop of a cemetery on a rainy day.

"Tell me, Mr. Kincaid, do you have a permit to carry a handgun?"

"As a matter of fact, I do and you've found my Colt .45 in the tire well. I have a Pennsylvania permit but I wasn't sure about New Jersey's handgun laws, so I stuck it in the trunk."

Kincaid had purchased the semi-automatic four years ago after a truck driver went postal, declaring that domestic violence was none of the newspaper's business. Kincaid published the story anyway.

Fronk removed a pair of latex gloves from his jacket pocket and snapped them on. He bent over Kincaid's trunk and pulled up a handgun Kincaid had never seen before.

"Ain't no .45 here. Just this 9 millimeter. Your stepfather was shot with a 9. You've got some explaining to do, Kincaid."

5

TUESDAY, SEPTEMBER 23, 2003

CAMDEN, NEW JERSEY — "You comfortable?"

Police Detective Charles Fronk's sarcasm was unintended. He just wasn't that subtle.

Kincaid perched precariously on a dented metal folding chair. A quarter of a cheek hung out over each side. He sweated in rain-sodden clothes.

Harriott left to fetch Cokes, leaving Fronk and Kincaid alone and seated on either side of a cigarette-scarred table in the interrogation room, which was tiny, no more than 10-feet square. The glorified closet stank of cigarette smoke and piss.

That was appropriate because Kincaid was pissed off and could have used a smoke. He quit 15 years ago at Alice's insistence. She didn't want him to get cancer and die. Kincaid still wondered at that little piece of irony.

"So tell me again how the 9 got into your trunk?"

"I haven't the faintest fucking clue."

"Nice mouth."

"I was polite the first five times you asked me. I thought the profanity might enhance your comprehension. I may or may not have left my car unlocked last night, I just can't remember."

Fronk smiled and changed direction. "I knew your old man, or at least knew of him. He retired six months after I joined the force. He was a legend around here. He was one of the good guys. Be a damn shame if his stepson killed him."

Sweat trickled down Kincaid's ribs. He wiped his hand across his forehead and then across the front of his shirt.

"You guys turn up the heat in here just to make me sweat?"

Fronk ignored the question. "What do you know about JFK?"

Harriott banged open the door and plopped Cokes down in front of Kincaid and Fronk. He took a seat at the end of the table

THE COMPASS ISLAND INCIDENT 21

to Fronk's right and Kincaid's left. "They dusted the 9, and I walked it down to ballistics. It'll be a couple of days before we get the results."

"Any prints?" Fronk asked.

Harriott nodded toward Kincaid. "You sure you want to discuss that now?

"Why not? We're all friends here."

"Gun was wiped clean. No partials. No latents. No nothing, unless you count gun oil. Somebody cleaned it up real good. Yessiree."

"Figures," Fronk said.

"You got a gun-cleaning kit," he asked Kincaid.

Kincaid nodded.

"Where?"

"At home."

"Figures."

Fronk smiled and nodded at Harriott. "I was just asking our friend here what he could tell us about JFK. And he hasn't answered yet."

Kincaid still couldn't fathom where Fronk was headed, but the question made him uncomfortable. He wasn't sure why. "He was the 35th president, right? Fell right between Eisenhower and Johnson. Lee Harvey Oswald assassinated him in Dallas, Texas, on November 22, 1963. People have been arguing ever since about whether it was a conspiracy or whether Oswald acted alone."

Kincaid popped the tab on his Coke and took a sip. "I met him once, you know." He bit his tongue. He hadn't meant to open that can of worms but he was desperate to divert Fronk's attention from the gun in his trunk."

"Who did you meet, Oswald?" Harriott giggled, underlining his wit.

Fronk rolled his eyes.

Kincaid stated the obvious. "I met Kennedy."

"Really," Fronk said.

He leaned forward in his chair.

"Yeah."

Kincaid pulled out his handkerchief and mopped sweat off his brow to buy time to plot a course through a psychological minefield. "It was Nov. 16, 1963, less than a week before Kennedy was assassinated. I was in the Navy at the time, a journalist mate aboard a navigational research ship, the USS *Compass*

Island. We were steaming off Cape Canaveral and Kennedy landed on the helio deck on the stern of the ship."

Kincaid took another sip of Coke, hoping he'd said enough because some of the details of Kennedy's visit were still classified, as far as he knew.

Fronk wouldn't let it go. "And . . ."

"And nothing. He stayed aboard for a half hour. I got to shake his hand, and he ordered a test firing of a Polaris missile by the nuclear submarine *Andrew Jackson*, which was lurking nearby. I covered it for All Hands Magazine. Took lots of pictures, even got a chance to talk to the president."

"About what?"

"I dropped my notebook right in front of him, and he told me to relax, or something like that. Then I told the president my stepfather had worked to get him elected."

"Is that so?" Harriott interjected.

"Yeah. Jacob was an Irish Catholic just like Kennedy. He thought JFK was the best thing that ever happened to this country and he was devastated when he was assassinated and then Bobby, too."

"You say anything else to Kennedy?" Fronk wanted to know.

"Nothing else I can remember, but he signed my notebook and I gave his signature to Jacob. That scrap of notebook paper was one of his treasured possessions. It's still framed on a wall in the dining room, as far as I know," Kincaid said.

"Hey! We missed that!"

Fronk held up a finger to silence his partner while he thought. "Shh!"

"Anything unusual about Kennedy's visit?" Kincaid felt the blood drain from his face.

Fronk noticed. "You feel OK?"

Kincaid lied. "Yes. I'm feeling fine. And no, there was nothing unusual about Kennedy's visit."

Fronk pulled at his left earlobe. "Curious. Listen. We've kept this out of the papers, but I can't find a reason not to tell you. Your stepfather left a message before he died."

"What sort of message?"

"This is unpleasant. It was written in blood on the kitchen floor."

Kincaid shuddered. "What did it say?"

"'I killed JFK.' We're not sure whether he wrote it or his murderer did, but there was blood on your stepfather's right index finger. What do you make of that?"

Kincaid exhaled explosively.

"I have no idea."

"Neither do we, Mr. Kincaid. Neither do we. And that, for the moment is the $64 question in this murder investigation. That and how the fucking 9 got in your fucking trunk."

He made a pistol of his thumb and forefinger and pointed it at Kincaid.

6

TUESDAY, SEPTEMBER 23, 2003

CAMDEN, NEW JERSEY — Mike Kincaid studied his feet through the rich amber of three fingers of his third Old Forester bourbon which were slumming it in a cheap motel-room tumbler. There was, he noticed, a hole in the toe of his right sock. His big toenail needed clipping. Somehow, attending to routine personal hygiene had become more of a chore since Alice died.

Kincaid sprawled on one of the two queen-sized beds in Room 204 of a Motel 6. He occupied the bed closest to the door for a reason sublimated by a psychological imperative. Without even thinking about it, he always took the bed closest to the door in motel rooms . . . to protect Alice from intruders.

Kincaid didn't intend to move until it was time to pour his fourth Old Forester. He rationalized an extravagance his physician would have frowned upon with the excuse that he'd had a hard day.

"You're as strong as an ox, Mike, but you're twenty pounds overweight and you drink too damn much," Dr. Foley had said, during Kincaid's most recent physical. "If you don't slow down, you'll be diabetic within five years and dead within 10."

Foley had uttered those words without grasping the toll the relentless pressure of grief had exacted from his patient. But today, anyway, Kincaid possessed a gold-plated excuse for excess. Someone had framed him for his stepfather's murder, but who, and why?

In fact, every day had been a bad day since Alice got sick. Despite their fervent prayers, or maybe (perversely) because of them, the biopsy of a pea-sized lump in Alice's right breast had tested positive for cancer; more ominously, so had two lymph nodes nearby. Her physicians were optimistic that the mastectomy and regimen of radiation and chemotherapy had the cancer on the run.

For a while, it appeared the doctors were right. They started to breathe, again. Then, two years post-op, a follow-up MRI confirmed every cancer survivor's worst fear. Alice's cancer had recurred in an aggressive and virulent form in her liver. Surgeons removed the larger lobe of her liver, but the cancer shrugged off a concentrated bombardment of radiation and a steady stream of chemicals that left Alice glowing like a lava lamp. It galloped through her body and Alice was dead in six months.

Kincaid had been dying ever since, in small increments measured by the jigger. His anger was directed without prejudice at God, fate, physicians, clergy, hell, all of humanity when you got right down to it. He also was furious at Alice, although it was difficult for him to admit that. She had abandoned him—left him alone to deal with his demons.

And so he drowned his sorrow and his rage in Old Forester. But God damn his guilt! It knew how to swim. Guilt crawled across the surface of his drunkenness like a swimmer in the calm waters just beyond the breakers.

His guilt lay in that, even with the outcome of the battle a foregone conclusion, Kincaid had insisted upon an aggressive treatment for Alice's cancer. His motives were selfish. He was determined to hang onto his wife for as long as he could because a sick and dying Alice was better than no Alice at all. At his direction, the nuclear and chemical warfare on the temple of her soul continued unabated until almost the very end, even though he knew full well that compassion and kindness lay on the side of just letting her go.

The sin of selfishness was bad enough, but Kincaid was tormented by yet another demon. In the last two weeks of her life, Alice bobsledded into dementia as the cancer metastasized to her brain. Late one Sunday evening, after the interminable how-is-she-doing phone calls had subsided because the clock had expired on compassion, Kincaid summoned his last reserves of courage. He gave Alice a massive overdose of morphine. Then, ignoring the stench of vomit, urine and feces, he climbed into the hospital bed Hospice had installed in their den and held her close as her ragged breathing slowed and then stopped. His eyes were clenched against the relentless pressure of his tears, but against the dark backdrop of his retinas, an image appeared.

Amoeba like and luminescent, it coalesced until Kincaid imagined he was gazing upon the joyful countenance of his wife.

"Thank you, Mikey," she said.

And then she was gone.

There was no getting around it: in the eyes of the church and of the law, he had murdered his wife. Yet Kincaid knew that his sin lay in not effecting this final kindness sooner.

Alice was dead, for two years now, but he could still hear her voice in his head in times of reflection as he laid aside the cares of the day and allowed his mind to float in free fall in that altered state of consciousness that precedes sleep. In those times, she told him not what he wanted to hear . . . that all was well with her, although he was certain for reasons he couldn't fathom that it was. She told him what he needed to hear . . . that all was not well with him.

Her exact words were ephemeral and never survived his awakening. But Kincaid could remember the soft inflection of her voice; he could feel the gentle brush of her light brown hair on his cheek as she bent close to whisper in his ear, and he reveled in the smooth, familiar lines of her jaw, her chin, and her brow and the sparkle in her deep blue eyes. In those moments, everything was as it had been before the cancer had beaten her senseless, raped her and left her for dead. While he welcomed her visits, as he had come to call them, he was forced to consider the notion that Alice was not pleased with him; that there was something she wanted him to do, something he should have done and done often during their 29 years of marriage. He knew what it was, even though it was difficult for him to articulate it.

Alice wanted him to rise above the fundamental reticence that had made their marriage more of a monologue than a dialog. She was tired of talking and she wanted to listen while Kincaid laid bare those significant portions of his soul that he had kept hidden from her through all their years together. Kincaid was terrified of that prospect. It was as if an essential part of him was locked away in a vault and he didn't know the combination. When he tried to open the door and gaze upon those hidden aspects of himself, a smooth-skinned, brown-haired man, wearing a windbreaker over a shirt and tie, confronted him. "Remember what you promised," the man said. "Never breathe a word of this to anyone. Anyone!"

That man's name was John Fitzgerald Kennedy and he looked just as he had looked on Saturday, Nov. 16, 1963, the first and last time Kincaid had laid eyes upon the 35th president of the United States.

Was he crazy?

Kincaid didn't think so, but he had felt uncomfortable when the two police detectives tried to establish a connection between JFK's assassination and Jacob's murder.

"I killed JFK."

"What the hell does that mean?" Kincaid asked the walls of his motel room.

They didn't answer.

Kincaid had gone over his recollections of the president's visit to the USS *Compass Island* so many times that it was difficult to separate his genuine memories of the event from the puff piece he had written for All Hands Magazine.

But he remembered a conversation with the ship's executive officer as if it were yesterday.

"I can't put this through to the old man!" shouted Lieutenant Commander Jonathan Briggs. "If this bull shit makes it up the chain of command, your ass will be grass."

"What do you want me to do? Pretend like nothing happened?"

"Of course something happened. The president of the United States visited our ship and observed the launching of a Polaris missile by the *Andrew Jackson*. That's what your story should say, and nothing more."

Kincaid shook his head in frustration because he couldn't articulate, even to himself, why Briggs had been so upset with him. Nor could he fathom why he had become so uncomfortable when the police detectives asked if he understood Jacob's final confession. How could JFK's assassination be related to his stepfather's murder? God, he needed another drink. He staggered from the bed and started toward the tiny alcove just outside the bathroom where a fresh bottle of Old Forester and a bucket of ice awaited.

He was diverted from his intended path by a knock on his hotel room door.

Kincaid stumbled to the door and peered through the peephole at two figures standing on his doorstep. "Now what?"

Kincaid unlatched the security chain and threw open the door. A short man stepped forward into the canopy of light that unfurled from his motel room.

Kincaid stared at the man. "What do you want?" His social graces were blunted by a boozy bad mood.

The man stepped forward with his hand outstretched. "Is that anyway to greet an old shipmate? It's me, Mike. It's been forty years, but I'd recognize you anywhere."

Kincaid's memory retrieval circuitry chunked along at a snail's pace, addled by alcohol, but he accessed the appropriate file. "Skeeter! If there was a God you'd be dead by now, you son of a bitch!"

7

THURSDAY, NOVEMBER 15, 1962

HAMILTON, BERMUDA — The USS *Compass Island* fought its way home to Brooklyn through a fierce nor'easter having been relieved of blockade duty in what would become known as the Cuban Missile Crisis. Mike Kincaid had pulled the 0800 to 1200 day watch in CIC with a second-class electronics technician named Bailey Cooper, known almost inevitably as "Coop."

Kincaid, a journalist mate striker, was saddled with CIC watches underway because there was a Navy wide shortage of radarmen. There were no new contacts to track and Coop was using the down time to catch up with some routine maintenance on the Loran Alpha receiver, which triangulated radio transmissions from a worldwide network of transponders to determine the ship's exact position.

The Loran receiver was installed above the chart table in CIC and was consulted periodically by the duty quartermaster who reported its data to the ship's navigator, Lieutenant Richardson. Coop had the cabinet of the Loran console open and was working through steps enumerated on a laminated PMS card, short for planned maintenance system. Coop tapped his finger on the glass plate of a voltage meter and muttered to himself. "God damn reading is off spec. It must be the goniometer, but I just replaced that son-of-a-bitch!"

Kincaid puzzled over the word goniometer but decided not to ask. He was seated in a chair facing the primary radar repeater, which was welded to the floor facing the compartment's starboard bulkhead. An illuminated chronometer was positioned above the repeater so the operator could time his range and bearing readings. Kincaid checked the time: 0843, another three hours and 27 minutes to go before his watch was over and he could join the crew queuing up for lunch on the mess deck.

Like most 17-year-olds Kincaid could set his watch by his stomach and breakfast was already a fleeting memory. After a month at sea, he was acclimated to the rhythmic cadence of shipboard life, and he found heavy weather exhilarating.

The buzzer on the bridge phone sounded. Kincaid grabbed the phone. "CIC!"

He effected a gruff baritone to obscure an adolescent voice still prone to cracking.

"Any new contacts to report?

The speaker lisped. The voice was effeminate and recognizable as that of the executive officer, Lieutenant Commander Jonathan Briggs.

Kincaid was annoyed by the question. If there had been any contacts to report, he would have reported them.

"No sir, contact Gulf, is past CPA and almost off the scope."

"Well, keep your eyes open. We are answering a distress call and, according to the position report, the contact should be on the screen somewhere around 030, relative, range 10,000 yards, OR LESS!"

The XO's 'or less' had some bite to it and Kincaid sat up straighter in his chair.

"Aye, aye, sir!"

Kincaid hung up the phone.

"Aye, aye, sir?" Coop mimicked. "Aren't we being formal?"

He pushed the Loran Alpha receiver back into its housing and tightened the thumb screws that held it in place.

"Cut me some slack, Coop. XO has the bridge and we're closing on a mayday."

"That explains the course change."

Coop took a seat at the backup radar repeater. "Hey, what's that?" he asked.

"I don't see anything but noise."

Kincaid knuckled his eyes to clear his vision.

"Try turning up the gain on your repeater."

Kincaid blushed. He had turned down the gain at the start of the watch to minimize "noise," a blotchy luminescence on the CRT caused by radar waves bouncing off the ocean surface. It was more pronounced in rough seas.

"See? It's right there, at 2 o'clock . . ."

Coop spun the bearing and range finder dials. "Shit! I lost it!"

Kincaid fiddled with the gain. "No! You're right, there is something there, but it wasn't there just a moment ago."

Kincaid bent even closer to the CRT. "Outline's fuzzy. Damn it! It's gone again."

"Did you get the position marked?"

"Yep, for all the good it will do us. Wait! There it is again." The tiny blip peeked through the noise again, blinking brightly. Then it was gone. "Shit! Better phone this one in to the bridge."

Kincaid picked up the phone.

"Bridge, CIC," he said.

"Go ahead CIC."

Kincaid was relieved. He recognized the voice of Lieutenant Junior Grade Randolph. He wouldn't have to deal with the priggish XO after all.

"We've got a tentative contact, designated H-Hotel, bearing 023, range 8,500 yards. Contact is intermittent and we don't have a plot, but we're working on it."

The bow of the ship pitched upward, following the lead of a huge wave, and Contact Hotel flared more brightly. Kincaid ignored the elevator feeling in his stomach and glanced at the chronometer, marked the spot with his grease pencil and read off the range and bearing to Coop.

Five minutes crawled by on the ship's chronometer and Kincaid spun the dials and called out the contact's current range and bearing. Coop went to work at the chart table, muttering to himself.

He looked up. "Contact is dead in the water, although she's drifting a bit to the west. I'd recommend a course of 040 true to intercept."

Kincaid called it in to the bridge and it wasn't long before the ship turned to starboard and the noise and vibration level generated by the ship's screw rose. Soon, they heard the familiar thumping the drive shaft made when the engine room answered full speed. The ship's speed indicator situated above the chart table in CIC climbed to 14 knots, a bone-jarring pace in heavy seas. Coop hooked an ankle through the support rungs of his metal chair. He pursed his lips and whistled for a moment or two before Kincaid recognized the theme song from the television show Bonanza.

"Ride 'em cowboy!"

Kincaid grinned like a kid on his first roller coaster ride as the ship bucked sideways into a monster wave and Coop's voltage meter skittered across the chart table.

Coop cursed, leapt to his feet and kicked his chair out of the way. He made it to the chart table just in time to catch the meter before it crashed to the deck. He smiled and gave Kincaid a thumbs-up.

"Better stow this in the electronics shop. I'll be right back."

Coop banged open the door to CIC and headed down the passageway behind the bridge to the electronics shop, a small compartment just off the port bridge wing.

The ship's 1MC system hissed to life and the XO lisped:

"Attention all hands, rig for heavy rolls. We're changing course to intercept the schooner Curlew, foundering off Bermuda with six hands aboard."

For the next two and a half hours, Kincaid and Coop monitored the radar screen as the *Compass Island* sped to the scene then slowed and maneuvered through heavy seas to close with the stricken yacht. The heavy weather discouraged other traffic and the radarscope was otherwise absent of contacts.

At 1150 hours just 10 minutes before the watch was due to change, Radarman 1 Richard Slovensky sauntered into CIC. "Hey Kincaid," he said. "You're relieved. Captain wants you on the bridge, pronto."

"Shit!

Kincaid worried that he was due a dressing down for not sighting the contact sooner. He made sure his shirttail was tucked in. He rubbed the toes of his brogans on the back of his utility trousers and squared his belt buckle, wishing he had thought to polish it. Kincaid dragged his fingers through his hair and felt the bile rising in his throat. His breath probably was bad, too, he thought as he opened the door that led to the passageway behind the bridge.

Shutting the door quickly behind him so daylight didn't corrupt Coop's vision in the amber light of the CIC, Kincaid squared his shoulders and walked four or five steps to the starboard side entrance to the bridge. The bridge windows were spattered with salt spray but Kincaid could see the bow rise to meet a 30-foot swell bearing down like a blitzing linebacker. The *Compass Island* was no scat back. Evasion wasn't her running style. The ship plowed ahead, and Kincaid widened his stance and bent his knees.

The bow buried itself in the crest of the wave and shook off frothy foam like a Labrador retriever emerging from a lake. Before the bow could rise again, the crest of a following wave crashed on the forecastle and the entire ship shuddered as the screw drove it ahead against the onrush of tons of seawater. Kincaid had to brace himself against the navigator's chart table to keep his feet. The quartermaster stumbled but was able to catch himself without spinning the ship off course.

"Right standard rudder. Aye, aye sir," the quartermaster repeated into the mouthpiece of his sound-powered headphone set. He spun the ship's wheel and added:

"My rudder is at right standard, sir."

Lieutenant Junior Grade Randolph, looking green about the gills, raised his head from the black rubber skirting fixed about the bridge radar repeater to make its signal more visible in the daylight.

"Skipper's turning us broadside to the waves AGAIN. Rig for heavy rolls, men," Randolph said. Noticing Kincaid's presence, he added:

"Captain's on the starboard bridge wing."

Kincaid took a deep breath. "Got any idea of what he wants?"

Randolph smiled through his seasickness.

"Relax sailor. You're not on the carpet. I think he wants you to take some pictures. Fucking O'Malley's so goddamn seasick he can't push the shutter button."

Kincaid made his way to the sliding door leading to the bridge wing. He paused to tug on a heavy foul-weather gear coat hanging on a hook next to the door. He buttoned the coat and pulled the hood tight around his ears before pulling the door open.

Stepping outside, he turned his back to the storm and pulled the sliding door closed to protect the bridge watch from the raging elements. The wind whipped, tugged and screamed. Droplets of seawater and rain stung his face and eyes. The ocean snarled about the ship.

Commander Julius Earnhart didn't seem impressed by Neptune's ferocity. His right arm was crooked about the stanchion for the azimuth instrument and he was leaning forward over the rail studying the roiling sea below. John Carpenter, a quartermaster striker, huddled at the captain's starboard elbow, manning the sound powered phones as Earnhart maneuvered the *Compass Island* ever closer to the yacht. Earnhart was so intent upon this task that he didn't recognize Kincaid's approach until he was standing right next to him.

"Oh, there you are," he said, stepping back from the precipice. "Be glad you're aboard this beauty in a sea like this."

Earnhart waved his hand and Kincaid inched forward and looked over the rail of the bridge wing. Foundering in the ocean below them about 60 yards to starboard was a three-masted ship of about forty-five feet in length. Her sails were rolled and strapped to her masts, to avoid being ripped away by the gathering gale. It was clear the Curlew was finding little comfort in the protection of the hulking Navy auxiliary ship. Her masts snapped back and forth as successive walls of water assaulted the hapless yacht. Her puny screw, powered by an auxiliary diesel could find little purchase as the ocean rose and fell at Neptune's whim beneath her hull, but her crew hadn't surrendered. Three men were huddled at her stern struggling with a heavy hawser connected to something on her deck that Kincaid couldn't make out. A fourth man was visible in the ship's pilothouse, wrestling with the wheel.

"They're trying to rig a sea anchor, for all the good it will do, the poor bastards!" Earnhart shouted above the gale.

Kincaid wasn't sure what a sea anchor was. He nodded his head and saved his breath.

"All ahead, one third!" Earnhart shouted and Carpenter relayed the order to the helm. Thirty seconds later, he amended the order. "Ahead slow! Rudder amidships!"

"Kincaid?"

"Aye, Aye, sir!"

"A rescue at sea, in a God damn gale? All Hands eats that sort of shit up," he said, referring to the Navy's official magazine. "Get your ass down to the main deck and take some God damn pictures!"

"Aye, Aye, sir!"

Kincaid hurried off to the ship's tiny photo lab one deck below the bridge where he grabbed a two-lens Rolleiflix camera. His fingers were thick and clumsy with anxiety, but he managed to load the camera with a 36-exposure canister. He shoved a second roll in his pocket, although he had no clue how he'd manage to reload outside on the main deck buffeted by the raging gale. He made his way via the internal stairs through the ship's superstructure to the main deck bouncing off the bulkheads like a pinball as the ship pitched, rolled and corkscrewed across an angry sea.

Just inside the superstructure at the quarterdeck he paused next to the 1MC box and caught his breath. He noticed for the first time a bronze plaque riveted to the bulkhead next to the 1MC. Bending forward he read the inscription:

"SS Garden State Mariner, delivered to the Maritime Administration on 24 October, 1953, built by the New York Shipbuilding Corporation, Camden, N.J."

"Son of a bitch," Kincaid thought. "Pop may have worked on this ship."

He had to push hard on the starboard side door to open it against the force of the gale, which slammed the door shut behind him of its own volition. Turning his back to the sea, he dogged the door tight, holding onto the door lever to maintain his balance on the slippery treacherous deck. Only then did he allow himself to look over the bulwark at the sea, which glowered at him like a gray-green gargoyle.

"Here, tie yourself off, asshole!!"

Kincaid's vision was obstructed by the hood he had pulled tight about his ears, so he was startled by the approach of BM2 Brian McBride.

McBride handed him a coil of a one-inch rope, one end of which was rigged to a heavy hawser the deck apes had tied off to stanchions fore and aft as a safety line.

McBride screamed against the fury of the storm. "Don't just stand there! Wrap it around your waist and tie yourself off with a bowline. They still teach knots in boot camp don't they?"

Kincaid had strung his camera about his neck, underneath his foul-weather parka to protect it until he was ready to shoot. He shifted the camera out of the way and looped the line about his waist. Actually, he had learned to tie the bowline in Boy Scouts. Muscle memory took over. He made quick work of securing himself to the safety line alongside four other sailors waiting to assist the crew of the Curlew. It was as if the ship, now turned broadside to the march of the waves, was dancing with the ocean, moving back and forth to its lead. Walls of water crashed over the bulwark and left a frothy trail across the deck before dissipating in the scuppers.

Protecting his camera as best he could, Kincaid shot off a roll of film framing the Curlew against walls of water. He also took pictures of the deck crew of the *Compass Island* struggling against the elements to rig cargo nets to be lowered over the side of the ship to facilitate the rescue of the sailors aboard the yacht, should it come to that. Then, leaving the deck crew to its vigil, he returned to the photo lab and re-stowed the Rolleiflix. He didn't want to be responsible for damaging one of O'Malley's precious cameras, and it was clear that the saga of the Curlew would play out over the course of hours, rather than minutes.

Relieved of his radar watch and with the workday modified due to heavy weather, Kincaid had little more to do than hang around the bridge and listen while successive watches helped shepherd the Curlew toward the safety of St. George Harbor, Bermuda. Kincaid ate dinner, watched the movie at 2000 hours on the mess deck and went to bed. Sleep eluded him, and at 0300 hours he climbed from his rack, dressed, collected a camera from the photo lab, and made his way to the quarterdeck. Kincaid donned foul weather gear and pushed open the watertight door against the force of the gale. He was confronted once again by McBride.

"What the fuck do you think you're doing, Kincaid?"

"Captain wants a story on the rescue of the Curlew," Kincaid shouted back.

"Why are you still here?"

"Captain wants the yacht's crew rescued," McBride replied.

Kincaid lost his wink in the dark.

Kincaid tied himself off on the safety line and huddled next to the bulwark. The deck apes had rigged spotlights to illuminate the deck and a 50-yard patch of angry ocean just beyond the bulwark. He watched as a big wave slammed the yacht against the side of the Compass Island. He could tell that the yacht's crew was preparing to abandon ship and began taking pictures. The yacht's bowsprit and foremast splintered and were carried away by the raging sea. McBride and one of his men climbed over the side on the cargo net to help catch the crew of the Curlew as they leapt from the stricken yacht.

One after another, the yachtsmen struggled up the cargo net and were hauled over the rail and deposited in the river of salt water sluicing across the Compass Island's decks. The sixth sailor leapt toward the cargo net as the time interval between successive waves shortened. He was slammed by an aggressive wave into the side of the ship and by a stroke of luck managed to crook an elbow through the cargo netting before the retreating water could suck him away from the ship and into the embrace of the next wave.

"Hold on tight boys!" McBride yelled to his shipmates. He grabbed the back of the yachtsman's life jacket, dropped a looped safety line around the man's head and shoulders, and tugged it up beneath his armpits, all while hanging up-side-down like a monkey dangling from a tree. A confluence of interests, the upward struggle of the stricken yachtsman, the muscle power of the *Compass Island* sailors tugging on his safety line, and the arrival of a monster wave starboard amidships conspired to hurl the yachtsman up and over the rail. The young sailor landed on the deck and skittered along for several feet on his buttocks before crashing into Kincaid's ankles, tangling both men in an undignified heap on the deck. Regaining their feet the two men hugged each other as briny water cascaded over them.

The newcomer's teeth were chattering, but his eyes laughed as he said: "Petty Officer Third Class Emilio Sanchez. Reporting as ordered. Permission to come aboard, sir!"

Kincaid laughed back and supplied the enlisted man's de rigueur response:

"Sir, hell! I work for a living

8

FRIDAY, NOVEMBER 8, 1963

BROOKLYN, NEW YORK — Mike Kincaid went to sleep with the acrid ozone smell of a welder's torch and the fecund stench of his own feces permeating his olfactories. The *Compass Island* was laid up for repairs alongside Pier K of the Brooklyn Navy Yard and the engineering department had been hard at it all day, cutting and welding in the head just aft of his berthing space.

Kincaid owed his present circumstances to a mistake he had made eight hours earlier. Hurrying to relieve the watch on the quarterdeck, Kincaid had paused to relieve himself. He figured (wrongly as it turned out) that the snipes had knocked off for the day, so he ducked under the "head-closed" sign taped across the doorway and answered nature's call in the third stall.

As he was leaving the head, Kincaid passed by his friend Radioman Second Class Emilio Sanchez, who had been a part of the ship's company ever since his rescue a year ago from the Curlew, which he was crewing while on leave from the United States Navy.

His explanation of how he came to be aboard the Curlew was vintage Sanchez.

"Guy I know offered me two grand to help sail the old tub down to the Caribbean for the tourist trade. I had 30 days' leave coming and I needed the cash."

"Haven't seen you for a week Skeeter. What have you been up to?" Kincaid asked.

Sanchez winked. "Detached duty."

"Again?"

Sanchez's frequent absences from the ship were often discussed on the mess deck. There were whispers that he was being trained for the Navy's new elite fighting force called the SEALs.

"Head open?" Sanchez asked.

"Appears to be. I just used it anyway."

Sanchez ducked under the head closed sign. "Well, see you around. Duty calls."

Kincaid headed forward to stand the first leg of the dog-watch. A big black hull technician second class named Bill Petry steamed by at flank speed. Petry's face was shiny. Water dripped from his hair and his dungaree shirt was soaking wet.

Realizing what had happened, and feeling more than just a little guilty, Kincaid followed Petry to the head.

"Sum sumbitch must think this is the fucking poop deck!" Petry roared.

He ducked under the head-closed sign and charged Sanchez who was preparing to drop trousers in one of the toilet stalls.

"You asshole!"

Petry's fists were clenched as tight as his jaw. "Can't you fucking read? This head is closed!"

Petry was a solid six-footer and towered over Sanchez with the glowering demeanor of a circus strong man dispatched to quell a riot in the dwarfs' tent.

There was ice in Sanchez's reply. "Back off Bill."

Watching from the doorway, Kincaid shivered.

"I just got shit on and you tell me to back off?"

Petry launched a swift right cross at Sanchez's jaw. Sanchez wasn't there when Petry's fist arrived.

In a blur, he slipped the punch, spun Petry around and slammed him into a toilet stall.

"Like I said Bill. Back off."

As a subdued Bill Petry emerged from the toilet stall, Kincaid decided it was time to fess up. "You're beef's with me Bill. I was in a hurry to relieve the watch and I didn't take the time to walk forward to the other head. It was a stupid thing to do. I'm sorry."

Petry gathered up the loose ends of his pride and shouldered his way past Sanchez and Kincaid.

"Paybacks are a bitch, Kincaid. Remember that." He stalked out of the head.

"What was that, judo?" Kincaid asked.

"Something like that," Sanchez said. "I'd watch my back if I were you Mike. I don't think Petry will come after me again. He's learned his lesson, but he'll be laying for you."

Sanchez's words were prophetic. When Kincaid returned to his rack at 2330 hours that night, having lost fifteen dollars in a stud poker game in the enlisted men's lounge, he found a pile of what he hoped was his own shit simmering atop his mattress. It didn't take much imagination to figure out who'd put it there.

Sighing, Kincaid gathered up his bed sheets and mattress cover and made his way forward to the head where he flushed the turd and scrubbed the worst of the smell out of his bed linen in one of the showers. He wadded the wet bed sheets and mattress cover, which still smelled faintly of shit, into his drawstring laundry bag, and hung it on the end of his rack for pick up by the laundry crew the next morning. Then he kicked off his shoes, crawled clothes and all under his one wool blanket and went to sleep.

At 0300 hours, the claxon sounded and the 1MC wailed. "Fire! Fire! Class alpha fire in the forecastle. Fire party assemble on the quarterdeck!"

Kincaid dropped to the deck and kicked his feet around under his rack until he encountered his brogans. Stuffing his feet into them, he headed forward and above to the quarter deck, where the petty officer of the watch, Quartermaster Third Class Philip Ambrose, handed him an oxygen breathing apparatus and told him to join the fire party gathering at the forecastle.

BM 2 Brian McBride already was on station when Kincaid arrived.

"Well don't just stand there. Gear up," McBride said.

"What?"

"Put on your breather, asshole."

Kincaid donned the harness, draped the hose and mask across one shoulder and waited while two of McBride's deck hands laid a two-and-a-half-inch canvas service line from the fire station just forward of the superstructure.

McBride tested the watertight door leading beneath the forecastle with the knuckles of his right hand. "Warm but not hot," he announced. "Phillips!"

The deck ape hurried forward. "Yeah."

"You don't have a breather so you'll have to stay outside, but keep a firm hold on the hose. Kincaid's going to need some backup. Understand?"

Phillips nodded.

McBride slipped the straps of the face mask over his head and pulled the tabs tight, motioning for Kincaid to do the same. He yanked the lanyard on his breather, activating a chemical reaction that produced oxygen.

Kincaid followed suit.

"You got air?"

McBride's voice was muffled by his face mask.

Kincaid nodded.

McBride picked up the nozzle and Kincaid settled in behind him crooking the limp canvas hose in his left elbow.

"This bastard will be heavy as hell when we get it charged," McBride said. "I'll need your lard ass right behind me weighing it down. Don't want this ankle breaker to go whipping around the deck. Charge it!"

The hose writhed like a giant anaconda and Kincaid almost lost his grip. McBride was right the bastard was heavy.

Phillips swung the door open.

McBride stepped into the dark smoky compartment beyond. Kincaid followed behind him, tugging the heavy canvas hose over the threshold.

The ship's emergency lighting system cast an eerie glow over a familiar space. The heavy smoke descended upon them like the reaper's shroud. Dread assaulted Mike Kincaid and he stopped in his tracks.

"Come on Kincaid! Work with me here!" McBride yelled.

They struggled forward. McBride opened the door of the sail locker, which spewed even thicker black smoke. He tugged back on the bail of the nozzle and loosed a high-pressure stream of water into the sail locker. Sparks flew at them like enraged fireflies.

Ignoring the stench and the sparks, McBride pressed forward. He adjusted the nozzle, dampening the stream of water to a fine mist, which he directed at a heap of canvas and lumber scraps the deck crew had piled against the portside bulkhead. Through the thick fog of smoke, Kincaid could see two, five-gallon cans of paint, and more ominously, a five-gallon jerry can of what he assumed was paint thinner, left behind by a work party that had been making repairs the day before to the captain's gig.

McBride beat back the worst of the fire and then shifted the nozzle to the paint thinner can and paint buckets, dousing them with water to forestall an explosion.

"Those sum bitches blow, we'll be knee deep in shit quicker than you can say toilet paper," McBride yelled.

He redirected the spray to the canvas pile once again as the fire hissed and spit. He adjusted the nozzle for a steady stream and beat folded canvas drop cloths apart with the force of the water, scouring the sodden debris for any hot spots. Cold water sloshed about their ankles and the smoke thickened as the fire succumbed to the inevitable.

"That should do it. Uncharge the line!" he screamed.

The hose went limp.

McBride dropped the nozzle to the deck and Kincaid let go of the hose. "Go tell Lieutenant Richardson that the fire is out while I kick apart the debris just to make sure. "He'll want to assemble a work party to clean this mess up. We're going to find someplace to hide. I'd say we've done our part."

Kincaid grinned under his mask.

As he left the sail locker, the emergency lights flickered and the smoke roiled like steam in a witch's cauldron. An annoying buzz permeated the forecastle. Kincaid's hair stood on end and danced to the oscillating cadence of an electric charge whose source he could not identify.

The buzzing built and on it rode an eerie, yet familiar, voice, which seemed to come from nowhere and everywhere at the same time: "If there's one thing this life has taught me it's that you have to pay for your mistakes."

"Who said that?" Kincaid yelled. "Who said what?" McBride screamed.

Kincaid didn't answer because in the glow of a battle lantern the roiling smoke coalesced and assumed a human form. Shit! What was that? Kincaid rubbed at the eyepieces of his breathing mask and tried to convince himself that he wasn't staring at a huge man leaning against the bulkhead. But he was. The man's features were obscured in the swirling smoke. His right leg was bent at the knee and his foot was propped against the bulkhead with the nonchalance of a man waiting for a bus.

"I've made my mistakes, Mikey me boy. And I'm sorry for them. Truly I am."

The apparition dropped his right foot to the ground and turned to face the solid bulkhead behind him.

"What's that you say? It's time? Praise be! It's time."

The solid bulkhead beneath the battle lantern shimmered and assumed the luminous fluidity of a backlit aquarium.

The apparition looked back over its shoulder at Kincaid. "I'll be leaving now," he said. "Seems I'm getting another chance. But all this makes you wonder, doesn't it boy?"

Kincaid's pulse was a bass drum throbbing in his own ears. "Wonder what?" he croaked past dry spit that tasted like stomach acid and soot.

"Is this world for real or for pretend?"

Just then McBride stuck his head outside the sail locker and yelled.

"God damn it Kincaid. Quit screwing around. Report to Richardson."

When Kincaid returned his eyes to the spot where the apparition had loitered, a tendril of smoke swirled and dissipated, carrying with it a question that seared his soul.

"Is this world for real or for pretend?"

Kincaid wasn't so sure, at least not anymore. He fled the forecastle as if hornets pursued him.

9

SATURDAY, NOVEMBER 16, 1963

CAPE CANAVERAL, FLORIDA — It was a blustery November day off the coast of Florida. Mike Kincaid sweated in his dress blues but it never occurred to him to doubt the judgment of Captain Earnhart who had ordained that they wear their winter uniforms in the tropics.

Kincaid and a dozen or so squared-away sailors assembled on the helio deck at 1000 hours to greet President John F. Kennedy. Chief Boatswain's Mate George McCain led a detail of eight side boys, who would form a human corridor through which the president would pass as he disembarked Marine One. McCain wore his boatswain's whistle on a starched white lanyard around his right shoulder. Kincaid noticed that McCain's lips were raw, probably from practicing for the moment he would pipe the president aboard the ship.

The entire ship's company, at least those not involved in engine room or bridge watches, stood shoulder to shoulder along the rails. The crew was exhausted from two weeks of hard labor preparing the *Compass Island* for the president's visit. Kincaid had never seen the old girl look better. The bridge brass gleamed. The decks, sides and superstructure wore a fresh coat of Navy gray. The tile in the passageways was spit shined and the porcelain in the heads had a Pepsodent gleam.

At about 1020 hours, Captain Earnhart and Rear Admiral James Gallagher, the Navy's director of Special Projects, arrived on the helio deck. The ship's executive officer, Lt. Commander Jonathan Briggs, trailed along behind like a pledge eager to join their fraternity. Briggs, for some reason, was wearing a sword.

The captain took off his cap, scratched his head and took a long look at his ship. "By God Briggs, we're as gussied up as a thirty dollar whore on festival day. The boys did a fine job, wouldn't you say?"

A lookout sighted the helicopter as it crept over the horizon and raised the alarm. The 1MC's loudspeakers hissed to life:

"Marine One. ETA five minutes."

The helicopter's screaming turbines and whomping rotors soon overpowered the sounds of water rushing past the hull and the restless shifting and snuffling of 200 men sweating in the hot sun. The signalmen ran the president's flag up the mainmast as Marine One settled on the helio deck right on time. The rotor wash tugged at Kincaid's uniform. A side boy's hat blew off and plastered itself to Kincaid's chest. Kincaid grabbed the hat and returned it to its relieved owner.

The helicopter's engines wound down and stopped, but Kincaid's ears buzzed with the aftershock.

The stairway unfurled and two Secret Service agents in suits took station on either side of the doorway, ready to grab an arm should the president stumble.

Kincaid snapped off four quick shots with his Rolleiflix camera as Kennedy ducked, stepped off the helicopter and made his way through the side boys toward Captain Earnhart and Admiral Gallagher. Studying Kennedy through his viewfinder, Kincaid decided that he looked too young to be president. His skin was tight; his smile assured. A thin navy blue necktie secured his starched white shirt tight at the collar. The president's charcoal suit was travel-rumpled. He wore tortoise-shell sunglasses. Kincaid captured several shots of Captain Earnhart first saluting the president, then shaking his hand as the announcement was passed over the 1MC "United States, arriving!"

The sun, the sea, the assembled ship's company, imbued the moment with magic. The boatswain's whistle startled Kincaid from his reverie. He crouched to frame the president and Admiral Gallagher against the enormous American flag, which strained against its halyards in a brisk breeze on the fantail. As Kincaid arose from his crouch his notebook fell from the waistband of his pocket less trousers and landed at the president's feet.

Kennedy and Kincaid bent at the same time to pick up the notebook and almost banged heads.

The president, ducked, picked up the notebook and laughed.

"I am so sorry Mr. President," Kincaid stammered.

"What's your name, son, and where are you from?"

Kincaid regained his composure. He had thought about what he would say if given the chance to speak to the president and he responded in a rush

"Journalist Mate Third Class Mike Kincaid, sir. I'm from Camden, New Jersey. It's an honor to meet you, sir. My stepfather, Jacob Manley, is a Democratic committeeman. He helped turn out the vote for you in Camden in 1960."

Kennedy smiled and returned Kincaid's salute. "I carried New Jersey handily."

Kennedy pulled a pen from his shirt pocket and scrawled something in Kincaid's notebook. He handed the notebook and his pen to Kincaid.

"Give this to your stepfather, in appreciation of his hard work on my behalf."

Kincaid glanced at the pen, noting that it bore the presidential seal. He scanned the note and grinned. It read: "To Jacob Manley, loyal Democrat, with deepest appreciation from the former sailor he helped elect president of the United States."

"The *Andrew Jackson* will be on station in just a few minutes, Mr. President," Gallagher said. "There's just enough time for a quick tour of the bridge."

10

FRIDAY, DEC. 6, 1963

FORT EUSTIS, VIRGINIA — "You could make this a lot easier on yourself if you'd just cooperate," Emilio Sanchez told Mike Kincaid.

The two men were sitting knee to knee across a narrow table in an interrogation room in the stockade at Fort Eustis. The Navy had transferred Kincaid there for debriefing as investigators backtracked President John Fitzgerald Kennedy's activities during the last month of his life. That anyway was the cover story that would go in his file, if he cooperated.

The choice Sanchez offered him was simple. He could sign off on the official version of Kennedy's visit to the USS *Compass Island* on 16 November 1963, and rejoin his ship with a promotion to petty officer second class. Or, he could insist on telling the truth at a court of inquiry to convene on 13 December 1963, and face a general discharge from the Navy on the grounds that he was psychologically unfit to serve.

"I thought you were my friend," Kincaid said.

"I am your friend that's why I'm here you asshole. All you have to do is shut up!"

"It's a matter of journalistic integrity. What happened to Kennedy on our ship should be a part of the official record of his assassination!"

"Don't trot out that bull shit! You're not a civilian journalist, Kincaid. You're a sailor in the United States Navy and you've been given a lawful order to keep your fucking mouth shut! Besides you promised the president you'd never breathe a word about what you witnessed. Kennedy himself classified it as top secret for Christ sakes!"

"Yeah? Well that was before he was assassinated," Kincaid said. "People need to know what happened because it might have something to do with his death."

"The right people know and believe me it has been investigated. We just have to keep this out of official channels because it's a black mark on the entire U.S. Navy and the brass want it buried . . . they want it buried real deep."

"The brass or the CIA?" Kincaid asked.

Sanchez was startled into momentary silence. "That's a question you'd be better off not asking," he said, finally. "Besides it amounts to the same thing, as far as you're concerned. Cooperate and you'll be rewarded. Don't and you'll be punished."

"So the president of the United States gets . . ."

"Shut up Mike! I know what happened, I was there, too, remember? The incident had nothing to do with Kennedy's assassination. Period! We've investigated it thoroughly."

"We? Who is we? Are you some sort of spook Skeeter?" Kincaid asked.

Sanchez puffed his cheeks in exasperation.

"You are, aren't you? I can't think of any other reason they'd kick you free of duty on the CI so you could visit with me."

Sanchez answered the question with a question. "Do you have any idea how hard it will be to find a job in the civilian world with a general discharge on your resume?" he asked.

Kincaid swallowed and looked away.

Sanchez made a V of his index and middle fingers and held it in front of his eyes. "Look at me Mike! Right here! You make the wrong choice and this will dog you for the rest of your life. You might make a splash in the national press, but you'll always be looking over your shoulder wondering."

"Wondering what?" Kincaid asked.

"Wondering whether some special ops guy is going to cap you and put your body somewhere only the fishes will be able to find," Sanchez said.

Kincaid snorted. "Yeah! Right!" But it was bravado and Sanchez knew it. He dove like a peregrine to the kill.

"You're fucking with some powerful people," Sanchez said. His voice was stiletto sharp and as menacing as a garrote. "Shut up and stay shut up. That's your only viable alternative."

Kincaid shuddered. Someone was walking on his grave. "I'll shut up," he said.

The ignominy of surrender bubbled and rose like acid from the depths of his gut, burning his throat with shame.

Sanchez sat back in his chair and studied Kincaid for several long seconds over hands arrayed as if in prayer. He leaned forward. "You've made the right choice, buddy. Really, you have. I'll kick this upstairs and it won't be long before you're back on the CI with another stripe on your sleeve."

With that, Sanchez arose, shook Kincaid's hand, and left the interrogation room.

That was the last time Kincaid saw Sanchez, until he turned up outside Room 204 of the Motel Six in Camden, New Jersey, forty years later.

11

FRIDAY, SEPTEMBER 12, 2003

HAMPTON ROADS, VIRGINIA — The cursor leered at Gale Johnston from the top of a blank Microsoft Word document, but she
was too damn mad to succumb to its obscene provocation to fill
the page with the latest drivel the assignment editor had shoved
her way. The words would sound pretty if she wrote them, but
she didn't give a damn about the three-legged goat that had
survived a coyote attack and given birth to triplets, no kidding.

Truman Burke told her it would be the most read story in
the next day's paper and he probably was right, but she wasn't
going to write it. She had told him so in no uncertain terms
right before she quit. She had often quit.

Burke laughed, infuriating her even more. "Here we go again.
Just do the damn story, Gale, and shut up."

With that, he turned on his heel and stalked off to the Page
One meeting in the executive editor's office, which seethed still
with the malodorous miasma of her rage. Bill Harrington's attempts to open his office window were ongoing and futile. It was
painted shut. It amused her that Harrington, without realizing
it, was trying to clear his office of the lingering smell of his own
fear before the Page One meeting convened.

Gale Johnston was a formidable adversary, and while Harrington had won the loud argument in his office several minutes earlier, his prestige lay in tatters on the battlefield. The
newsroom would be tittering about their encounter for weeks
to come.

Let the little prick sit there and sweat, Johnston thought
to herself. The ball less bastard had just pulled the plug on a
story that could have won her (and the newspaper) a Pulitzer
Prize. Her expose on the JFK assassination was dead. Kaput.
Shot at dawn. In the interest of national security. That feckless

subterfuge frosted her shorts. That's why she blasted Harrington with both barrels.

"That's bull shit Bill and you know it. You must have checked your testicles with the sheriff when you rode into town. Tell them to take the Patriots' Act and shove it. What does JFK's assassination have to do with national security after all these years? Not a God damn thing and what's worse, you know it."

Having said that, Gale Johnston stormed out of Harrington's office.

The executive editor was right about one thing, though. Emilio Sanchez was playing her. He was trying to use her to punish his former employer, the Central Intelligence Agency. But Johnston didn't mind being used in the interest of a good story. Sanchez was a gold-plated source. He was a CIA agent with a grudge who had been uniquely positioned to observe the intelligence agency's frantic investigation and self-examination in the weeks and months following Kennedy's assassination on November 22, 1963.

She'd show the bastards. She'd quit, for real this time, and go find a newspaper with the cojones to publish the truth. She picked up the phone, and without thinking about it punched in the numbers for Sanchez's cell phone. He surprised her by answering on the second ring.

"Hola, Gale," he said, without preamble.

"The ball less bastards have killed the story," she blurted out.

Jillian Richardson, the office wag, was hanging on her every word from just within earshot but Gale didn't care.

"That doesn't surprise me, given the corporate ownership of your newspaper. In fact, I rather expected it. To tell the truth, I offered the story to you first, just to twist their beard."

This was news to Johnston and it stunned her to silence.

"I've told you all along that the way to tackle this is to help me write a book," Sanchez said. "That way we can lay the whole thing out there rather than trying to serialize it in a bunch of sanitized news stories that would be vetted and diluted by more lawyers than you can shake a stick at."

Sanchez's voice was warm, Hispanic and oozed testosterone. It would have melted the panties off a lesser woman, or at least of one who batted from the conventional side of the plate. His tone merely annoyed Johnston.

"If you're so damn smart, why don't you just tell me who killed JFK and have done with it!" she shouted.

She stabbed a one-fingered salute Jillian's way.

"You've given me bits and pieces, clues and innuendo, but I want more. At the end of the day, so did my editors."

The phone line was silent for a while, buzzing subtly with the electronic essence of all of the other conversations riding alongside hers in cyberspace. She thought she heard the rustling of papers somewhere in the background and the line was alive again.

"How would you like to take a road trip?" Sanchez asked.

"Where to?"

Sanchez ignored the question. "There's someone I'd like you to meet. Someone who can confirm an essential element of the assassination conspiracy and explain why your editor killed the story."

"What's this source going to tell me?" Johnston wanted to know.

"He's going to tell you how a U.S. Naval officer socked President John F. Kennedy in the jaw aboard a U.S. Navy ship on November 16, 1963 and got away with it."

"November 16? That's just a week before the assassination," Gale observed. "OK, you've got my attention now."

Jillian Richardson circled nearer as the decibel level of Gale's conversation dropped.

"What else will he say?"

"He'll say that I'm a dirty son of a bitch and he'd rather submit himself to a colonoscopy without anesthesia than cooperate with me. But if we talk to him nice he might confirm the name of the naval officer."

"And who might that be?"

Gale made a pistol of her thumb and forefinger and pointed it at Richardson, who back pedaled a step or two and glowered at her like a dog warned off shitting in her yard.

"Hugh Patterson."

The name was a revelation. Hugh Patterson was the absentee owner of the Virginia Pilot, and a half a dozen other medium-sized dailies sprinkled along the East Coast. No wonder the JFK story had been killed.

"No shit! Where do you want to meet?" Johnston asked. Sanchez told her and Johnston hung up the phone. She jotted some notes to herself in her reporter's notebook. Then she arose and stalked unannounced into the Page One meeting that had convened while she was on the phone.

She affected a faux southern accent that oozed contempt. ""I hate to interrupt y'all's little circle jerk. But fuck all you timid little pricks and upshove this job assward."

With that convivial adieu she left them to pore over a news budget that featured a three-legged goat giving birth to triplets, which was more or less their speed. JFK's assassination was way out of their league.

It was typical for her to confront adversity head on. She'd worry about the consequences later, stew over her lack of health insurance, and wonder how she'd pay her bills until she landed her next paying gig. For now she was consumed with frenetic purpose.

It was a pattern of behavior familiar to her long-suffering dad. Hiram Johnston had always laughed when the apparent misspelling of his daughter's name came up in conversation.

"Maggie never did know how to spell," he'd tell whoever was unfortunate enough to ask. "But she might have gotten it right after all. Gale lives up to her name. One minute all is calm and the next batten the hatches we're in for a blow!"

Gale Johnston winced every time she heard that story because there was a lot of truth to it. The turbulence that overwhelmed whichever of her enterprises fate had frowned upon sprang from a source she could not explain.

She had been frustrated as a child by her inability to articulate a wide range of feelings, emotions and memories that didn't seem to belong to her. They assailed her at night as she slept. Ghostly memories of them formed a spectral entourage about her during her waking hours. Her parents worried because she seemed forever distracted by things no one else perceived.

In time, her verbal skills caught up with the sophisticated images her brain had been processing for years. She became enraged when adults refused to understand that things were never what they seemed to be; that reality was stacked upon itself like blocks in the nursery of a careless child; that it was possible to be a man forever sheathed in a woman's body. That was her cross to bear. Her instincts were masculine and yet society insisted she sit down to pee. Well piss on them! That's what Gale Johnston had been doing for thirty-five years, pissing on them. And she hadn't been sitting down to do it.

People were afraid of her because she was a storm waiting to happen. Bill Harrington's windblown office was evidence of that. The hapless executive editor was still inventorying the emotional damage 30 minutes later as she blew out of the office of the Virginia Pilot for the last time.

12

MONDAY, SEPTEMBER 22, 2003

ALEXANDRIA, VIRGINIA — Dr. Sharon Albright ignored the phone twittering in the receptionist's vestibule and continued working. The office had closed two hours ago at 5 p.m., but she had stayed late to work on a psychological evaluation for a custody hearing the next day before the Juvenile and Domestic Relations District Court of Falls Church, Virginia.

The phone rang seven times and the caller hung up without leaving a message when the answering machine kicked in. Albright shrugged and continued typing. Her fingers clicking over the keys of her Dell laptop sounded like a dog's claws on a hardwood floor.

Albright was 42 years old, tall, willowy, auburn-haired and brilliant. She held a medical degree from Thomas Jefferson Medical School. She was a forensic psychiatrist with a secret that propelled her career in another, unusual direction.

Albright had lived before, not just once, but many times. She was certain of that. The many people she had been constantly clamored for her attention. They called to her from a rich and vibrant déjà vu that shimmered about her perception of everyday events. There was nothing she hadn't seen before.

Her unique perception of reality drew her to past life therapy. Employing hypnotic regression, Albright helped her patients understand that issues left unresolved in their previous lifetimes affected their behavior and sometimes their mental health in this one.

Her cell phone rang from the depths of her purse, which rested on the floor next to her feet. She was careful with her cell number, so this call commanded her attention. Albright dug the phone out of her purse and glanced at the digital display, frowning when she didn't recognize the number of the incoming call.

"Hello. This is Doctor Albright."

She used the voice she reserved for telemarketers and Mormon missionaries.

"In another life, I kept bears for baiting at Elizabethan fairs." The voice was rich, mocking and possessed the musical lilt of a native Spanish speaker.

She recognized the caller at once. Emilio Sanchez. Her sometime employer, the Central Intelligence Agency, had referred him to her for treatment.

She affected an English accent.

"In another life, I fed bear baiters to their own bears," Albright responded.

Emilio Sanchez's laugh was baritone, sexy and menacing all at the same time.

"I've got a case you might be interested in, Doc."

Albright took care to imbue her response with ambivalence. "Oh really."

"How would you like to putter around in the psyche of a man who has been brainwashed by our mutual employer?"

"There is no such thing as brainwashing."

"Forgive me for being imprecise," Sanchez said. "I'm talking about behavior modification. I have his file. I can show it to you. They used drug and aversion therapy to trigger panic if he tried to relate an incident my former employer preferred he forget."

Albright was intrigued despite herself. "When?"

"Forty years ago." Papers rustled. "His treatment started in December of 1963."

"That's a risky strategy forty years ago when the pharmaceutical options were much more primitive. It's unlike our friends to be that cavalier with secrets. I would have expected a more vigorous therapy," Albright said.

Sanchez laughed. "Good girl, doc. You catch on quick. Maybe there's a career in this line of work for you after all."

The phone line hissed while Sanchez thought. "Look. The guy was a friend. OK? I recommended a gentler handling back when my recommendations carried more weight. And now? Well, let's just say the statute of limitations has run out on this particular secret. I want him to remember. In fact, it's critical that he remember!"

"Critical to whom? To you or to your former employer?"

"In this instance our interests intersect."

"How can I be certain of that?"

"You'll just have to trust me. Besides, this guy needs your help."

"Just what is it that he needs help remembering?" Albright asked.

"Not on an open phone line."

"You're not a very good salesman."

"Listen. I'll pay your usual rates, plus travel expenses if you come up here and see him."

"Where's up here?" Albright asked. She bit her tongue, cursing herself for giving him false hope.

"He's settling his late stepfather's affairs at the moment in a funny little place called Fairview. It's in Camden, New Jersey."

Albright gasped as one of her former selves whispered in her ear: "We used to live in Fairview, dear."

"What's wrong, Doc?"

"Nothing," Albright replied. "Apparently, I once was someone who lived in Fairview."

"And I once was someone who raised bears for baiting at Elizabethan fairs."

"This is where I came in."

Albright hated herself for even considering his proposal, however; once she delivered the psychological profile in the custody case the next morning, her calendar was clear and by design. She intended to escape for two weeks to her favorite seashore resort, Rehoboth Beach, Delaware, where the weather would still be warm, and the beaches, shops and restaurants would be gloriously absent the usual summer throngs and thongs. It was all part of her master plan. She was going to wind down for two weeks before commencing a yearlong sabbatical to write the book she'd been outlining. The working title was The People We Have Been.

Sanchez sensed surrender in her silence. "Well how about it, doc? I'll make it worth your while." Albright surprised herself by saying yes.

She agreed to meet him at 7 p.m. the next evening in the parking lot of a Motel 6 in Camden, New Jersey. She wrote the address and Sanchez's cell phone number on the pad next to her desk blotter and hung up the phone. She dug a Kleenex out of her purse to wipe away the sweat accumulating on her brow and upper lip. What had she gotten herself into?

Sharon Albright knew Emilio Sanchez as intimately as a lover. She had helped him defuse a landmine buried in his psyche forty years earlier. Over the course of their therapy, Sanchez shared many dark secrets; for the most part without enough context for Albright to make much of them other than he was a remorseless killer who for some reason had developed a conscience.

One therapy session did stand out in her mind, however; even though she tried to suppress it because it was the sort of information that could get you killed.

13

ALEXANDRIA, VIRGINIA — Emilio Sanchez wriggled about until he'd carved out a comfortable space on the overstuffed couch in Dr. Sharon Albright's office. When he propped his feet up on an ottoman, Albright noticed that there was a hole in the sole of his left shoe.

"You comfortable?"

"Your tone indicates you might actually care. So yes, for the record, I am comfortable," Sanchez said.

He smiled and tapped his right temple with his right forefinger.

"I know all sorts of secrets. Secrets that could get you killed. You sure you want to go poking around in here again?"

"My clearances are in order," Albright replied. "So what do you want to talk about today?"

"I've killed 26 people. How's that for starters?"

Albright didn't flinch. "Is that the best you've got? If it is you're wasting my time."

A vein throbbed in her neck, belying her anxiety.

"OK. Try this one on for size. I know who killed JFK."

"What does that have to do with your showing up drunk for work . . . or not at all?"

"Nothing, but it's a hell of an ice breaker."

Albright didn't reply.

"Come on doc. you've got to be dying to know," Sanchez said.

"I'm more interested in what's bothering you. Your supervisor reports that you kneed a colleague in the balls. That's not appropriate conduct for the chief of the Latin America desk."

"My supervisor is an asshole and my colleague deserved to be kneed in the balls. Just like JFK deserved to die, the son of a bitch," Sanchez said.

"What do you mean by that?"

Albright bit her tongue. She hadn't wanted to get sucked up in Sanchez's transparent attempt to divert her from his real problem, whatever it was.

"Kennedy left a lot of good people swinging in the wind, in the interest of getting re-elected. So how about it, doc, want to know who killed him?"

"Lee Harvey Oswald."

Sanchez grinned. "Yep. He pulled the trigger, but I'm talking about the guy who pulled Oswald's trigger. Funny thing is, the man behind the curtain is the ancestor of the U.S. senator from New . . ."

"Enough!" Therapists don't usually shout at their patients, but Albright had had enough.

Sanchez curled his lip like a dog deprived of a bone. "OK doc, but I know you're trying to fill in the blanks. New Mexico, New York, New Hampshire . . ."

"Enough," Albright repeated, calmer now. The teacher had lost her composure for a minute, but she was determined to restore order to her classroom.

"I think the root of your problem lies in what we were talking about last session. You mentioned a little girl killed in a bomb blast. What was her name?"

"Maria," Sanchez said.

"That's right, Maria. The subject of Maria seemed to make you uncomfortable. I think the key to your problem may lie in your relationship with Maria."

"I didn't have a relationship with Maria. I met her right before the bomb went off. She wasn't supposed to be in the room. She was collateral damage. I was trying to kill her father, not her."

Sanchez's voice was thick with phlegm. He swallowed the lump in his throat.

"Sometimes we know people we don't think we know," Albright said.

"What the hell does that mean?" Sanchez asked.

"I think you know what that means. Don't you?"

Albright imbued her words with a gentleness that Sanchez wasn't expecting. He took his feet off the ottoman and sat forward on the couch. His eyes darted back and forth as if he was looking for an exit in a smoke-filled theater.

Albright broke the tension. "Let's forget about Maria for the moment. Sit back and let me tell you a story. I had a client once who came to me because she was troubled by a lack of intimacy in her relationship with her new boyfriend," she said.

Albright layered her speech with the calm, kind inflections she used when she hypnotized a patient. "She was certain she had found her soul mate, which in a way, I suppose, she had. But her new friend wasn't interested in consummating their relationship. In fact, he took great pains to avoid physical intimacy."

"What was he, queer or something?" Sanchez asked.

He was sitting back on the couch now. He crossed his legs, affecting nonchalance.

Albright sighed. At least he seemed to be engaged in her story.

"No, he wasn't gay."

She paused, weighing the risks and benefits of what she was about to say.

"Anyway, I hypnotized this client and asked her to recall encounters with her boyfriend that she considered compelling. It wasn't long before she stumbled on a memory of an incident that had occurred a long, long time ago."

"A long time ago? I thought you said the two had just met," Sanchez interrupted.

"That's right. They had . . . in this lifetime. My client was relating an incident that had happened in another lifetime."

"Does the CIA know you're a kook?"

She was ready for the question. "Nope, but they're certain you are. That's why you're here, remember?"

Sanchez laughed out loud. "Touché, Doctor. Touché. Now get on with your story."

"My client recalled strolling through a crowded market, holding hands with a young boy. They were laughing and talking about the fine muttonchops they were going to buy from the butcher. I asked her to look deep into the eyes of her companion and when she did, she began to cry."

Albright paused for effect.

Sanchez shrugged. "OK Doc. I'll play along. Why did she cry?"

"She cried because in that moment she recognized that she was peering into the eyes of her son . . . and of her new boyfriend at the same time. She realized that a physical relationship with her new man was doomed from the start because he had been her son . . . in another lifetime and physical intimacy between them in this one was out of the question."

"Why? Was he queer or something?" Sanchez repeated the question just to piss her off.

Albright didn't rise to the bait. "Come on Emilio. You're not stupid. Your IQ puts you in rare air. You're smarter than I am, on paper. But if you insist, I'll state the obvious. He recognized their previous relationship on a subliminal level and he couldn't bring himself to have sex with a woman who had been his mother."

"How's that relate to me?" Sanchez asked. "I've had sex with my mother and she was a lousy lay."

Albright laughed. "Here's how, Mr. Oedipus. My patient was drawn to this man by an attraction she couldn't understand. She was walking down a busy street and was compelled by an impulse to go into a bookstore. She had no interest in books, but she followed her compulsion inside where she met the man who had been her son."

Albright paused, collecting her thoughts and Sanchez waited her out.

"I've noticed similar phenomena many times over the years. There is a natural attraction that draws people together if they've had a relationship in a previous lifetime. Kindred spirits seek each other out."

"So you're saying that maybe I knew Maria in another lifetime and that our meeting again was preordained by some sort of mystic magnetism?" Sanchez asked.

Albright was gratified to note his voice bore wonder, not derision. "Baby steps," she told herself. "Baby steps."

She nodded. "That's right."

"How can you prove that?"

"Eureka!" She had him. "Well, I could hypnotize you."

Sanchez proved to be a pliant subject. Maybe it was because a steady psychic barrage of regret had beaten down his defenses, or maybe it was because he already knew the truth and needed an excuse to admit it to himself.

Albright had him move to a leather recliner in the corner of her office. She drew the drapes and dialed down the rheostat until the room had a comfortable glow and nothing more. Using a remote control, she selected a Yani CD and adjusted the volume to cover any ambient noise that might sneak in from the world outside.

"This will work if you take it seriously. Are you prepared to do that?"

Sanchez nodded.

Albright sat next to him in a wing chair.

"OK. I want you to relax. Concentrate on your breathing. Breathe in for 15 seconds. Breathe out for ten. Count it out in your head. Nothing else matters. Just breathe."

Albright fell silent. She watched Sanchez's chest rise and fall, counting the seconds silently along with him.

Good. He was spot on. He was engaged.

She allowed the music to wash over them for two minutes. Any longer and there was a danger he might fall asleep.

"Emilio."

"Yes."

"Let's talk about your encounter several months ago with a young girl named Maria."

"OK."

"I want you to imagine that you are sitting in a dark movie theater watching that meeting on the screen."

Albright allowed the memory to build before him for 30 seconds or so. "What's happening now?"

"I'm in Carlos's study. He says I can have five kilos within the week, but he wants to see the cash."

"What cash?"

"The money for the drug buy. I've got a quarter mil in counterfeit bills in the briefcase at my feet, along with a pound of plastique and a radio controlled detonator. The briefcase has a false bottom."

"Are you two alone in the room?"

"Yes. No. Wait a minute.

"What's happening now?"

"A little girl just came into the room. Carlos says 'Maria what are you doing here? Where's Delma? Maria says: 'Don't be cross with her Daddy. Delma had to go pee and I couldn't wait to show you the lovely picture I've colored.'"

"Describe Maria to me," Albright said.

"She's little, five years old or so with raven hair and chocolate eyes. God she's cute."

Albright counted off ten seconds. "What's happening now?"

"Carlos looks at Maria's coloring book and tells her it is pretty but that she'll have to go find Delma because Daddy has to talk business with this nice man. Maria is on her way out of the room now . . . she's stopping beside the couch where I'm sitting. 'Would you like to see my picture too?'"

Sanchez paused as the memory played out on the big screen only he could see.

"It's a Mary Poppins coloring book. Burt and his sidewalk paintings. She's written something in red crayon at the top of the page. It's a heart encircling the words 'I love Daddy.'"

Sanchez paused again, giving Albright an opportunity to frame this memory.

"Emilio?"

"Yes."

"Take a close look at Maria. Stare into her eyes. Her eyes are the window to her soul. What do you see there?"

There was a long silence. Albright counted it off. One one thousand; two one thousand. She got to eight one thousand when she realized that Emilio Sanchez was weeping. Tears leaked from the corner of his closed eyelids and coursed down his cheeks.

"Emilio? What's wrong?"

"It's Bonita. I see Bonita in Maria's eyes."

"Who's Bonita?"

"My third cousin. The only woman I ever loved. I killed her forty years ago. And then I killed her again."

14

THURSDAY, MAY 25, 1961

COJIMAR, CUBA — The fear was an affront to his Latin machismo and he dreaded its arrival like an abused child dreads the approach of his abuser. He fought it fiercely, but still the fear had come to him each morning since April 15. That was the day he had witnessed the death of his best friend, Jose Mendez.

One moment he and Jose were running side by side through viscid sand, roiling with the death throes of spent bullets. The crazy physics of the battlefield eerily disconnected the sounds of machine gun fire from the hot lead streaming their way. It was if they were actors in a movie whose sound and video were out of synch. Their hands were clasped tightly about their rifles, which they carried at port arms just as their instructors in Nicaragua had taught them. Their throats were raw with battle cries, or were they screams of terror? Emilio Sanchez glanced over to see if his friend was as terrified as he was.

In that instant, Jose's head exploded, loosing a red froth in the air, which settled on Sanchez, sticky and warm like paint from a spray gun. But it wasn't the gore that unsettled him as he reflected on the moment and as he struggled not to reflect upon it. It was the look of surprise that lit up his friend's face in the instant the bullet struck and then the absolute vacancy in his eyes as the essential elements of Jose Mendez were set free of their container and loosed on an empirical world so governed by cause and effect that it knew no regret.

The fear materialized so gradually in his bedchamber that he was uncertain of the exact time of its arrival. He strained to hear any creak or bump in the night or to feel a gust of air foreboding its approach. That was the horror of it. He dreaded the terror that would soon sweep him up like a hurricane toying with a small ship at sea. But the dread was almost as bad as the storm itself. In a perverse way he welcomed the onset of the tremors. He longed to be tossed about on the sea of his emotions amid towering waves of terror so he could say "There. It has happened. It can get no worse, and I am surviving!"

And then it was upon him. He tossed and groaned and called out in his sleep. "Jose. Jose. I am so sorry. Why did the bullet strike you and not me? You are the lucky one my friend. Where you are, there is no fear."

And he wept the tears not of a man but of a boy, alone in the world and bereft the solace of a mother's love. It was then that she came to him with the tears not yet dry upon his face. It was then that his third cousin Bonita Salvadore slipped into his bed and held him tight.

"Shh. Shh," she said, tenderly drying his eyes with the hem of her night skirt. "It will be all right. You are safe, now. You are not alone. You are with friends."

His terror subsided, to be replaced by something else. But what was it? Gratitude? Certainly, but there was something more. Lust. Oh God help him! His penis was as hard as a rock and it jabbed at Bonita with the insistency of a small boy trying to get his mother's attention in the cacophony of a crowded marketplace.

Rather than being revolted, Bonita was amused. "So what have we here man child?" she murmured, "and what are we going to do with it? Do you think if we rub it, it will go away?"

Her laugh was warm and throaty and it carried not a hint of derision.

His fear rushed out of the room as if it were late for an appointment.

"Perhaps if we put it someplace safe and warm it will leave us alone," Sanchez observed.

"Tch. Tch. Don't be in such a hurry. These are matters that must be handled delicately," Bonita whispered.

She pushed away from him and stood up. In one fluid motion, she pulled her nightgown over her head and dropped it on the floor next to the bed. It was dark in the room save for a bit of moonlight leaking through an open window. But in that meager light Sanchez saw all he needed to see to inflame him further. Her head was turned to one side accentuating the sleek line of her neck as she looked down on him. He imagined a variety of emotions at play in that look. Affection, amusement, pity, lust?

They were all there, but in what proportions? He decided he didn't care.

Bonita broke her pose and sat on the bed beside him. He reached up and ran the backs of his fingers gently along her jaw from her ears to her chin. He traced the line of her neck, and fluttered his fingertips across her shoulders and her collarbone. He brushed the backs of his fingers along the swell of her breasts and then trailed his hands down across her hipbones. Her body surged toward him and he drew her close and into a lingering kiss.

Breaking the kiss, she murmured. "Who has taught you boy? I was almost certain you were a virgin."

In truth, he was inexperienced. His hasty coupling with a whore, although it had ended his virginity technically, had taught him nothing about how to give pleasure to a woman. He was reacting to the moment instinctively. Her presence in his bed had restored his machismo and he drew her nearer. He circled the areola of her right breast with the tip of his tongue and then nibbled the nipple.

She gasped, fell back in bed and raised up her hips. "Help me off with these."

He knelt beside her like a supplicant before the altar of her sex. He tugged her panties down past her knees and then her ankles. Enthralled by the moist tangle of her pubic hair, he paused like a swimmer deciding whether the water was warm enough to jump in.

Bonita kicked off her panties and raised her arms to him.

"Come to me boy. It is time," she said. She spread her legs, and he knelt between them, unsure of how to proceed.

Bonita solved the problem for him. Reaching up, she clasped both hands about his neck and pulled him toward her, opening her legs wide to receive him.

Penetration was swift and sure because she was wet with arousal. His adolescence caught up with him then. He ejaculated.

Bonita smiled. "So you were a virgin after all," she said. "No matter. The nice thing about virgins is that they recover so quickly. Get off of me and lie on your back, so I can show you how a man pleasures a woman."

He did as she instructed and before his tumescence could subside, she sat upon him and guided him into her once again. Moving her hips in a slow circular motion, she bent low and pushed her tongue into his ear. He groaned and surged toward her. Recognizing that their coupling could now proceed with more vigor, she began raising and lowering her hips with ever increasing urgency. Her breath came in short gasps and Sanchez strained forward, taking her left nipple in his mouth while rubbing her other breast in a circular motion with the palm of his hand.

Her hip action became ever more urgent and he felt as if he were on a sled ride with the bottom of the hill nowhere in sight. She stiffened and moaned as if she were in pain. Sanchez was taken aback, fearing that he had hurt her. He grew still and held his breath in anticipation of what might happen next. She was soon recovered and her hips began to move in a circle once again, but with less urgency.

"Come dear one," she whispered. "Lose yourself in the moment. She bent low and took his right nipple in her mouth, nibbled at it and then began suckling as if he were the woman. He responded by thrusting upward, arching his back. She cried out, but he now was attuned to the sounds of love and he didn't stop until the little death claimed him a second time and he collapsed beneath her spent and sated.

"Come with me please," he said. "We'll make room for you in the boat."

"Shh. Shh, my love," she replied. "I have work to do here. We will be together again soon enough."

Three days later an hour before the sun arose, Bonita walked with him to the boat, kissed him one last time and watched as he and his fellow castaways made themselves as comfortable as they could in the meager space available.

As the boat pulled away from the dock, he kept his eyes locked seaward and refused to look back as they slipped away into the pre-dawn darkness. Emilio was forever sorry for that act of petulance because that was the last time he saw the woman who had looked into his soul and dissipated the horror of the Bay of Pigs.

15

CAMDEN, NEW JERSEY — "That's a hell of a way to greet an old shipmate," Emilio Sanchez said.

He grabbed Mike Kincaid's arm and steered him back into his room at the Motel 6.

He applied enough pressure on Kincaid's elbow to turn the big man around so he could sit on the edge of the bed.

"Come on in, Doc. I think we can persuade him to be reasonable."

Kincaid lost his balance as he sat and flopped back onto the bed, banging the back of his head on the headboard as Sharon Albright stepped into the room.

"Shit!"

Kincaid sat up and swung his feet onto the bed, resting his back against the headboard.

"Who's that?"

Albright stood at the foot of the bed staring at him with the intensity of a dog watching her master eat.

"Someone who can help you," Sanchez said.

"The best thing I could do to help him right now, is to get him a cup of coffee and a couple of Tylenol," Albright observed.

Her voice was rich and low-pitched and startled Kincaid from his befuddlement.

Sanchez noticed Kincaid's surprise.

"Disconcerting, isn't it" he asked. "Her voice changes to fit the circumstance. Sometimes I think there are a bunch of people living inside her."

"There are in most of us," Albright said. Her accent was English now.

Kincaid shook his head like a swimmer trying to clear his ears of water. "So how is an impersonator going to help me? She know who killed my dad? The police seem to think I did."

Kincaid's voice was thick with bourbon.

Sanchez cocked his head like an attentive spaniel.

"I knew your stepfather had been murdered, but I didn't know you were a suspect. So that's why Tweedledum and Tweedledee met you at the cemetery and took you to police headquarters. What was it they took out of your trunk?"

"A gun. Police think it might be the murder weapon, but I have no idea how it got there, or how the hell they knew to look for it. Hey! How did you know that?"

"I was spying on you. Isn't that what spies do?"

"Are you sure you want to go there?" Albright asked. Her voice had assumed a masculine timbre again.

Turning toward her, Sanchez said: "It's OK, Doc. Mike knows what I did for a living."

"Yeah, and that knowledge landed me in the nut house," Kincaid said. "They stamped nervous breakdown all over my military jacket and I never got that promotion to E-5 that you promised me."

Sanchez shrugged. "Apparently it wasn't mine to promise," he said.

"You son of a bitch. You ratted me out didn't you?" Kincaid asked.

"You were a loose cannon. I was ordered to tie you down."

"I told you I would keep quiet, damn it."

"But I could tell you were lying and I wanted to keep you alive. My superiors thought killing you was a better solution."

"So they injected me with drugs, smeared my military record and made me an emotional cripple. I couldn't even cry when my wife died." Kincaid's voice was sharper now, as even the Old Forester faltered under anger's assault.

"You're alive. And you're welcome," Sanchez said.

Kincaid glared at him and struggled to rise.

Sanchez stepped forward, menacingly. "Relax Mike. You're big, but you're impaired and I'm a pro. This is no time to settle old scores."

Kincaid thought better of it and settled himself back on the bed. "So what are you doing here? Have you come back to torture me some more?"

Sanchez stroked his nose with a forefinger, and then pulled at his chin. "Actually, and this is rather embarrassing, I now have a considerable stake in your remembering what we forced you to forget all those years ago.

"And what was that?" Albright interjected.

"I need him to remember what happened on November 16, 1963, in the passageway behind the bridge on the USS *Compass Island*."

"And what was that," Albright repeated.

"I need Mike to remember that Lieutenant Commander Hugh Patterson punched the president of the United States in the jaw and then got thrown down a flight of stairs and paralyzed for his trouble."

Kincaid's face suddenly lost its Old Forester floridity. "I never forgot it," he croaked. "I just can't talk about it. Look at me now! I'm hyperventilating for Christ's sake. Shit, it's hot in here."

Kincaid yanked at the collar of his T-shirt and scrunched his eyes tightly shut like a terrified child standing in line for a roller coaster.

"He OK, Doc?" Sanchez asked.

Albright stepped forward and bent over Kincaid. She put the index and middle fingers of her right hand on his throat and looked at the watch on her left wrist.

After about 15 seconds, she replied: "His heart's racing and he's sweating profusely."

"I can see that by looking at him. Tell me something I don't already know."

"He'll live," she said. Albright stepped away from Kincaid. "Now what's all this about President Kennedy getting socked in the jaw?"

Sanchez's cell phone chirped. He pulled it from his jacket pocket and held up his hand for silence. "Hola. Yes. We're all here. Room 204. OK, bye."

Who was that?" Kincaid and Albright asked, almost in unison.

"A friend."

"You have a friend?" Kincaid asked.

Sanchez bared his teeth. "Actually, she's a business associate, who's going to help me write the definitive book on the Kennedy assassination."

Albright headed for the door. "You may have crapped in the nest with our mutual employer, but I still have a contract and I intend to keep it," she said.

"You've already burnt your bridges behind you," Sanchez replied.

"What do you mean?"

"I mean, all I have to do is let my former superiors know that you met me here and why and your credibility with them is caput."

"Are you threatening me!" she said. Her voice was shrill now and hers alone.

"I didn't sign on for a book project. I thought I could help someone who had been harmed by their government."

"You can still do that, but is that really why you showed up?" Sanchez asked. "I got the idea that you had some sort of fatal attraction for Fairview, New Jersey. Isn't that why you're really here?"

Albright's shoulders slumped. She pulled the chair from beneath the hotel room desk and sat on the edge of it as she struggled with the flight/fight reflex.

Just then, there was a knock on the door.

16

WASHINGTON, D.C. — Wiley Patterson, the junior senator from New Jersey, was at his desk in the Hart Senate Office Building at 9:15 a.m., scanning the front page of the Washington Post when his personal assistant, Jamie Sheaffer, buzzed him on the intercom.

"Can you take a call from your brother?" she asked.

"Sure." He punched the button for his private line. "Talk to me Al."

"Big bro, we have a problem."

"What sort of problem?"

"Nothing we can talk about on the phone. Can you come home?"

"This is a really bad time for me to be out of Washington. I've been put on alert that Dubya may want to talk to me about being his running mate in 2004!"

The excitement in his voice crackled over the phone line and Al Patterson rose above sibling rivalry and actually felt sorry that he'd have to burst his older brother's pretty balloon. Al Patterson had never been one to sugar coat. That's why their father, Hugh, had elevated him to chief executive officer of the family's media empire.

"If this blows up in our face, all the razor cuts and three thousand dollar suits in the world won't mean spit. Dubya will flush you down the nearest shitter like yesterday's turd," Al said.

"So what's the problem?"

"Emilio Sanchez. He wants more money. Significantly more money. He's threatening to sell his story if we don't pay up and . . . he's been talking to a reporter at the Virginia Pilot."

Wiley Patterson's enthusiasm took two turns around the toilet bowl and disappeared down the drain.

"Christ! The cheeky bastard! That's one of our newspapers."

"Yeah, he picked the Pilot just to piss us off."

"What's Dad say?"

"He says you're an ugly son of a bitch and he's always loved me more."

"Ha. Ha. That joke was funny. The first hundred times you told it."

"He says for you to get your ass home!"

"OK. OK. Can you have the Lear at Ronald Reagan in, say, two hours?"

"Done."

The senator hung up without saying goodbye and pushed the button on his intercom. "Jamie. What's up for today?"

"You're supposed to greet the sixth-grade of Sarah Jackson Middle School at 10 a.m. in the Capitol Rotunda. You're to meet with Senator Blust and the Black Caucus at 11:30, but it's a cattle call. You could skip it if you need to. You're on for lunch with Stan Picola, executive director of the South Jersey Shore Chamber of Commerce. He wants to twist your arm about federal funding for beach restoration. The afternoon is mostly clear but the majority whip wants to talk to you about Senate Bill 340.

"What's 340?"

"Base closure."

"That won't clear committee for another three weeks. What's Sam thinking?"

Wiley sighed and drummed his fingers on the desktop. "OK here's what I want you to do. Get Francis to cover the sixth-graders. Have Joe lunch with Stan. Joe can tell Stan that I agree. The beach at Ocean City's as narrow as a spinster's ass, and I MIGHT be willing to get behind a proposal for beach restoration."

"What about Sam Ulrich?" Jamie asked.

"Tell Sam I'll vote with him when 340 clears committee.

Then call Chuck and have him bring the car around. Something's come up I have to deal with. Right now."

"Where we headed boss?"

"Me, not we. Sorry."

"O-KAAAY. Where are YOU headed?"

He gritted his teeth and softened his voice. There was a lesson here. Never sleep with the help.

"Sorry babe. It's family business. I'm off to Philadelphia. I have to confer with the old man."

17

WEDNESDAY, SEPTEMBER 24, 2003

CECLITON, MARYLAND — The day had proceeded at an altogether satisfactory pace: Reveille at 6:30 a.m., just like always, a quick shower, then a leisurely breakfast of orange juice, black coffee, wheat toast and raisin oatmeal, which Robert Cabot consumed as he poured over the papers. He read The New York Times first, just to get his blood boiling. Next came The Washington Post. Then, finally, he got the "real" news from The Washington Times and the Wall Street Journal.

Cabot, 70, a retired intelligence officer who had reached the pinnacle of his career as a deputy director of the Central Intelligence Agency in Ronald Reagan's second term, was enjoying the good life on a modest horse farm, situated in the northeastern most part of Maryland. He had sold off the last of his standard breds in a fit of pique three years earlier after his best trotter had failed to place at the Hambletonian; this despite the trainer's assertion that Cabot's Juggernaut was a sure thing. Cabot missed the sounds of the horses snorting and cavorting in his paddock, but he didn't miss the expense. He diverted the extra cash into other games that amused him much more, such as affecting the outcome of beltway politics by means both overt and covert.

Cabot was far enough away from the nation's capital to maintain some objectivity as the political winds swirled about the beltway, yet close enough to exert influence when exertion was of the essence.

Cabot lived alone, although he did employ a man Friday who occupied the gatehouse on the edge of his little 15-acre slice of Eden. He was fit in his 71st year because he had always eschewed the excesses of his hard-living colleagues in the inteligence service. He followed a regimen of regular exercise religiously, harkening back to his days as a midshipman at the Naval Academy.

He was short and slight and manicured. He maintained his snow-white hair with the same care he maintained his waist-line. And he took inordinate pride in a cholesterol reading of 145 and a PSA of .7. He knew a lot of 40-year-olds who would kill for those numbers.

Although he had retired 10 years ago, Cabot still offered his services as a consultant to his former employer at bargain basement prices. His willingness to work cheap was construed as patriotism by some and to be fair, he was patriotic. But his patriotism was bundled about a hard core of self-interest. Cabot was eager to maintain his influence in the agency he had done so much to mold.

Consulting work aside, Cabot often took on special projects of his own initiative when he saw opportunities to affect government in a fashion in keeping with his own political proclivities. Cabot was a Spartan among Athenians. He paid lip service to the trappings of democracy, but he knew that the way of life he enjoyed could be preserved in one fashion alone—the exercise of absolute power by an elite ruling class. George W. Bush, with the not-so-subtle influence of Dick Cheney had done much to restore the imperial presidency destroyed by those traitors Woodward and Bernstein. But Cheney was too old to perpetuate the dream and Bush was too damn stupid; a younger, smarter, champion was necessary and Cabot was putting his money on Wiley Patterson, the junior senator from New Jersey and son of his protégé at the Naval Academy, Hugh Patterson.

That afternoon, Cabot planned to give a review of Stephen Ambrose's three-volume biography of the great Richard Milhous Nixon at the Cecilton Branch of the Cecil County Library. It mattered not that he would be addressing a captive audience. The library hosted his lectures because he was a patron with deep pockets. The friends of the library would make sure that the seats were full. That people who abhorred his politics would occupy many of them bothered him not one bit. There was little to be gained by preaching to the choir.

Cabot was standing in his foyer dressed in his signature outfit of British tan slacks, white shirt, wingtips and blue blazer and ready to head off in his meticulously maintained 1984 Ca-dillac Seville when the phone rang in his study.

He thought about ignoring the phone but, glancing at his watch, he decided that he had enough time to tell whoever was calling on his private line to go to hell. Cabot always arrived at appointments an hour early just to case the venue for suspicious activity that might imperil his mission. Old habits die hard. Dropping his keys on the lowboy in the foyer, he hurried into his study and caught the phone on the fifth ring, just before his answering machine would have picked up.

"I'm late for an appointment," he said. "So this had better be good."

"It's not good, but it demands your attention," Al Patterson replied. "Sanchez is demanding another million dollars, five hundred thousand now, and five hundred thousand when he delivers the documents. If we don't pay up he's going to go public with what he knows."

Cabot plopped down in his padded leather swivel chair, and spun it around so he could stare out the window at his empty paddock.

"What's your Dad make of that?"

"Dad won't pay one dime more. He's already ponied up a million and has a bad case of buyer's regret. He thinks that since Wiley is two generations removed from the organized crime stigma, we'll be able to ride out any negative publicity Sanchez might be able to stir up," Al Patterson replied.

"Your Dad may be right but we can't take the chance that he's wrong. How is Sanchez proposing that we pay him the money?"

"He wants it deposited in a bank in the Cayman Islands. He's given me an account number."

Cabot sighed. Sanchez was playing a clever game; Cabot had to give him that. He was pretending to go after the Pattersons, knowing full well that Cabot had an even bigger stake in suppressing what he knew about the Kennedy assassination. There were two possible revenue streams and Sanchez was trying to tap both of them.

"Give me the account number," he said.

Al Patterson read off a nine-digit number, which Cabot jotted down on a note pad beside the phone.

"I'll make the deposit, but damn it! This puts a serious dent in my discretionary budget and I may have to take some decisive steps to recover the money once Sanchez has been neutralized. You can't get squeamish on me."

"Just because Dad's got cold feet doesn't mean I have. You've just got to give me . . . Wiley deniability. No malfeasance can be traced back to the senator!"

"Malfeasance! That's a puny word for what I have in mind. I'm willing to do your dirty work, but I'll own your souls. Remember that."

Al Patterson changed the subject. "What about Dad? Are we cutting him out of the loop?"

"Your father has lost his nerve," Cabot said. "He doesn't need to know our plans. In fact it's much better that he remain in the dark. Understand?"

"Yes. I understand. Not a word."

"Luco Pepitone's on the job, isn't he?" Cabot asked.

"Yes. He's got a team watching Sanchez and he's reporting an unusual confluence of personnel."

Cabot already knew this, but he feigned ignorance. Al Patterson had no need to know that Cabot was pulling the old mobster's strings.

"What do you mean by that?"

"Sanchez is in Camden, New Jersey. He's established contact with Mike Kincaid and he's coerced the lady shrink to join them. And here's another thing . . ."

Patterson paused for dramatic effect.

Cabot lost patience. "Out with it man! I haven't the time to dilly dally!"

"Sanchez is sleeping with the enemy."

"What do you mean by that?"

"He's been in touch with a reporter at the Virginia Pilot. Offered her the definitive story on the Kennedy assassination. Apparently they've had several meetings. We've killed the story, of course. But I had to put the editor's ass in a sling to do it."

"The Virginia Pilot? Subtlety was never Emilio's strong suit," Cabot said.

"Yep. Pepitone thinks we should wipe them all off the table right now. I told him to wait until I conferred with you."

"Pepitone always has been . . . decisive. What he proposes is tempting, but the documents are still out there somewhere and only Sanchez knows exactly where they are. So it's safer to stick to the original plan. Stay close to Sanchez. Let him retrieve the documents. He brought Kincaid, the reporter and the doctor on board just to get our attention. If I know Sanchez, he'll take care of them. Then Pepitone and his boys can take care of Sanchez."

"That's a hell of a body count, are you sure you can . . . contain the situation?"

"I'm an expert at hiding bodies," Cabot said.

"And you'll take care of the money?"

"Yes. I'll take care of the money." Cabot hung up the phone without saying goodbye, and glanced at his watch. He still had a half an hour to make the 15-minute trip to the library so he decided to meditate for five minutes, restore his pulse to an athletic 60 beats per minute and chase the doubt from the corners of his mind.

As he meditated, he reflected upon his first meeting with Midshipman Hugh Patterson forty nine years earlier. Patterson, a lowly plebe, was struggling with the rigors of calculus, and Cabot, a firstie in his final year at the academy, was assigned as his tutor. Cabot by then was resigned to his sexual orientation and thought he recognized similar proclivities in the young plebe. Patterson was tall and slight and his voice had a slightly effeminate timbre.

Alas, from Cabot's perspective anyway, Patterson was decidedly heterosexual. He took well to Cabot's tutoring and diplomatically rebuffed his mentor's subtle attempts at seduction before they could reach a level impeachable by the authorities at the Academy. For that Cabot was eternally grateful. He had kept his sexual orientation under lock and key ever since, mindful of Patterson's gentle reproach when he had allowed his hand to linger too softly and too suggestively on the plebe's shoulder for too long.

"A pederast is never welcome in a society of righteous men."

How Cabot's cheeks had burned with shame. Patterson, displaying discretion unusual in one so young, had not even looked up from his book. The moment had passed without doing either man irreparable harm.

Cabot was able to repay that kindness nine years later. By then a commander in naval intelligence on special assignment with the Central Intelligence Agency, he had been dispatched by his superiors at Langley to help Patterson put his life back together and tend to the damage control that had been ordained by the 35th president of the United States. Patterson was a broken man both physically and mentally, but Cabot had fixed him.

That was his gift. He was a fixer. And now some more fixing needed to be done to clear Wiley Patterson's path to the White House and to save America from itself.

18

WEDNESDAY, SEPTEMBER 24, 2003

CAMDEN, NEW JERSEY — Three cups of coffee, a quart of orange juice and three Advils restored Mike Kincaid to some semblance of normalcy, but he turned down an invitation to join the others for breakfast at Dennys. His stomach was too queasy for bacon and eggs.

A long hot shower beckoned. Afterward, a bracing lecture completed his recovery. His late mother, Kathleen Kincaid Manley, incarnate once again as his conscience, delivered it. She spoke to him from the swirling mist that gathered in the Motel 6 bathroom where the exhaust fan was inoperable.

"Shame on you for being a drunk, but quit walking around like a whipped puppy. Your stepfather taught you to be stronger than that," she said.

"But he's dead now, Ma. And the police have all but accused me of killing him—just like I killed you."

"Pish Tosh. You didn't kill me. A bungling surgeon did. Quit beating yourself up over not delivering that phone message from the doctor. Jacob took me to the hospital anyway."

"He would have got you there sooner if I'd told you that the doctor had called about your white blood count."

"The surgeon would have been just as incompetent if I'd arrived at the hospital two hours earlier. Put that nonsense out of your mind. And don't worry about the police, either. You were two hundred miles away when Jacob was murdered, with witnesses to prove it. The police are the least of your worries."

"So what's the worst of them?"

Kincaid already knew the answer but his mother told him anyway.

"The worst of them is that you feel responsible for my death and for Alice's death. I've already absolved you in my death and

God has forgiven you for killing Alice. I know it because he told me so."

Wondering whether he was crazy, Kincaid smeared shaving cream on his face. He used a hand towel to wipe the steam from the bathroom mirror. He took up a disposable razor and tackled the coarse hair beneath his lower lip first, just like always.

"Anyone with half a brain knows that Jacob was his own man," his mother said. "He wouldn't move from Fairview no matter what, so you can't stop feeling guilty about that, too."

Kincaid bent close to the mirror to tackle the tricky spot on his Adams apple. For reasons he couldn't fathom, he felt as if he'd just turned a corner. This day portended a clean break in the unrelenting tedium of his life. That prospect excited him, but it also scared him because there is some comfort in the tedium of a routine—even one that's rooted in remorse.

He was dressed and sitting at a table with a game of solitaire spread out in front of him, when the breakfast crew came back from Dennys. Kincaid saw them approach through the window, but he stayed put. Sanchez had taken one of Kincaid's motel room swipe keys with him and opened the door without making Kincaid get up. He stepped back to allow first Gale Johnston and then Sharon Albright to enter the room.

The three of them encircled Kincaid like football players surrounding a teammate who had just taken one in the nuts.

"You can play the six of diamonds on the seven of spades," Albright observed.

"Jesus guys. Give me some room. I'm starting to feel claustrophobic."

Kincaid threw up his arms in exasperation.

Albright and Johnston retreated to the back of the motel room where they perched uneasily on opposite ends of the second bed. The animosity between the two women was palpable. He glanced at Sanchez wondering what might have happened at breakfast to set the two women at odds.

Sanchez shrugged his shoulders. "Oil and water," he said.

"Huh?"

"They don't mix."

Kincaid fielded the allusion and nodded.

"I was talking to the Doc over breakfast and she seems to think she can help you defuse the psychological landmines laid by the shrinks at Walter Reed all those years ago," Sanchez said.

Albright's voice was brisk and business like. "Emilio showed me your file. Their methods were pretty sophisticated for the time, but crude by today's standards. They drugged you and laid down a subconscious suggestion to make you feel extremely uncomfortable whenever you think about your encounter with John F. Kennedy. They established a subconscious link between Kennedy and a very unpleasant event in your life. I would imagine that you feel pretty uncomfortable whenever the general topic of Kennedy is brought up."

"What was the suggestion?" Kincaid asked.

"I think you know the answer to that question, although it may be difficult for you to articulate it," Albright replied.

Kincaid pretended to concentrate on his game of solitaire. He played a ten of spades on a jack of hearts and counted off three cards to continue his game.

"Eight of hearts. No help."

He counted off three more cards.

"They drugged you and then suggested that Kennedy's visit to the *Compass Island* was fundamentally related to a traumatic event in your life," Albright prompted.

"Care to guess what that event was?" Sanchez asked.

Kincaid pulled at the loose skin along his jaw line. Beads of perspiration popped out on his forehead.

"Do you remember a phone message you forgot to relay?" Albright asked.

Kincaid jerked his head like a boxer slipping a punch and his eyes welled up with tears. He swept the cards into a pile and busied himself with turning them all the same way. He wiped his eyes with the backs of his wrists.

"It was my senior year in high school," he said. "I'd just played my final game of football. I caught seven passes for 130 yards and the head coach at Rutgers talked to me after the game. Said he'd be offering me a scholarship, a full ride."

Kincaid's eyes lost focus and he stared off into space.

Albright rose to her feet and approached Kincaid tentatively, like a cat stalking a squirrel. "And?"

"Mom wasn't home when I came home from school. She hadn't been feeling well and she left me a note saying she'd gone to the pharmacy for some medicine."

Kincaid scrubbed his face with both hands.

"The phone rang and I answered it. It was Doctor Fuller's office calling. The nurse asked for mom and when I told her she was out at the pharmacy, she said: 'Tell your mom not to take any over the counter laxatives and have her call us right away. Her test results are in.'

Kincaid wandered off into a labyrinth of regret. Albright steered him toward the exit.

"You forgot to deliver that message didn't you, Mike?" she asked.

Her voice was gentle, soft and calming, but Kincaid took little solace in it.

The emotional dam broke. Tears streamed down his face. "I went off to meet my girl friend, Sue Fletcher, at Barney's Luncheonette. I wanted to tell her all about my scholarship offer. And I was in such a hurry that I forgot to leave a note on the message board. Mom came back from the pharmacy, took her laxative and eight hours later she was dead."

Kincaid threw the cards against the window and shoved back his chair. His eyes stabbed wildly about the room before settling on Sanchez. "I got drunk and told you that story and you used it against me. Fuck you Skeeter. I thought you were my friend."

He took two quick steps toward Sanchez and threw a crisp overhand at Sanchez's jaw. The CIA agent could have countered it easily but he sensed Kincaid's need for catharsis. Instead, he rolled with the punch and went crashing onto the bed, having slipped much of its impact. Sanchez sat up and rubbed his jaw.

"Try that again and I'll kill you," he said.

His words were delivered with a flat inflection that was chilling. It was as if a demon had peaked from behind the curtain of Sanchez's soul and offered a glimpse of the horrors that lay within.

Kincaid backed up as his fight/flight meter redlined on flight.

Albright saved his honor. She took him by the arm and led him back to the table.

"Sit," she said.

Kincaid sat, like a well-trained basset.

Albright took a chair opposite Kincaid and took his left hand in both of hers over the table. "Listen. The hacks at Walter Reed implanted the hypnotic suggestion that you think about your mother's death every time the subject of John F. Kennedy arose. They suggested that the way to escape your guilt was to suppress certain aspects of the president's visit to your ship. I think

I can restore your memory. Give me a few more sessions and we could resolve some of your other issues as well."

"What issues?"

"The issues that led to your consuming the better part of a bottle of bourbon last night."

"What do you propose?" Kincaid asked.

"I propose injecting you with sodium pentothal and seeing if we can sever the psychological tether linking your guilt over your mother's death with your memories of Kennedy's visit to your ship."

She paused, staring deeply into Kincaid's eyes. He stared back, mesmerized. She blinked in slow motion, allowing him to peer into a private room within her soul. "You OK with that, Mikey?"

There was something familiar in the inflection of her voice. Sanchez was right; she was a vocal chameleon. Her words carried a familiar subtext that he couldn't quite place. Then it hit him. Whether by design or by accident, her voice had taken on tonal qualities he associated with his mother.

His voice was thick. He had to force the words out past the lump in his throat. "Mom used to call me Mikey. How did you know that? ESP?"

"I really don't know. Sometimes things just come to me and I say them. I've learned to trust those instincts as a therapist. Mikey just seemed to fit," Albright said. She patted his hand. "Now, would you like me to treat you?"

"Sure," he heard himself saying. "When do we begin?"

"As soon as I chase these two out of the room. Come on guys; we discussed this over breakfast. Psychiatry isn't a spectator sport."

When neither Sanchez nor Johnston moved, she added: "Go back to your rooms and I'll call you when I'm done."

Gale Johnston glowered.

"God damn it Emilio. I don't like this one bit. If you want this book to have moral authority, you can't keep any secrets from me."

Sanchez pulled at his lip.

"Are you going to tape this like you do all your shrink sessions?" Sanchez asked. "That way we'd have a record to satisfy our resident journalist."

Albright nodded. "I planned to do that, with Mike's consent of course. "You OK with that Mike?"

Kincaid nodded.

Johnston followed Sanchez out of the room. She banged the door closed behind them.

Albright arose and turned on the lights in the vanity alcove, using the rheostat to dim them to cocktail lounge intensity. She closed the draperies and turned to face Kincaid who had been enjoying the view of her behind as she reached for the drapery cord. Kincaid blushed as if he'd just caught himself having carnal thoughts about his sister.

"Why don't you stretch out on the bed Mike? You'll be much more comfortable there."

Kincaid arose and started toward the bed closest to the door on knees suddenly stiff with indecision.

"Use the other bed, please. I want to sit in a chair between the beds so I can use the nightstand," Albright explained.

As Kincaid settled in, situating the pillows just so against the headboard, Albright moved a chair close to the bed and put her handbag on the nightstand. Perching on the edge of the chair she studied Kincaid's face as if she was concentrating on the instructions for a new digital watch. "Do you understand the concept of aversion therapy?" she asked.

"More or less. I did a story on it once. It's often used to treat alcoholics and drug abusers, isn't it?"

"That's right," Albright said. "It's particularly effective for behavior modification in subjects who are susceptible to hypnosis."

"Can't everyone be hypnotized?"

"Actually only about 20 percent of the population is susceptible. It's that 20 percent that the lounge hypnotists single out when they take their acts to colleges, coffee houses and clubs. You're lucky you fall within that 20 percent."

"Why?"

"If you weren't, even drugs wouldn't have been enough to plant such a strong and lasting aversion. It's quite remarkable, actually."

Albright shivered as if she were chilled. She added: "and inordinately lucky from your perspective."

"What do you mean by that?"

"Sanchez is right. He probably did you a favor. From what he tells me, you witnessed an event that threatened the careers of some important CIA operatives. I'm surprised that they didn't opt for a more permanent solution to the security risk you then presented."

It was Kincaid's turn to shiver. "Do you know what I saw?"

"In outline, I didn't want to prejudice my treatment of you by asking too many questions of Emilio. We need a true record of what you remember seeing, not one contaminated by my expectations of what you should be remembering. Make sense?"

"I guess so."

"You ready for this?"

"What the hell. I'm pretty sure you aren't going to shoot me up with a heroin overdose and it will be a relief to get this monkey off my back."

Albright rummaged about in her purse and withdrew a miniature tape recorder, a vial of medicine, a small foil pouch, a packaged disposal syringe and a short length of red rubber tubing, which she laid out in a neat row on the nightstand. "Give me your arm."

Supporting his arm with her left hand she smacked the inside of his elbow sharply three times with the fore and middle fingers of her right hand. "You've got nice veins."

Releasing his arm, she ripped open the foil pouch to reveal a white pad that reeked of rubbing alcohol. She swabbed off a spot in the bend of his left elbow and tossed the pad into the waste can.

She looped the red rubber tourniquet about his bicep and pulled it tight. Next she took up the syringe, tearing it from its sterile packaging, which she also deposited in the trashcan.

"You travel with that stuff?" Kincaid asked. Nerves lent his face the chalky patina of a corpse.

"I suggested this intervention over breakfast, and we stopped by a pharmacy on the way back." Albright picked up the medicine vial and loaded the syringe. She squirted a quick shot through the needle to clear it of air and looked at Kincaid appraisingly. "You ready?"

Kincaid nodded.

Albright punched the record button on her tape recorder and jabbed the needle into the prominent vein in the crook of Kincaid's left arm.

"Ouch!"

Albright grinned. "Best to do it quickly. Sometimes the anticipation is more painful than the needle stick. Now relax, in a minute or two we can begin."

She pushed the plunger.

Within seconds, Kincaid was as loose as a $10 whore.

"How are you feeling?" Her words floated by like subtitles in a French language movie. Kincaid had to concentrate to read them.

"Relasched." The word came out in a mumble as if he had a lip full of Novocain.

"What's your favorite vacation spot?"

"Rehoboth Beach."

Albright smiled. Talk about your serendipity.

"Good. Now I want you to imagine yourself lying on a beach towel at Rehoboth Beach. It's a warm August day. You can feel the sun playing tag with a cloud. You can smell sunscreen and the vinegar on Thresher french fries. You can hear the sea gulls screech, the rumble of the surf as the waves crash and the delighted squeals as the surf chases a four-year-old back to his mother. How do you feel?"

"Good. Peachful."

"We're going to talk about some things that may make you feel uncomfortable. Should you feel panicky, just race back to that beach towel and pretend that you're observing something that's happening to someone else. You're relaxed. Happy. Safe."

"Safe."

"Now I'd like you to count backward from five and when you hit one, I want you to let go. I want you to melt into the mattress and remember what happened on November 16, 1963."

"Five. Four. Three. Two. One."

Oblivion.

19

CAMDEN, NEW JERSEY — "At the time of John F. Kennedy's visit to the USS *Compass Island*, I was a journalist mate third class, an E-4, the equivalent of a corporal in the Army," Mike Kincaid said.

Kincaid was comfortably arranged before a small round table in front of the window of his motel room. He was pushed back from the table with his legs crossed, for all appearances at peace with his world, save for an intermittent twitch of his left eye as he spoke.

"We were steaming along the coast of South Carolina on our way to participate in a test firing of a Polaris missile by the submarine USS *Andrew Jackson* when the skipper, Commander Julius Earnhart, called me to his stateroom to iron out the details of how we were going to handle the president's visit. He wanted a story and plenty of pictures for All Hands Magazine."

"Why does he keep twitching like that?" Johnston asked.

Albright bristled. "It's a post hypnotic suggestion. I told Mike that he could dissipate his anxiety by twitching his eyebrow. It'll work, too, if you keep your damn mouth shut."

Johnston looked daggers at Albright who was seated next to her on the bed closest the window. Johnston didn't rise to the rebuke, but she extended and retracted the point of her pen in an annoying fashion.

Click. Click. Click. Click. Click.

"Give the God damn pen a rest it's getting on my nerves," Sanchez said.

He was sprawled out on the other bed, obscured from Kincaid's view by the two women.

"It's OK Sharon, I can take care of myself," Kincaid said. "Now do you want to hear my story, or don't you?"

His left eye twitched.

"I've got another idea Mike. Why don't I just play the tape of your hypnosis session? It will save you a lot of time and probably some pain as well. I've got the tape queued up to the critical part on the bridge of the *Compass Island*. Is that OK with everyone?

Kincaid nodded. Johnston and Sanchez looked at each other and shrugged.

Albright punched a button and the tape recorder faithfully disgorged the sounds of Mike Kincaid shifting on the bed and of a car driving by in the parking lot outside.

"Turn it up. I can't hear." Johnston clicked her pen. Albright cranked up the volume. "Where are you now?"

"On the bridge."

Mike Kincaid's voice sounded far away and dreamy. The tape spit and hissed.

"Who else is on the bridge?"

"The helmsman Maurice Brothers and Chief Erving; he's quartermaster of the watch."

"Anyone else?"

A pause as if Kincaid were counting on his fingers.

"Yes. Lieutenant Richardson, the OD, and Lieutenant Junior Grade Jerry Brown. He's the JOD"

Sanchez signaled Albright to stop the tape.

He explained: "OD stands for officer of the deck. JOD means junior officer of the deck."

He nodded to Albright who restarted the tape.

"Is that all?"

The tape hissed as Kincaid relived the moment.

"Lieutenant Commander Patterson. He's here, too."

Johnston shifted on the bed.

"Can't we move this along?" she asked. Albright held a finger to her lips. "What's happening now?"

"We're all gathering around the helmsman. Admiral Gallagher asks Kennedy if he'd like to steer the ship."

Long pause.

"Kennedy says: 'Damn admiral this thing certainly is bigger than a PT boat.' We all laugh."

The toilet flushes in the background and the tape records the sound of Kincaid shifting on the bed.

"It's OK Mike, it's just the toilet."

In real time, Kincaid observed:

"Damn toilet does that sometimes. Flushes itself. It's annoying as hell. Wakes me up at night."

Back to Memorex.

"Refocus Mike. What's happening now?"

"Captain Earnhart says: 'Mr. President. There's someone I want you to meet.'

Pause.

"Mike?"

"Sorry. Yeah. Earnhart motions Patterson to come on over. He does, but you can tell he has an attitude."

"How so?"

"Patterson's a tall guy, but he's all stooped over. He salutes the president, but he's glaring at him. I can tell that Captain Earnhart is pissed. He tries to cover for Patterson. He says: 'Lieutenant Commander Patterson is in charge of our special operations department. We had to call him back from bereavement leave to oversee today's missile shot. His mother died unexpectedly.'"

Tape hiss. Squeak. Squeak. Squeak. A maid passes by outside the room pushing a trolley with a wheel in need of some grease.

"Patterson says: "Mom asked to be remembered to you sir . . . in her suicide note. She met you at a Princeton football game in 1935. She was a freshman at Bryn Mawr College at the time.'

Gale Johnston clicked her pen and edged forward on the bed. The tape hissed some more.

"Kennedy says: 'What was your mother's name?'"

Sounds of the bed shaking and laughter.

"What's so funny Mike?"

"Patterson says: 'Oh come on now Mr. President how many girls from Bryn Mawr College did you fuck in 1935?'"

More sounds of laughter.

"Mike?"

"Admiral Gallagher is as red as a fire engine. 'Captain Earnhart,' he says. 'I want this man locked up in the brig for gross insubordination. I expect you to handle his punishment at Captain's mast."

Tape hiss.

"Skeeter?"

"What?"

"Emilio just came onto the bridge. He's waving a piece of yellow teletype paper. He says: 'Mr. President, I have an urgent dispatch."

In real time, Sanchez said: "Stop the tape there for a minute will you Sharon?"

Albright punched the button.

"That dispatch still is top secret because it relates to the president's assassination. I'll explain how later. For now, let Mike continue with his story."

Sanchez nodded at Albright who restarted the tape.

"Kennedy is reading the dispatch. He hands it back to Sanchez. Then . . ."

"Yes Mike?"

"The president embraces Patterson. He says: 'I do, of course remember your mother. She had a kind heart. I am so sorry she is dead.'"

Another long pause.

"Mike? What's happening?"

"Kennedy tells Gallagher and Earnhart 'no further action regarding this matter is warranted. As far as the Navy is concerned this case is closed. 'Do you understand gentlemen?' Gallagher and Earnhart agree. What choice do they have?

"Kennedy says: 'Very well. Admiral, may I suggest that we take up station for the missile launch? This dispatch tells me the *Andrew Jackson* is awaiting my order to fire.'

"Captain Earnhart nods at me and motions toward the port side door at the rear of the bridge. Guess he wants to take the interior stairs down through officers' country. I walk through the door, turn left and take a couple of steps down the passageway toward CIC to clear the way for the president. Skeeter comes through the door and stands beside me."

In real time, Kincaid filled in the blanks. "CIC stands for combat information center."

Another pause.

"What's going on now Mike?"

"I'm reloading my camera. It's a narrow passageway. Earnhart, Gallagher and the secret service agents, step back to allow the president to go down the stairs first. I focus my camera on the president . . . No. I can't do this."

On tape, Kincaid's voice sounds desperate.

Albright punched the stop button.

"This is the specific incident the CIA wanted to obscure in Mike's memory. Without the sodium pentothal, he would never have been able to articulate it. She glanced at Kincaid, who was still sitting at the table. "You OK with this Mike?"

He nodded, but his eyebrow twitched.

"Yeah. It's still uncomfortable. But a part of me is relieved that this is out in the open now. The pressure's gone. I feel like, like . . . I'm me again."

Albright smiled at him.

"OK. Here we go."

She pushed the play button.

Sobbing. Kincaid is sobbing. The tinny quality of the tape can't obscure his despair.

"I can't do this . . . it hurts. The devil is inside me. He's screaming at me to shut up. Shut up. Shut up. Make him stop. My ears are bleeding. Mom I'm so sorry I killed you."

More sobs. Then Albright's voice, clearer now because she's moved closer to the microphone.

"Mike. Mike. It's all right. Remember what I told you. No one can hurt you here. If you're scared just twitch your eye. That's right. You're safe. You're among friends. Twitch your eyebrow. That's right. Twitch. There, see? Everything is fine. Now tell me what happened next."

Residual sniffles. Kincaid blows his nose.

"I'm looking through the view finder and focusing on Kennedy, but in my peripheral vision I see movement. Patterson elbows Earnhart and Gallagher out of the way. He says: 'God damn it, that's not good enough!' I punch the shutter button on my Rolleiflix just as Patterson socks the president of the United States in the jaw."

Kincaid's words arrive in a rush:

"The president stumbles back against the bulkhead. A Secret Service agent dives at Patterson but misses. Patterson runs toward the stairs. He trips on Captain Earnhart's feet and careens headlong down the stairs. The secret service agents go flying after him. Kennedy regains his feet and calls down to them:

"'Be careful, you fools! Can't you see that he has a neck injury?'

"I'm standing right next to the president. So is Skeeter. Kennedy whispers: 'Please don't hurt him. Please don't hurt my son."

20

WEDNESDAY, SEPTEMBER 24, 2003

CAMDEN, NEW JERSEY — Emilio Sanchez arose from the bed, crossed the room and took a seat across from Kincaid at the hotel room table. He pulled a flask from his sweatshirt pocket, unscrewed the top and took a long pull from it. His Adams apple jumped up and down as he drank.

He set the flask down on the table and looked at Kincaid, appraisingly.

Want a drink?" he asked, motioning toward the flask. Kincaid winced.

"No, I don't suppose you do."

Sanchez took another short pull on the flask and wiped his mouth with the back of his hand. "Well now. How would you folks like to know who really killed John F. Kennedy."

Sanchez set the flask carefully in the center of the table without bothering to replace the cap.

"Quit screwing around Emilio and tell your story," Johnston said. "That's why we're all here, isn't it?"

Sanchez grinned like a wolf. "Yes, I suppose it is." He took a deep breath. "Would it surprise you to know that John F. Kennedy was killed on Nov. 22, 1963 in Dallas, Texas, by Lee Harvey Oswald."

Johnston exhaled explosively. "Jesus Christ! For this I quit my job at the Virginia Pilot!"

"Sorry Gale." Sanchez didn't seem contrite.

"The bigger question of course is who was behind the conspiracy to kill JFK. I've been piecing that story together for years and, now, with Mike's input, and Gale on board as wordsmith, I'm ready to share that story with the world."

"And collect a nice fat check to comfort you in your old age," Albright said.

Sanchez took no offense, or pretended not to. "Money's a good thing. But even more important, once we put the story out there, my former employers, finally, will get what they deserve."

"Are you saying the CIA was behind Kennedy's assassination?" Kincaid asked. "That theory is old hat."

Sanchez shook his head. "The CIA had no direct role in the planning or the execution. What I am saying is that the CIA allowed the president to be killed and to this day has good reason to obscure the truth of its negligence."

"Go on," Johnston said. "You've told me some of this before, but I'm interested in seeing how you're going to tie this in with the story Kincaid just told us. So Kennedy fathered an illegitimate son who assaulted him on a U.S. Navy ship at sea a week before his assassination. I don't think we can hang an entire book on that."

Sanchez looked at the flask on the table, but didn't pick it up. "I'll connect the dots. I promise you." He pulled at his nose. "At the time of Kennedy's assassination, America was embroiled in the Cold War. But the Kennedys, Jack and Bobby, his attorney general, were engaged in another war much closer to home. Anyone want to guess who they were fighting?"

Johnston started to say something and Sanchez held a finger to his lips.

"Shh! Gale, keep quiet, you already know the answer."

Kincaid and Albright looked at each other and shrugged.

"Poverty?" Albright asked.

Kincaid smiled. "You're showing your age . . . or lack of it. That was Lyndon Johnson's war . . . that and Vietnam. God must love irony."

Kincaid thought for a moment. "Organized crime?"

Sanchez nodded vigorously. "That's right! Bobby Kennedy had a hardon for organized crime. Meanwhile, JFK had a peculiar passion of his own."

He saw Kincaid's eyes twinkle and quickly added: "And no, I don't mean Marilyn Monroe. John F. Kennedy was mortified by the failure of the Bay of Pigs invasion of Cuba in 1961. Considered it a blot on his presidency, even though the planning for that fiasco was carried out largely by the Eisenhower administration. The president was obsessed with bringing down Fidel Castro."

Sanchez paused and studied the faces of his audience.

"Not many people know it, but right before his assassination, Kennedy signed off on a second invasion of Cuba. D-day was supposed to be December 2, 1963. We were locked and loaded and then . . ."

Sanchez smacked the tabletop with the palm of his right hand, sloshing some whiskey from his flask onto the tabletop.

"The ball-less bastard lost his nerve!'

Sanchez swiped the spilt whiskey onto the floor with the blade of his right hand and picked up the flask. His hand was shaking as he took a deep draught. He set the flask down and rearranged its position until it occupied the exact center of the table.

"Why don't you give the whiskey a rest?" Albright asked. "I thought we'd drowned those demons."

"It's not whiskey. It's rum. Cruzan rum, distilled in Saint Croix. And I need a little fortification. This story makes my blood boil."

Albright sighed and shook her head.

"Anyway. Working through an emissary named Enrique Ruiz-Williams, Jack and Bobby persuaded Cuban Army General Juan Almedia to kill Castro and his brother, Raul, and assume control of the government," Sanchez said. "The Kennedys promised the overt support of the United States government to neutralize the 20,000 Russian troops still occupying Cuba," Sanchez said.

"To make the coup more palatable to the Cuban people and to sell its authenticity on the world stage, my mentor Ruiz-Williams, Harry we called him, was poised to lead a second invasion of expatriates."

Sanchez's eyes lost focus. "I fought with Harry during the first invasion in 1962. He was horribly wounded but saw to the comfort of his men before he accepted any quarter from our captors. God, what a man."

"You fought at the Bay of Pigs? You never told me that," Kincaid said.

"There are a lot of things I didn't tell you, such as what I really was doing aboard the Curlew when you rescued me."

Gale Johnston clicked her pen.

"I hate to detour this little trip down Memory Lane, but what in the hell are you talking about?"

"Forty one years ago I was a crew member aboard a two-masted schooner called the Curlew, which foundered off Bermuda in a heavy storm. Mike's ship, the USS *Compass Island*, answered our mayday. That's how we met," Sanchez said.

"And what were you really doing aboard the Curlew?" Kincaid asked.

Sanchez smiled.

"An interesting schooner, the Curlew. She's still afloat, you know. She was salvaged after the storm and is doing charter service somewhere on the West Coast."

Sanchez turned his head and stared out the window at the parking lot.

"The Curlew was built in 1926 at a shipyard in Maine, originally for a rich member of the New York Yacht Club," Sanchez said. "She was owned variously by the Merchant Marine Academy, and the U.S. Coast Guard. Ironically, Kennedy himself is reputed to have captained her during her Coast Guard days when she was stationed not far from here at Cape May."

Sanchez turned to Kincaid.

"By the time you plucked me off her decks, she was serving an entirely different master. Care to guess who?"

"The CIA?" Johnston blurted out.

Sanchez nodded. "She belonged ostensibly to a Philadelphia lawyer named Berto Rinaldi who specialized in keeping organized crime bosses out of prison. But Gale is right, Rinaldi was fronting for the CIA, which had dispatched me to return to Cuba and plot the assassination of Fidel Castro. That nor'easter blew that plan way off course."

Gale clicked her pen some more. "All this is interesting back story, and it will add to the credibility of our book. Master spy reveals all. That sort of thing, but what does this have to do with Kennedy's assassination?"

Sanchez's voice was heavy with sarcasm when he said: "Almedia was a man of principle. He didn't mind being America's whore in Cuba but he wouldn't stoop to murder. That, at least was the coward's rationale. The truth is that the bastard lost his nerve at the last minute and cost Bonita Salvadore her life."

"Who is Bonita Salvadore?" Johnston asked.

She sat up straight on the edge of the bed. It was clear that Sanchez was wandering into unfamiliar territory.

Sanchez didn't reply. He stared at the parking lot. A bird flew by and spattered shit on the window.

Albright answered the question for him. "Bonita Salvadore was his distant cousin . . . and his lover. She hid him from Castro's troops after the Bay of Pigs invasion and she stayed behind to continue the resistance when Emilio fled back to Miami."

"And how would you know that?" Johnston asked.

"I'm his therapist," Albright said.

"Aren't you violating some sort of professional code by telling us that?" Kincaid asked.

Albright wiped her forehead. "I think I'm on safe ground; I'm not revealing that he likes to wear women's underwear or anything like that."

Sanchez's reverie shattered like a dropped dish. He laughed. "I'm a boxer sort of guy."

Sanchez shifted his gaze from the parking lot. He knuckled moisture from the corners of his eyes. "Bonita Salvadore was a Cuban patriot and the only woman I ever truly loved. She became Castro's whore so she could provide the CIA with intelligence from his inner sanctum, and she agreed to help murder the bastard when Almedia backed down."

Sanchez studied the faces of his companions, looking for what? Evidence of empathy from the women? Or, perhaps, for contempt in Kincaid's demeanor, because a strong man had been reduced to tears by a mere woman?

"The message I delivered to Kennedy on the bridge of the *Compass Island* originated with Bonita," he said. "I know because I was her CIA handler."

"What did the message say? You promised you'd tell us," Johnston reminded him.

"The beard can be shaved in Cojimar. Location confirmed until noon EST," Sanchez said.

"The beard? Kincaid asked.

Sanchez nodded. "That was the rather obvious CIA code name for Fidel Castro."

"Did the message say anything else?" Johnston asked. She scribbled something in her notebook.

"Yeah. It included the exact latitude and longitude for a villa overlooking the fishing village of Cojimar, Cuba, where Fidel Castro was in residence."

Kincaid took a logical leap. "Jesus Christ, Skeeter. Are you saying that Kennedy took a pot shot at Castro from the decks of our old ship?"

"Yep. But he missed."

"Obviously," Kincaid said.

"Wait a minute," Johnston interjected. "There's a hole in your story big enough to sail a ship through."

"What's that?" Sanchez asked.

"Why would Kennedy order an attack that could be traced back to him so directly?"

"Megalomania. Kennedy wanted to pull the trigger himself. His advisers told him that there would be no way to prove that the Polaris missile he had test fired from the *Andrew Jackson* had anything to do with the death of Fidel Castro."

"How so?" Johnston asked.

"The *Compass Island* harbored some of the most technologically advanced electronic gear in the world. It manufactured a false telemetry good enough to fool the best brains in the business, but even more than that, the *Andrew Jackson* didn't fire a Polaris missile that morning."

"It sure as hell fired something. I was there. Remember? I saw a missile go swoosh! Hell, I took pictures of the son of a bitch, which you confiscated, I might add," Kincaid said.

"Describe the missile the *Andrew Jackson* launched."

"It was . . . I don't know forty feet long or so and had a tail fin. It looked like a jet with no wings."

"Polaris missiles don't have tail fins," Sanchez said. "The *Andrew Jackson* fired a Russian P-5 cruise missile salvaged from a Soviet sub that sunk off the coast of Finland in 1961. So any analysis of the bomb debris at the site of Castro's villa would bear the indelible stamp of Soviet Russia. The plan was almost foolproof. The idea was to kill Castro and force the Soviets off balance, defending themselves against false allegations of their complicity, while the American-backed expatriates took control of Cuba."

"So that's why you confiscated my film of the missile launch."

Sanchez nodded.

"Yep. Captain Earnhart was pretty pissed at you. Said he gave you explicit instructions. No pictures of the missile launch. But you took them anyway.

"I was caught up in the moment," Kincaid said.

"And that was another good reason to obscure your memories of President Kennedy's visit to the *Compass Island*," he said. "So Kennedy fires at Castro and misses," Johnston said. And one week later, Lee Harvey Oswald fires at Kennedy and doesn't miss. I can't see a relationship between the two."

"You have to consider the two events in the context of Lieutenant Commander Hugh Patterson's parentage," Sanchez said.

"He was JFK's son. We know that," Johnston said.

"I'm talking about his mother," Sanchez said. "Her maiden name was Rinaldi."

"Wait a minute isn't that the name of the mobbed-up Phila-delphia lawyer who owned the Curlew?" Kincaid asked.

"Bingo. The CIA had been plotting to kill Fidel Castro for several years before Kennedy took office. Organized crime was a willing accomplice because Castro had cut off the flow of money from the vice trade in old Havana. The second invasion of Cuba was no secret to Berto Rinaldi because the army of expatriates the CIA had recruited for the second invasion had been thor-oughly infiltrated by the mafia, which shared similar interests.

"By 1963, Bobby Kennedy's war on crime was hitting the mob where they were most vulnerable . . . the pocketbook. And three of the mafia's most influential bosses took it upon them-selves to kill the president," Sanchez said.

"What were their names?" Johnston asked.

"Luigi Amato, Giovanni Valenti and Frederico Scarlata. Their plan was to make the Castro-loving Oswald their pawn in an assassination that inevitably would be blamed on Castro. Berto Rinaldi argued against the plan. Said that it was too risky. Amato, Valenti and Scarlata didn't want buck him because they would need all the legal help they could get if the plan went south."

Kincaid moved forward on the edge of his seat.

"Then, Rinaldi's grandson was paralyzed in that fall aboard our ship . . ." Kincaid said.

Sanchez nodded vigorously and finished Kincaid's sentence:

"And Rinaldi changed his mind. The president had con-tributed to the suicide of his daughter and the paralysis of his grandson. Rinaldi decided that Kennedy needed to die for rea-sons personal as well as professional. He told Amato, Valenti and Scarlata that America's failed attempt on Castro's life pre-sented the perfect opportunity to sweep the president off the board, with impunity."

"Wait a minute Skeeter. How could Rinaldi have known of the missile attack on Castro?" Kincaid asked.

Sanchez hesitated.

"Good question. Sophia told him. Like many in the freedom movement she had ties to organized crime. Her father operated a rum distillery that laundered money for the mafia during the bad old days of Batista. Her family lost a fortune when Castro nationalized the distillery. Bonita wanted revenge. And it got her killed."

21

CONJIMAR, CUBA — Juan de Jesus awoke to the sound of birds chirping just outside his bedchamber. The French doors leading to the veranda were open and a gentle breeze ruffled the mosquito netting which rose above him like the vault of a gossamer cathedral.

Juan was visited anew with the peculiar sensation that he was living inside another man's skin. The 35-year-old sargento de segunda (sergeant second class) in the Cuban Revolutionary Army had been a fisherman before he was conscripted to the military service. He was more familiar with the smell of gun oil, testosterone and fish guts, but his bed this morning bore the scent of a woman's perfume, and he could taste the essence of a fine cigar, salted sardines and expensive rum on his mustache and beard.

He scratched violently at his cheeks, dragging his fingernails roughly across his skin beneath the wispy black beard he had lately cultivated in keeping with his current assignment that of surrogate for the Comandante en Jefe of the Revolutionary Army. His job was to impersonate Fidel Castro, to eat his food, to wear his clothes, to sleep in his bed and perhaps, although no one said it, to take an assassin's bullet. This was the first time, however, that he had fucked the dictator's woman. That should have been a warning that the stakes in this game had suddenly doubled or trebled. Alas, Juan was oblivious to such nuance. He was not the smartest of men although, in his defense, he was addled this particular morning by too much rum the night before.

A woman's voice startled him from the other side of the bed. "What's the matter, patrocinador? Have you been lying with the dogs?"

Arising on one elbow, he turned toward Castro's whore, Bonita Salvadore, who had aroused him (eventually) at 2 a.m.

as he slept in drunken stupor and entertained him for a while before both of them had fallen asleep tangled in sweat sodden bedclothes beneath the mosquito netting.

Juan's head pounded with the inevitable consequence of too much rum, and he replied sullenly: "No, but I have been lying with a chucha."

She sat up and studied his profile critically. Then she reached out with both hands as if to straighten his beard which had been pushed off to one side in his sleep.

She yanked his beard with both hands. And she spat on him.

"I should have known! You make love like a pescador. So this is what Fidel thinks of me? He lures me to his bed to yoder su pendejo."

"To fuck his fool?" Juan repeated her words, incredulously. "I'll show you a fool."

He lunged at her, but she moved too fast. Slipping under the mosquito netting, Bonita padded across the hardwood floor on cat's feet, collected her clothes, which were discarded in a heap at the foot of the bed and darted into the bathroom.

When she emerged fully clothed, Juan swung his legs over the bed

"Where do you think you're going chucha? She picked up his under shorts and pants.

"Won't that make a picture for your army buddies out in the courtyard, the great Fidel's fool chasing after his puta with suendeble pene flapping in the breeze. I don't think the great man would have approved of your performance last night, either. You fuck like a chicken with your little chicken dick."

Juan made a rude gesture, but thought better of chasing after Castro's whore. He settled back into bed to nurse his hangover as well as his bruised pride. "Go then woman, and good riddance. Your tits are too small for my liking anyway."

Juan was delighted with himself for finally offering a repartee.

Unlike Castro's surrogate, Bonita Salvadore was no fool. She was university educated and came from a family recently fallen on hard times thanks to the Goddamn communists. The fanatics of Che Guevara's commerce ministry nationalized the Salvadore Rum distillery in 1961, and her father had been shot when he protested the seizure of his property too vociferously.

Ernesto Salvadore's death was a blow to his family, certainly, but it had ramifications spreading beyond Cuba to another family, one known as la casa nostra. For years, the Salvadore distillery produced a profit disproportionate to the production of its rather pedestrian rum because it was, in fact, a front for the Caribbean interests now represented by Giovanni Valenti. The organized crime boss, based in Miami, nurtured the Mafia's interests in gambling and prostitution in Havana, and had long used Salvadore's distillery as a front for money laundering.

Bonita was a willing conscript in the plot to dethrone Castro whose regime had so drastically altered her lifestyle. Castro was no fool. He knew of her lineage and must have suspected her motives. It amused him to sleep with the enemy.

Castro on several occasions had summoned Bonita to early morning liaisons in a villa lent to him by his friend Agustin Cruz. The villa occupied a hilltop in the picturesque village of Cojimar, reputed to be the setting for Ernest Hemmingway's classic novel, The Old Man and the Sea. The novelist, in fact, had maintained a house there until politics drove him back to Key West.

Bonita wasn't surprised when she received a phone call from Castro on the afternoon of November 15, 1963, asking her to join him in his bed early the next morning. His instructions were specific. She was to arrive at the villa a 2 a.m. The company of Revolutionary Army soldiers stationed there would be expecting her and would let her in. She was to enter Fidel's bedchamber, strip off her clothes and join him in bed. She was to arouse him from sleep and to tumescence by fellatio. Bonita dutifully reported their pending assignation, leaving out the part about fellatio, to her CIA operative in Havana.

After fleeing de Jesus' bed the next morning, she had one thought in mind. She must tell her CIA contact that imposters were being used in the ongoing game of cat and mouse between Castro and those plotting to kill him.

As she sped toward Havana in a 1957 Ford Fairlane with bald tires and a noisy muffler on gas specifically rationed for Castro's whore, the laughter of the company of soldiers stationed in the villa's courtyard burned her ears still. Meanwhile, 150 miles away just off Cape Canaveral, Florida, a missile arose from the ocean on a flat trajectory and just a few minutes later deposited 500 pounds of high explosives at Longitude W82 17'59.64 and Latitude N23 09'49.32.

The missile's telemetry was, in fact, 25 yards off, but that didn't matter much to Juan de Jesus and the 20 men loitering in the courtyard of Agustin Cruz's villa at Cojimar. They were incinerated instantly as the warhead detonated.

22

SATURDAY, NOVEMBER 16, 1963

HAVANA, CUBA — "Ah Bonita," Fidel Castro said. "I asked them to treat you gently, but apparently you put up too much of a fight. You should not have kneed Ramon in the balls. And now look at you. I am so sorry."

Bonita Salvador squinted at her patron through narrow slits. Her eyes were swollen from the beating she had taken at the hands of Ramon and his friends. Battered though she was, she was angrier with herself than with her assailants. Escape had been within her grasp. She should have gone straight to the family's old vacation spot along the coast. There she had secured a boat equal to the task of spiriting her to Florida.

But, consumed by a false sense of duty, she had visited the dead drop first, hoping to send a message to her handlers, telling them she had been compromised; that Fidel still lived, despite the best efforts of the U.S. Navy.

Her contact, that snake Ramon, had been waiting for her with two dangerous-looking young men, wearing the uniforms of Castro's elite police. They jumped out at her from the bushes as she put her note beneath the loose brick on the garden wall. How could she have been so stupid?

Ramon taunted her like a bantam rooster confronting the weakest hen in the barnyard. "Bonita, you fool. I was a patriot all along. Everything I told the Americans, I also told Castro. And now look what your treachery has won you."

He spat at her feet contemptuously.

"I'm not the treacherous one, you filthy pig," Bonita replied.

One of Ramon's comrades had her arms pinned to her sides from behind so he must have felt secure as he stepped forward and ran his tongue along the line of her jaw.

He wasn't expecting a knee to the balls. It was almost worth the beating she endured to see him doubled over and retching in the grass. The bastard!

And now she stood, defiantly, in front of the great man himself in his favorite suite in the Havana Hilton. Castro groomed his beard as he studied her, exuding a surprising degree of compassion.

"Bonita, Bonita. What am I to do with you?" he asked.

"Why the charade? You'll order me killed, of course, because you haven't the cojones to do the job yourself!" she exclaimed.

Castro laughed. "That's exactly why I kept you near. You have fire! I'm like a moth attracted to your heat and light."

He scratched his nose. "But I'm afraid you're right. Compassion is a hallmark of a great leader, but in this instance I can't afford to be merciful. Your offense was too flagrant. Twenty-seven good men died in the attack on my friend's villa. I would have died, too, had not Ramon reported your correspondence with the Americans. And here is further proof of your treachery."

He waved the dispatch she had intended for her handlers.

Glancing at the note to refresh his memory, he recited: "The beard lives. We have failed. I can trust no one. Look for me soon in Miami."

Castro shook his head. "I have always been amused by the CIA's code name for me. The Yankees are so unimaginative."

He sighed heavily. "Your death will be painless. I have arranged for a massive overdose of heroin. Your body will be left in a public place as a lesson for those who continue to plot against me. But you will feel no pain, my dear, of that I assure you. I owe you that much."

Bonita fought back her tears. She did not want to die. She was young and longed for the embrace of her lover even now. But she had been resigned to a painful death as soon as Ramon's treachery became apparent. She was relieved, almost grateful to Castro, who offered her a painless way out.

She would not die, as she imagined, screaming her lungs out while being eviscerated by one of the unholy death squads that roamed the capital offering grisly object lessons to those who opposed Castro's will.

"There is one other thing you could do for me . . . for old time's sake," Bonita said.

Castro was curious. He cocked his head to one side and smiled. He had always appreciated her wit and had treated her with the avuncular air of an adult captivated by a precocious child. When he wasn't fucking her.

"May I write a farewell note to my lover?" she asked. "Grant me the peace, at least, of knowing that I'm being mourned by one who loves me."

"Who is this man who has tamed a spitfire?"

"His name is unimportant, but rest assured he is beyond your reach. I can tell you where to send the letter so that he will receive it."

Castro motioned to the desk. "There is stationery and a pen in the top drawer. Write your note and address an envelope. I promise it will be delivered, as long as you don't call me a dirty dog, or try to reveal state secrets."

Bonita pulled out the desk chair and sat down. "What state secrets might I reveal? Perhaps that you curl your toes and arch your back when you come?"

"Naughty, naughty, girl. Now write your letter before I change my mind."

She was conscious of movement behind her as she finished her letter, but she resisted the impulse to turn and face Castro.

So she didn't see the revolver he pulled from the pocket of his bathrobe. And she never heard the snap of the hammer and the consequent explosion that sent a .22 caliber bullet into the base of her brain.

Castro as it turned out had the stones for the job at hand. Bonita's murder was calculated, designed to add to his mystique. The sound of the gunshot still hung in the air as two police officers stepped into the room and went about the business of hauling away Bonita Salvadore's body. Housekeeping wasn't far behind. Soon there was no evidence that Bonita had ever existed, save for the image of her burned onto Castro soul by the revolver blast.

Studying her letter afterward, Castro noticed that a single drop of Bonita's blood had landed on the letter right next to her signature. He blotted it with a handkerchief and smiled to himself when it formed a heart-shaped splotch.

23

WEDNESDAY, SEPTEMBER 24, 2003

CAMDEN, NEW JERSEY — "Can you prove beyond a reasonable doubt that Hugh Patterson is the illegitimate son of John Kennedy?" Johnston asked Emilio Sanchez.

"What do you want, counselor, cheek swabs from United States Senator Wiley Patterson and his great uncle Ted Kennedy?" Sanchez asked.

"Are you kidding me?!" Kincaid interjected. His journalistic juices were flowing now. "Wiley Patterson is JFK's grandson? I hear he's on the short list of candidates to replace Cheney as Dubya's running mate next year."

"He'll come off that list quick when I prove that Patterson's great grandfather, Berto Rinaldi, signed off on JFK's assassination," Sanchez said.

"Can you?" Johnston wanted to know.

Sanchez puffed out his cheeks. "I can prove that Berto Rinaldi's daughter Sophia had a son born August 17, 1936, and christened Berto Luca Rinaldi III. On June 6, 1937, Sophia Rinaldi married Baird Collins Patterson a scion of a powerful New England publishing family. It was a marriage of convenience. Baird was a queer."

Albright winced and glanced at Johnston who shot Sanchez the finger.

Sanchez returned the salute and continued with his story.

"Under pressure from his father in law, Baird agreed to adopt Sophia's son, whose name was legally changed to Hugh Collins Patterson. I have photocopies of the documents filed with the Delaware County prothonotary's office. But more important than all of that, I can prove that Berto Rinaldi had motive."

"How?" Johnston wanted to know.

"Hugh's mother left a note when she killed herself on October 14, 1963, the 28th anniversary of the first time she laid eyes on the love of her life, John Fitzgerald Kennedy. She begged her son to forgive her but she couldn't go on living. Apparently Kennedy sent her a terse letter telling her to back off. So she backed off, all the way off."

"No wonder Hugh snapped when he met Kennedy," Albright said. "I can only guess what it must have been like, meeting your father for the first time under such circumstances."

"Yeah," Sanchez said. "Now put yourself in Berto Rinaldi's shoes. By all accounts he doted on Sophia. So her suicide must have had him teetering on the edge. Kennedy's role in the crippling of his grandson a little more than four weeks later could have pushed him over the precipice."

"Rinaldi would have been enraged," Johnston acknowledged. She thought for a moment. "You paint a plausible picture, but you're thin on evidence. You wouldn't happen to have a copy of Sophia Rinaldi's suicide note, would you?"

"Well, not on me, but I know where I can find the original. It's hidden along with Sophia's diary, which details how she met and was seduced by Jack Kennedy. That's what his friends called him back then."

"And where are these documents?" Johnston asked. "Buried away somewhere in the CIA archives no doubt?"

"Actually, they are somewhat more accessible, if they're still where I left them," Sanchez said.

Kincaid was the first to ask: "Where's that?"

"I think I'll sit on that bit of information for a little while longer," Sanchez said.

Johnston weighed in. "At least tell us how you acquired Sophia's note and diary," she said.

"I thought it would be in the best interests of my employer if I tidied up Lieutenant Commander Patterson's stateroom after he was med-evaced from the *Compass Island*. The diary and the suicide note were shoved underneath his mattress . . . and I squirreled them away for safekeeping.

"Translation: You recognized their potential for blackmail so you saved them for your own profit," Albright said.

"How was I to know back then that Hugh Patterson would father a son who would aspire to be the vice president of the United States?"

"Then why hide the documents?" Kincaid asked.

"When Kennedy was assassinated, the brass went to DEF-CON Five trying to distance the agency from the fallout. I was a loyal trooper back in those days. I reported what I had found to my boss Robert Cabot and we decided that officialdom would be better served by avoiding a closer inspection of the events aboard the *Compass Island* on November 16."

"Such as why Berto Rinaldi wasn't identified as a threat to the president of the United States?" Johnston asked.

"That's right. Cabot was up to his armpits in the planning for the second invasion of Cuba and he was afraid that the agency would be blamed for not following up on a lead that could have saved the president's life," Sanchez said.

Kincaid asked the obvious: "Why didn't you?"

"Because the president told us not to . . . in no uncertain terms," Sanchez replied. "He was protecting his son."

"OK," Albright interjected. "So for the past year, you've been the disaffected spy, angry at your employer for a lack of loyalty. Why haven't you retrieved Sophia's note and diary if they're so accessible?"

"I tried to, about six months ago," Sanchez said, right after they cashiered me out of the CIA. "But the task was slightly more complicated than I had anticipated."

Sanchez paused as he noticed something in the parking lot. "Anybody expecting the police?" he asked.

24

THURSDAY, SEPTEMBER 25, 2003

CAMDEN, NEW JERSEY — The dream consumed Sharon Albright like a praying mantis feasts on her lover. Her bedcovers were sodden with sweat, even though it was, in fact, chilly inside her room at the Motel 6. Summer was not long gone and the management had yet to activate the heat even though the nights were becoming colder. She lay, still and sweating, burrowed under the covers enraptured by REM slumber so deep that hot and cold, cramped and comfortable had lost all meaning.

She was afraid to move because he might perceive movement as a sign she was awake and receptive to his drunken advances. So she lay there still as a rabbit trying to persuade a hawk-eyed predator that no meal was in sight. She scrunched her eyes shut, hoping that if she concentrated hard enough she could disappear. She mewed like a blind kitten deprived of its teat by a stronger sibling.

He was, of course, her abusive husband.

In her dream, she heard his key scratching at the front door downstairs and could tell he was too drunk to effect its coupling with the pins and tumblers of the lock whose brass face was much scratched by previous encounters. She bore similar scars. Soon he would be beside her, reeking of beer, sweat and testosterone, but too drunk to effect a coupling with her, without the added arousal of first smacking her around. Her mother had told her that sex could be painful. She hadn't warned her that it could be fucking excruciating.

She laughed in relief the first time the beer made him too flaccid to penetrate her and earned for her trouble a split lip and a bloody nose. He put his hands about her neck as if to choke her, but then his fingers relaxed and wandered lazily to her shoulders and then her breasts.

It made her want to puke, but to say so would have provoked another bitch slap and then she might cry out and wake the boys and drag them kicking and screaming into the nightmare that was her relationship with their father.

She was struggling now in her dream with the beer-sodden bastard who called himself her husband and with the covers, which were entwined, about her legs like a sea serpent trying to drag her below the surface of reality to the watery depths of hell. Suddenly there was a glow a fathom or so above her as if someone had opened the door into a fire lit room.

The tentative radiance brightened with her conviction that this was her salvation. She struggled to consciousness. The light was coming from the bathroom. The rheostat was dialed to dim so she could find the potty in the dark. She was not married. There was no need to protect the two small boys she had imagined were slumbering in the bedroom down the hall.

She arose unsteadily to her feet and headed toward the bathroom. On her way she tripped on a pillow that had fallen to the floor. She stumbled into the closet door, which was veneered with mirrors.

A mirror shattered. A sharp edge sliced the flesh of her right arm. She left a trail of blood on her way to the bathroom.

25

THURSDAY, SEPTEMBER 25, 2003

CAMDEN, NEW JERSEY — The little refrigerator in her motel room hummed and rattled. Outside in the grass beyond the parking lot a baby rabbit screamed in the jaws of a feral cat. Inside the Motel Six, Gale Johnston slept and dreamed.

In her dream, a manual alarm clock clattered on the night-stand. Befuddled, she swung her legs over the edge of the bed. She was startled by movement behind her and by a woman's voice, heavy with sleep. "Honey, please shut that thing off before it wakes up the boys.

She reached for the alarm clock, unsure of how to shut it off. It slipped from her grasp and fell to the floor. There was a crash and the ringing stopped.

"Shhhh!" the woman whispered. "Now, hurry or you'll be late for work."

As she sat up, she noticed tightness across her shoulders as pajama fabric stretched over an unfamiliar swell of muscles. She rubbed her chin and felt a sandpapery roughness. It was happening again. While she slept, she had crawled inside a man's skin. She was slave to his every whim. She struggled to sever the relationship, to awake and escape the dream. Testosterone won the day. The dream played on.

Was this world for real or for pretend?

He put his feet on the floor. Cold. The floor was cold hardwood. Sure felt real. As he/she stood, his/her feet bumped into something. He sorted it out. His slippers. Stabbing around with his toes in the dark he managed to get the appropriate slipper on the appropriate foot. The slippers were lined with fleece and felt right, comfortable and familiar.

He stumbled into the bathroom, flipped on the light, and stood in front of the toilet for a moment suddenly befuddled anew. He needed to pee. Of that he was certain. But it occurred to him that he usually sat down to pee. Instinct prevailed. Pull open the flap; pull out the penis; lift up the lid. Ready. Aim. Fire! That's right. Ahhh.

The dream lurched ahead in fast forward. A short man stood before him, waving his arms in agitation. He knew this man and part of him was certain he had no reason to fear him.

"You're a son of a bitch, John," the man said. "I never laid a hand on her. You broke her nose for Christ sake!"

"Fuck you Jacob! You've fucked her, I know you have."

"You're a fool. I'm not having an affair with your wife. I made love to her, sure, but that was a lifetime ago, long before you two were married!"

In the dream, Gale Johnston was suddenly overwhelmed by sound. Giant metal-hooked cranes moved mountains of metal overhead on rails of steel producing a discordant symphony of metal on metal. This world is for real and he belonged in it.

"Bang!"

Pain. Incredible searing pain. He grabbed his chest and fell backward. His spine jarred against a ribbed wall of metal. He stared at his assailant whose brown eyes were the size of teacups.

"Jesus, Burt," he heard someone say. "You shoulda let me handle it. The wire's quieter."

"Shadup, Jules. There's nobody around, and he's dead ain't he?"

His knees collapsed and he started to slip . . . downward. Someone caught him and pushed him upright again. He felt cold metal pressing in tight under his armpits and time lurched into fast-forward mode with events tumbling by so quickly he couldn't capture them. There was noise and the sound of distant voices. A bright blue light glowed in the darkness. Emerging from it was a woman's face. "Mom?" he said hoarsely. She wagged a finger at him in rebuke and he realized he must be dreaming within his dream.

"Your father was a son of a bitch, Johnny, but that's no excuse for you to be one, too. I raised you better than that."

Her words floated by like the subtitles in a French movie.

He heard the thump of a fastball striking the catcher's mitt and the voice of the umpire: "Strike three, you're out." There was movement. It was as if he was ascending then descending in an elevator.

For a long, long time, there was nothing.

Then, what was that?

Music?

It was faint at first, but soon it grew louder. Dolly Parton should have left Led Zeppelin alone. Was she climbing the stairway to heaven having descended to the depths of hell?

The cheap Motel 6 sheets clung to her like a feverish child. Her mouth was pasty. As Gale Johnston arose to start a new day, her dream escaped to the dark corners of her subconscious, ready to pounce upon her once again when she least expected it.

26

THURSDAY, SEPTEMBER 25, 2003

CAMDEN, NEW JERSEY — Mike Kincaid awoke with a start in the dark. His internal clock told him it was early morning, but that's not what woke him up. His bare feet were exposed and chilly and the room was dark. The mattress beneath him was flimsy. He could feel the sheet metal beneath it sag and then snap back into place as he rolled onto his right side. He brought his knees up to his chest to warm his feet beneath the too-short blanket. Befuddled with sleep, he cast about desperately for clues as to his present circumstances. The answer was a revelation. He was confined to a holding cell at the Camden County Prison. With any luck, he'd soon be released on bail.

Kincaid reflected on the events of the past day as he worked up the gumption to put is feet down on the cold concrete floor. His bladder needed attention, but he was reluctant to use the toilet which was in full view of the prison staff, should they wander by at an inappropriate time. Public urination and defecation were among the humiliations that had commenced with a cavity search and continued with the fluorescent pink sweats and T-shirt they had issued him. His new suit bore the county seal, and the word prisoner was emblazoned on the legs of the trousers. Kincaid figured that pink had been selected as an affront to the machismo, although he had to admit that someone clad in such garish garb would be immediately recognizable should he wander into polite society having escaped his jailers.

His arrest the day before was a blur. Charles Fronk and Tom Harriott chased Albright, Sanchez and Johnston from Kincaid's motel room and served him with a search warrant. They both donned vinyl gloves. Harriott looked in the closet and under the beds while Fronk went through Kincaid's suitcase rooting among his dirty underwear, and slightly used socks and shirts like a Rottweiler on scent of a skunk.

"What's this," Fronk said, pulling an envelope from the elastic pouch at the front of his suitcase. Fronk opened the envelope clumsily with vinyl-clad fingers and pulled out a folded piece of paper. Fronk unfolded the paper. "Well lookie here Tommy, he called out to his partner who was out of sight, searching the bathroom.

"It's a letter from the Ohio Mutual Insurance Company. It says Mike Kincaid is a beneficiary of a $250,000 life insurance policy."

Kincaid was stunned. He had no clue how that letter had made its way into his suitcase. He hid his confusion with bravado.

"There's a law against possession of a letter from an insurance company?"

"Nope, but there is a law against killing your stepfather to collect his life insurance. You claimed that you had no idea the policy existed. Hey! There's a smear of red on the corner of the paper. I'm betting it's blood."

"Bull shit!" Kincaid said.

He arose suddenly from the chair he had settled into, affecting an artificial calm while the two detectives searched his motel room.

"Easy bucko!" Fronk said.

Front shifted his shoulders and elbowed his jacket out of the way to reveal the .38 special nestled in a holster on his right hip.

The movement wasn't lost on Kincaid. He sat back down.

"I didn't kill my stepfather. I wouldn't have . . . couldn't have . . . I loved him."

Harriott emerged from Kincaid's bathroom.

"Hold on to your hankies ladies, I might just shed a tear," he said. "What do you think, Chuck? We got enough?"

Fronk pulled a Ziploc baggie out of his coat pocket and sealed the letter and envelope in it. He stared at Kincaid.

"Yep. Let's do this. Mike Kincaid, you're under arrest for the murder of Jacob Manley late of Fairview, New Jersey."

Kincaid's vision narrowed. The room closed in as if he were riding in a train that had suddenly entered a tunnel.

"On your feet!" Harriott said.

Kincaid arose, unsteadily, supporting himself on the back of the chair.

"Turn around and put your hands behind your back!" Harriott said.

Kincaid complied. Fronk read him his Miranda rights as Harriott snapped the handcuffs around his wrists.

The police detectives herded him outside onto the sidewalk where Albright, Johnston and Kincaid had lingered waiting to see what would happen next. They watched in stunned silence as the detectives shoved Kincaid into the back of the marked police cruiser they had checked out of the motor pool specifically for the arrest. It was all part of the mayor's new initiative to make community policing more visible among the masses.

"The letter from the insurance company's no reason for an arrest," Kincaid said. "I take it that the ballistic report confirmed the gun you found in my trunk was the murder weapon."

Kincaid was surprised by his own clarity of thought given the absurd circumstances he found himself in.

"Our murderer's a pretty sharp guy, isn't he, Tom?" Fronk asked from the passenger's seat.

It was Harriott's turn to drive.

"Not sharp enough to get rid of the murder weapon," Harriott replied.

He slapped the steering wheel with his left hand.

"You really think I'm that stupid? Come on guys!" Kincaid implored. "My Honda was parked unlocked overnight in the motel lot. Anybody could have stashed that gun there."

"So he thinks we should arrest anybody," Harriott said.

He slapped the wheel again, apparently in appreciation of his own wit.

"Prison is full of anybodies," Fronk said. "You'll get to meet some of them soon."

Kincaid decided that he had enough cop repartee. Exercising his Miranda rights, he retreated into silence. He was surprised when they pulled up to a multi-story building on Federal Street in Camden, which he recognized as the county jail.

"You're not taking me back to the police station?" he asked.

"Nope," Fronk said. "You've drawn a go directly to jail card. Tom and I think you'll be much more receptive to questioning after you've spent a night or two as a guest of Camden County. The gun and the ballistics report give us enough prima facie evidence to book you while we build the rest of our case. Don't supposed you've come up with a better explanation of how the Sig 9 that killed your stepfather ended up in the trunk of your car?"

Kincaid shook his head.

"And interesting weapon, the Sig 9. The version we recovered from your trunk was made of stainless steel. It's a unique weapon, typically issued to United States Special Forces. We're running the serial number through the system right now. So far nobody's fessed up to losing it, but the ballistics are irrefutable. It's the gun that killed Jacob Manley. Poor bastard. Shot by his own stepson."

Fronk and Harriott left him in the tender care of a big black guard, who manhandled his in-processing with the meaty savoir faire of an offensive lineman. Kincaid was given permission to make a phone call to his personal attorney the genteelly alcoholic William Fetrow back in New Bloomfield. Fetrow, typically, was indisposed. His secretary, Thelma Woods (who loved her boss far more than she loved her snuff-dipping deer-hunting husband), promised that Fetrow would get on Kincaid's case as soon as he returned from lunch.

The guard, whose name tag read Raymond Cruise, escorted him to the property department, where Kincaid signed a chit for his wristwatch, wedding band, wallet, pocket change, car keys, shoe laces, belt and suitcase, which Fronk and Harriott had stuffed roughly with his loose clothing and toted along to the hoosegow.

"What about bail?" he asked Cruise, as the property clerk sealed his wallet, money clip and loose change in a manila envelope.

"Bail?" the man had replied. "Won't be no bail. This is what the lawyers call a cap-i-tal crime. Your white ass 'l be mine for a long, long time."

Raymond stored him in a holding cell for about twenty minutes before returning to announce. "Good luck chump. Judge Steven is running ahead of schedule. We'll get your white ass arraigned then move it into more luxurious accommodations."

Raymond attached shackles to his legs and Kincaid dragged his chains down a short corridor sounding like Marley on his way to an assignation with Scrooge. He had to hold onto his pants, which without his belt threatened to fall below his knees. The corridor ended at a guard station manned by three

corrections officers. A buzzer sounded and the bars slid open. Raymond herded Kincaid down a hall to a doorway that opened into a twenty-foot square room dominated by a large screen television. A video camera was set up on a tripod next to the TV and pointed at a straight-backed chair.

Two corrections officers, a court reporter, and the public defender, a journeyman attorney named Bill Grisham, according to his name tag, sat at a table off to the right of the television screen. Fronk and Harriott had taken seats in the small gallery of chairs arranged at the back of the room on either side of the door. Kincaid was escorted to the chair facing the television screen and shackled to an iron ring welded to the floor.

"Is that really necessary?" Kincaid asked.

Raymond tugged on the chain to make sure the connection was secure. "Don't do the crime, boy, if you can't hack the time."

An image flicked on the television and District Judge Evan Steven's courtroom across town leapt into view. Off camera, the tipstaff intoned, "Hear ye, hear ye, the arraignment court of District 33, Camden County, now is in session, the Honorable Evan Steven presiding."

"What's the matter at hand?" Steven asked.

"Docket Number 14 of 24 September, 2003 —the arraignment of Mike Kincaid of New Bloomfield, Pennsylvania, on charges of homicide one in the shooting death of Jacob Manley, late of Fairview, New Jersey," the tipstaff said.

"Is there prima facie evidence to proceed with this case?" the judge asked.

Before anyone could answer, the judge added:

"I'm sure this is all pretty intimidating to you Mr. Kincaid. The gentleman to my right here is assistant District Attorney Paul Smith. He's handling the case for the state of New Jersey."

Smith, a tall well-upholstered man picked his pants from his butt crack. "Yes, your honor. According to the affidavit of probable cause, which should be in front of you, Detectives Charles Fronk and Tom Harriott of the Camden City Police Department conducted a lawful search of the defendant's car on Wednesday, September 24, and recovered a 9 mm Sig semi-automatic handgun from the trunk."

"I don't see any indication that the officers had a search warrant," Steven said.

He peered at the assistant district attorney over the top of wire-rimmed reading glasses.

"They didn't need one. The defendant gave his explicit permission for the search. The detectives, again with Mr. Kincaid's consent, tape-recorded his statement of consent to the search," Smith said.

Steven nodded. "Continue."

"The affidavit also includes the results of a ballistics report from the New Jersey State Police crime lab which proves conclusively that the handgun recovered from the trunk of the defendant's 2002 Honda Civic is the same weapon that was used to murder the defendant's stepfather, Jacob Manley of 640 Tuckahoe Road, Fairview, New Jersey, on the morning of Tuesday, September 19."

"Who is representing the defendant?" Steven asked.

"I am your honor," Grisham said.

This was news to Kincaid, who had yet to hear from the honorable William Fetrow, whose specialty in any event was wills and estate planning, when he wasn't drunk or chasing skirts worn by women other than his wife. Fetrow's one redeeming characteristic was he worked cheap.

"I didn't hire him!" Kincaid protested, interrupting the proceedings.

"Be quiet, sir. You will be given your chanced to speak," Steven intoned.

"Well, Mr. Grisham?" Steven asked.

"I have been employed by Mr. Kincaid's friends to represent his interests until his personal attorney can take over," Grisham said.

"If that's the case, don't I get a chance to confer with my attorney before you charge me?" Kincaid said.

He hated the peevish tone his voice had taken on.

"Mr. Kincaid," Steven said. "The purpose of this hearing is to formally arraign you on charges of criminal homicide and to reach an accommodation with the state on the matter of your bail. Nothing more, nothing less."

Steven shuffled through a pile of papers, found the one he wanted and studied it for a moment or two. He cleared his throat.

"I hereby find that there is sufficient evidence to hold the defendant, Michael Kincaid, on a charge of homicide in the first degree. Bail gentlemen?"

"The defendant is accused of murdering his stepfather with a handgun with the motive of collecting $250,000 in term life insurance from the Ohio Mutual Insurance Company. Given the heinous nature of his crime, the state requests remand," Smith said.

"Come now, your honor," Grisham said. "Mr. Kincaid is a newspaper publisher with no criminal record and the state has a real problem with the chain of evidence, not to mention the fact that I have recently talked with two eye witnesses who can confirm his presence in New Bloomfield, Pennsylvania on the day of the murder."

"These are issues you can bring up at the preliminary hearing," Steven said. "However, I must say that I am interested in the state's response to the issue of Mr. Kincaid's alibi."

Smith didn't seem in the least flustered. "The time of death has yet to be determined precisely," he said. "And New Bloomfield is little more than a three-hour car ride from Camden. The state feels strongly that the evidence and motive should be presented at a preliminary hearing."

Steven pulled at his lip.

"I'm not overwhelmed by your prima facie," he said finally. "I'm going to set bail at $50,000 and require Mr. Kincaid to surrender his passport."

"But your honor, I don't have a passport," Kincaid said. "Well in that case, you're not much of a flight risk, are you Mr. Kincaid? Preliminary hearing is set for October 24 in the Camden County Court of Common Pleas. That's it, gentlemen. Next case."

Steven banged the gavel down on his table across town, and Raymond shuffled forward to unshackle Kincaid and escort him to a cell.

"Excuse me," Grisham said. "I think I should be allowed a moment with my client. The correction officers seated in the video courtroom looked at each other, glanced at the police detectives and shrugged.

Grisham hurried up to Kincaid. "We've only got a minute," he said. "But I can tell you that a Mr. Sanchez already has arranged to post your in bail. It'll take a couple of hours, but you should be out by tomorrow morning. Given that, I'm going to insist that they put you in a holding cell rather than the general population."

"How did Sanchez swing that?" Kincaid wanted to know.

"Mr. Sanchez convinced a bail bondsman of his sincerity and of his ability to pay if you jump bail," Grisham replied.

"That's enough!" Raymond said.

He grabbed Kincaid by the elbow and propelled him toward the door.

Grisham stepped back and gave Kincaid a wink and a nod. "You'll be out soon," he said.

Kincaid was booked and fingerprinted, stripped and de-loused and searched so aggressively that his butt hole still hurt the next morning. He should have been humiliated, indeed that was the intent of the process, to dehumanize him so it would be easier to store him like so much cord wood in the public's locked shed.

His anger was his salvation. It was a crystal goblet, perfectly formed and impervious to the shrieking bedlam he had been consigned to by the crazy gods. Using the relaxation techniques Albright had employed as part of his hypnosis session, Kincaid retreated into himself. He was surrounded by drunks and pimps, drug addicts and pedophiles, burglars and robbers, thieves and wife abusers—victims all of the system that had trained them and now was punishing them for having learned their lessons too well, or perhaps not well enough.

He imagined that he was alone on an island surrounded by a sea of tranquility. And the hours crawled by slowly with the sounds of imaginary surf caressing the shoreline drowning out the cries of misery in the long cruel night.

Eventually, he slept, only to awaken with cold feet, a full bladder and a gnawing hunger that prison food would never sate. Rising from his bed, he made his way to the toilet and pulled down his pants. The toilet was barely visible in the uncertain light leaking from the guard station and he thought of sitting down to pee. Instead, he shot a stream off into the darkness and was gratified to hear splashing from the stainless steel bowl of the rimless toilet.

He was sitting on the edge of his bunk two hours later when Raymond Cruise appeared at the bars to announce that Kincaid had made bail. Disappointment was written all over the big black man's face. Cruise wouldn't understand himself in these terms, but he was dismayed to be releasing yet another miscreant to circulate freely in the polite society populated, in part, by his daughter, Belle, on whom he doted.

27

THURSDAY, SEPTEMBER 25, 2003

FAIRVIEW, NEW JERSEY — "Where are we going?" Mike Kincaid asked, as he settled into the passenger seat of Emilio Sanchez's plain white Ford Crown Victoria. Sanchez had bought the big boxy car because it was a favorite among police departments and it often suited his purpose to be mistaken for a police officer.

"Aren't you abrupt?" Sanchez said. "How about a thank you Skeeter for bailing me out of jail?"

"How about a fuck you Skeeter for fucking up my life?" Kincaid snarled. His gloomy disposition had not brightened during his night in jail.

Sanchez crinkled his eyes. "Oh come on Mike. I had nothing to do with your spending the night in jail. I sprung you, remember?"

Kincaid knew this was true, but he had lately learned to cultivate angst as meticulously as a constant gardener tends his roses. "Where are we going?" he repeated, filling the space that should have been occupied by an apology.

"Home," Sanchez said.

"Whose home?"

"Your home."

"In New Bloomfield?"

"No, in Fairview," Sanchez replied. "The women are waiting for us there in Albright's car. Johnston wants to see that note Kennedy autographed for your stepfather. So do I, for that matter. Plus, we need a quiet place to talk. I've checked us out of the Motel 6."

Kincaid stewed for several minutes in silence as Sanchez turned left off of Broadway onto Atlantic Avenue and followed the signs toward Interstate 676 and the Walt Whitman Bridge.

"The note might not be there," Kincaid said, breaking the silence.

"Why's that?"

"The police could have confiscated it as evidence."

"Why?"

"Well, it seems my stepfather left a message, written in his own blood on the kitchen floor."

Sanchez drew in his breath sharply. He spun the wheel, dancing the big car around one of the potholes endemic to the Camden area. "OK. I'll bite. What did the message say?"

Kincaid swallowed hard, almost choking on his truculence. "I killed JFK."

Sanchez glanced in his review mirror. He threw a look at Kincaid. "What the hell does that mean?"

"The police asked me the same question, several times," Kincaid replied. "I've racked my brain, but I can't come up with anything. Dad was a cop and he idolized JFK."

Kincaid imagined Sanchez was searching his memory for any allusion to Camden Police Sergeant Jacob Manley within his unofficial JFK assassination file.

Kincaid could see some sort of realization building behind Sanchez's eyes, but then the former spy shook his head, apparently discarding whatever memory shard he had been examining.

They drove for several minutes in silence, and then Sanchez, following Kincaid's instructions, took the Morgan Boulevard exit from Interstate 676. He turned left, crossed the bridge over Newton Creek and then turned left again onto Tuckahoe Road.

"It's the third house on left," Kincaid said.

"I can see that. The women already have arrived."

Albright's red Toyota Camry was parked in front of the house he had grown up in and which he had left at age 17 to join the Navy, eschewing a football scholarship to Rutgers University because of his guilt over his mother's death.

Kincaid battled ambivalence. He hadn't been inside the house since his stepfather's murder and had visited infrequently over the years. It wasn't that he didn't feel close to Jacob, who in many ways was the only father he had ever known. They had kept in touch through phone calls, letters, and later e-mails.

It was his mother's ghost that kept him away. In his mind's eye he could still see her standing at her kitchen sink up to her elbows in soapy water as she did the dinner dishes. Or he imagined her watching the Ed Sullivan show from her favorite wine-colored armchair. Her feet would be propped up on the matching hassock and her stockings would be rolled down to her ankles because her feet were always cold and her legs were always warm. That's what she said, anyway.

After her death in 1962, Jacob hadn't done much to change the look of the place. He kept things as they had been not because he wanted to enshrine Kathleen's memory but because he was a guy and guys didn't worry about things such as decorating or whether the fabric on the right arm of the BarcaLounger had worn through to show the ticking underneath.

In the spring of 1984, Jacob had bestirred himself, finally, to refinish the basement, so he could have his cop buddies over for Monday night football in front of a rousing game of seven-card stud. But typical of Jacob, he had not gone out to purchase a card table. He'd rescued a cigarette-scarred relic from the discard pile at the Pink Cat, which at the time was undergoing a modest renovation of its own.

"Are we going to sit in the car like bobble dolls or are we going to go inside?" Sanchez asked, breaking Kincaid's reverie. "The women have to be getting restless."

"Sure. Let's go."

Kincaid unbuckled his seat belt and swung the Crown Vic's door open.

The women, in fact, were not getting restless. They were lost in conversation. Their shoulders and hips were turned toward each other as they conversed. Kincaid wondered at the differences in the way men and women relate to each other. He and Sanchez had occupied the same spots in the front seat of a car only moments before, but Kincaid could not remember turning toward Sanchez nor Sanchez turning toward him to facilitate conversation.

"Women are weird," he said.

"You got that right, Mikey me boy," Sanchez replied. He affected an Irish brogue that Kincaid found irritating.

"Just yesterday they spoke to each other only in snarls," Sanchez observed. He tapped on the window of Albright's Camry, startling them into silence.

The women alit from the car, and they moved as a group toward the front door of Jacob Manley's house, which was still cordoned off with yellow crime scene tape.

"Maybe we shouldn't go in," Kincaid said.

"Nonsense," Sanchez replied, pulling a penknife from his pants pocket and slitting the tape the loose ends of which he stuck to either side of the doorjamb. "They gave you back your keys didn't they? And I'll bet they never said anything about not returning to the scene of the crime."

Kincaid nodded in agreement.

"Listen Mike," Sanchez said, "I know how these guys work. They've already been over this place with a fine tooth comb several times. If there was any evidence here, they've already compromised it."

Kincaid fumbled for the proper key on his key ring and inserted it into the lock. He twisted the key counterclockwise and tried the door. It was still locked. He turned the key the other way and heard the dead bolt slide open on the other side of the door.

He stepped into the small entryway of his old home, walking to his left past the stairs and into the front parlor as his mother had called it. His dad's BarcaLounger and mother's armchair occupied their same old spots on either side of a brocaded sofa. The furniture however was arrayed before a 42-inch rear-projection television.

"That's new," he said, looking at the TV. "It surprises me Jacob moved that aggressively into the 21st Century."

Those words were still hanging in the air when Sharon Albright collapsed on the little piece of worn Linoleum that had welcomed visitors to Jacob Manley's vestibule for sixty-five years.

"Jesus Christ!" Sanchez said. He caught Albright under the arms and struggled against her dead weight. "Give me a hand here will you Mike?"

Kincaid grabbed Albright's right arm. He noticed an unusual thickness underneath her sweater, as if her bicep was wrapped in a bandage.

Kincaid and Sanchez propelled the still-woozy Albright to the couch, laying her out like a mortician would a dead body on a slab in the morgue. Kincaid fluffed a threadbare pillow and propped it under Albright's head, while Johnston demonstrated her concern by wandering into the dining room where Jacob Manley had proudly displayed John Fitzgerald Kennedy's autograph.

"I'll be damned," she called out. "That sure does look authentic. You didn't tell me he'd framed the pen, too. Sure looks like the official White House seal."

28

THURSDAY, SEPTEMBER 25, 2003

FAIRVIEW, NEW JERSEY — The room was spinning like a dreidel. She was lightheaded, intoxicated by fragrantly familiar memories. This neighborhood, this house, this parlor, the way the September sunlight filtered through the dying leaves clinging to hope on the branches of the old oak tree outside, had her psyche singing like a tuning fork. She was vibrant and stimulated by sights, sounds, smells, tastes and textures of another lifetime.

Experience had taught her to take this much for granted: she had lived not once but many times. Her psyche, her soul, her essence, whatever convention cares to call it, coexisted, sometimes peacefully, and sometimes not, with the memories of all the people she had been.

Her consciousness was segmented into compartments arranged in a labyrinth fashioned by the same rollicking happenstance that is the fabric of the universe, at least as humans perceive it. Some of her memories crouched behind locked doors like gargoyles ready to spring to life and devour her. But if she was patient (and courageous enough) she could pick the lock, swing open the door and confront the memory lurking there. Other rooms stood welcomingly open and contained happy memories lined up like toys to be played with and then returned carefully to the shelves of an orderly nursery.

It was a testimony to her steel will that she was sane amid the cacophony of voices clamoring for her attention. She had modeled her behavior to meet the norm, to conform to the way she saw others reacting to what had to be a prevailing perception of reality. But she knew in her heart of hearts that the real world was not as others perceived it. Her reality was not constrained by time and place. Her life did not, as many imagined, stretch out before her like a straight ribbon of road in the desert. Her memories were not arranged like mileposts along that road destined to pop up and then fade forever into the past with little more than a fleeting glimpse of them visible in the rear view mirror.

The real world, as she perceived it, was a series of random events spinning about the nucleus of her consciousness. The protons and electrons (the positives and negatives) of her experience were not hers to keep alone. No man is an island. John Donne didn't attach quite the same meaning to this observation but he got it right nevertheless. Her memories in this lifetime and in others were free agents in the vast universe of human experience. They moved tangentially about the spheres of other souls whose proximity in both body and spirit ensured that her memories were not unique to her perception of them. They were part of a collective consciousness that would endure beyond the set of mileposts marking her progress on the linear road linking birth and death. And they would survive the unraveling of this mortal coil.

This place, this modest little two-story house in the village of Fairview was both alien and hauntingly familiar at the same time. She was absorbed by an anachronism. The rooms, the placement of doors and windows, were as right as rain, but the timing was all off. The television didn't belong there. Where was her old black and white RCA built right here in Camden in 1959? And the rug was both right and wrong. The wear pattern showing the high traffic path to the dining room and beyond to the kitchen was too pronounced. That carpet was new damn it. She and Jacob had installed it just a year ago, or was it two?

Her favorite armchair was slightly out of place. It took all of her will not to arise and nudge it over two or three inches so the legs resided squarely in the indentations worn in the carpet.

The analytical part of her operating in linear time recognized that police probably had moved the chair as they searched for clues to the identity of Jacob's murderer. Then, suddenly, somewhere in the labyrinth of her memories a door opened on squeaky hinges and Jacob's murderer stepped through it. Recognition arrived like an owl swooping down on a baby rabbit huddled in false security in the tall grass next to the tree line. Her soul screamed like that baby rabbit in extremis as the talons of a horrible certainty tore at her. "No," she said to herself. "This cannot be happening. Not again."

Her denial was hanging there like dialogue forever captured in the bubble above a cartoon character, but her brain had already moved on to the next frame. In that instant, she knew that a long-ago tragedy was bound to recur because the principal issue could be deferred but not resolved by the taking of a life.

A resolution could be effected only by the cosmic two-step of contrition and absolution. She was by her very nature, nonreligious. Her rich spiritual life could not be contained within the boxes that mankind had built up about the mystiques of Buddha, Confucius, Zoroaster, Abraham, Moses, Jesus, or Mohammad. But resident in all of those boxes were some universal truths, among them the healing power of forgiveness. Absolution salves the soul, indemnifying it from the cruel caprice of wrongs committed and of wrongs endured. She prayed she had the courage to apply that principle to the tragedy threatening to sweep her up once again. She could feel John Kincaid's rage gathering force beyond the horizon as a cloying stillness clinging to her skin like a gossamer shroud.

29

THURSDAY, SEPTEMBER 25, 2003

FAIRVIEW, NEW JERSEY — She could smell peppermint on his breath as he bent over her.

"You feeling better?" he asked. "Skeeter's called a meeting in the dining room and he won't start until you join us."

Sharon Albright swung her legs over the edge of the sofa and sat up, carefully. She rooted around in her purse, which Kincaid had deposited on the floor next to the sofa and pulled out a candy bar.

"I'm hypoglycemic," she explained. "I'll be better in a minute."

She ripped open the wrapper with her teeth and took a big bite of a 3 Musketeers' bar.

Kincaid sat down beside her at the far end of the couch.

"Take your time. Skeeter can wait. He needs to cultivate patience."

Kincaid smiled and made eye contact.

Albright felt an familiar tugging at her heart. *"He's a nice guy. Complicated, but still a nice guy."*

She wondered at the revelation. In her line of work, complicated guys typically were looking for someone to help tote around their emotional baggage. She was OK with that because that's what she did for a living, but she was emotionally wary of complications in her personal life even when they were wrapped about nice guys.

She didn't sense a desperate need for emotional support in Kincaid. He certainly came fully equipped with emotional baggage, but he bore his burdens stoically. His reliance on Old Forester was an issue that warranted watching, but her sense was that he was self-medicating, coping about as well as could be expected with the recent death of his wife and his arrest for murdering his stepfather. Her diagnosis, apart for the cudgeling of his psyche by the Central Intelligence Agency, was mild depression. She surprised herself by feeling something more than a professional empathy.

Here sat a man who came by his phobias and insecurities honestly, and they had absolutely nothing to do with cigars or with wanting to kill his father and sleep with his mother. Her sometime employer, the CIA, had defiled his sanctity of self, but he had survived apparently without professional intervention. She admired his self-sufficiency, although strong and silent was not a course she would plot for most of her patients.

"I'm ready," she said.

She pushed herself up off the sofa.

He arose, too, wincing and rather more stiff-kneed than he cared to show.

"Let's go then," he said.

Gale Johnston and Emilio Sanchez were sitting in chairs on either side of Kathleen Manley's cherry dining room table. Johnston had taken the framed note from John F. Kennedy off the wall and was examining it in the sunlight filtering through the dining room window. Both of them had cans of Budweiser sweating in front of them on stained coasters bearing the name and logo of the erstwhile Pink Cat. Jacob was never one to discard a thing whose utility was intact.

"Care for a beer?" Kincaid asked as Albright lowered herself into a seat across from Johnston. "Beer is the only thing left in Jacob's refrigerator that hasn't spoiled."

Albright shook her head.

"No, but I could use a glass of water to wash down the candy bar," she said.

Kincaid pushed open the swinging door between the dining room and kitchen and stepped through quickly to avoid getting clocked in the butt by the backswing. It wasn't long before he lurched through the door again, this time bearing a jelly glass full of Camden city tap water in which drowned three ice cubes.

Kincaid sat down and looked expectantly at Sanchez.

"How would you guys like to go on a cruise?" Sanchez asked.

"Why would we want to do that?" Gale Johnston replied.

"I just read a report on the Virginia Pilot Web site. On October 14, the former USS *Compass Island* will be towed from the James River Reserve Fleet across the Atlantic Ocean to Hartlepool, England, where it is to be scrapped by a company called Able Ltd. I propose to be on board when the CI leaves."

"Why would you want to do that?" Johnston repeated.

"Because forty years ago, I put Sophia Rinaldi's diary and suicide note, as well as dispatches and telemetry documenting the missile attack on Fidel Castro in a manila envelope and hid it behind the bulkhead insulation in the emergency radio room aboard the *Compass Island*. When I went to retrieve them earlier this year, I found that some yard knucklehead had welded shut the door to that compartment."

"What makes you thing they're still there?" Albright wanted to know.

Sanchez patted his chest. "Faith, and a feeling right here."

Johnston rolled her eyes. "For this I quit my day job."

"I think they're still there because if anyone had stumbled on them, there would have been a ripple of some sort in the intelligence community and given my association with the events on the ship all those years ago, I would have been consulted," Sanchez said.

"Unless some yardbird found them, didn't realize what he had and threw your precious papers on the trash heap," Kincaid said.

"That could have happened," Sanchez agreed. "But I'm betting that it didn't. At least it's worth taking a look. But we have to move fast."

"Shit," Johnston said. "I knew about the contract, of course. I reported on it five months ago, I just didn't realize Able was ready to proceed so quickly."

"Well they are," Sanchez said. "My plan is to stow away on the CI at least for a couple of days just after it gets underway."

"That's stupid," Kincaid said. "Why not just board the ship now while it's still moored?"

"There are just too many prying eyes about," Sanchez said. "Workers will be crawling all over the ship getting it ready for the voyage. We'll have to wait until they're done then sneak aboard at the last minute."

"Why can't you do that on your own?" Kincaid asked.

"I suppose I could, but I thought Gale might like to come along to document the chain of evidence," Sanchez said. "The experience would be a terrific back story for our book, wouldn't it, Gale?"

Johnston narrowed her eyes, like a poker player deciding whether to call or fold. She chucked in her chips. "I'm in."

"How about you, Mike?" Sanchez asked.

"Me? You're kidding, right? I don't want to default on your bail bondsman."

"You don't have to worry about that. Your next court date is a month and a half away. I'll have you back by then, I promise . . . for my own good as well as your own."

"Don't you think I should be preparing for my defense? I am, after all, facing murder charges."

"I've already talked with Grisham, who has consulted with your guy Fetrow back in New Bloomfield. Fetrow thinks you're better off letting Grisham handle it. His specialty, after all is criminal law," Sanchez said.

"Nice of those guys to talk to me first."

"Mike. This isn't a request. Consider it a condition of your release on bail," Sanchez said.

"You're saying you'll rescind my bail if I don't go along with this scheme?"

Sanchez nodded.

Kincaid flushed red-hot. He clenched his fists and glowered.

Sanchez smiled. "Consider it a cruise . . . at my expense."

Kincaid wasn't ready to surrender. "Suppose the bondsman gets an anonymous tip that I'm planning to jump bail. You'll lose your deposit real quick. What was it, 10 percent? You ready to walk away from five Gs, Skeeter?"

The look in Sanchez's eye was daunting. "You don't want to play that sort of game with me. You're not nearly tough enough."

Kincaid relented. "Then I guess it's up to you to get me back in time for my preliminary hearing."

"That would be in my own best interest," Sanchez agreed. He turned to Albright. "I'd like you to come along, too," he said.

Albright took a sip of water and shuddered. "Or what? What will you threaten me with?" she asked.

"Well . . ."

Albright cut him off. "I'll save you the effort. No I don't want you to tell the CIA that I've treated Mike. I'll come along, too, but not because you intimidate me. I want to see how this story ends."

30

SUNDAY, NOVEMBER 17, 1963

BRYN MAWR, PENNSYLVANIA — The Lincoln Continental was as black as the night it was driving through. The glare and blare of the City of Brotherly Love had given way to subdued suburbia. The pale illumination leaking from the stately homes of mainline Philadelphia was no match for the fuzzy cold gloom that had settled on the streetscape as the skies did their darndest to snow and failed, sullenly.

Inside the armored car, the heat was comfortably adjusted and the men in the back seat were glad they had shed their overcoats and stowed them in the trunk at the onset of their journey from Philadelphia International Airport. At the controls, his features glowing in the backwash of the dashboard's subtle radiance, sat a short slight olive-skinned young man with paper-cut sharp features.

The driver, whose name in his present incarnation was Martin Pauli, had the front seat shoved all the way forward, giving the passengers in the back plenty of legroom. Pauli had picked up his passengers at the airport a half hour earlier. In a show of strength belying his small stature, the young man had disdained the services of the Skycaps and lugged their heavy bags to the curbside without complaint or comment. He stowed the bags and their overcoats in the trunk of the Continental, which was purring like a content cat hunkered down beside a warm fire. The car was situated directly beneath a sign warning that unattended vehicles would be towed, but the airport cop patrolling that particular patch of asphalt merely tipped his cap and smiled as Pauli arrived with his passengers in tow. A fifty-dollar bribe had abrogated the rules with a wink and a nod.

The driver was young, in his early 20s at best, and physically unimposing, yet something about him exuded danger. Giovanni

Valenti's bodyguard, George Stephanos, sensed it. He sat forward alertly in the back seat next to his boss. Stephanos's head was thrust forward on a bull neck and turned sharply toward the driver as if some measure of security lay in keeping Pauli pinned in an angry glare.

"Take it easy George," Valenti said. "We're among friends here."

"You take it easy boss," George Stephanos said. "You pay me not to take it easy, don't you?"

Valenti leaned forward and patted Stephanos on his ample thigh. "You're right, of course. Stay vigilant old friend."

The Lincoln turned and made its way through a residential neighborhood of brick two- and three-story homes set well back from the street and sheltered by stately oak and beech trees. Turning again into a wide cul-de-sac, Pauli nosed the big Lincoln to a stop between brick columns standing sentry on either side of a gated driveway. "I'll take care of this Martin," Valenti told the driver. The rear window whispered open on electric power. Valenti stuck his head out and waved at the guard who, recognizing the occupant, busied himself with opening the gate. "Go right on in, Mr. Valenti," the guard said. "Mr. Rinaldi is expecting you."

The car stopped in front of the house and the driver alighted, opening the door for Valenti. Stephanos opened his own door, and crawled out, squinting in the glare of spotlights that illuminated the front of the house as if it were daytime. He heard a rustling in the bushes on the fringe of the property and reached into his coat, grabbing the butt of his pistol. Reacting to Stephanos's demeanor, Valenti instinctively crouched, putting the Lincoln between him and the street.

"What's wrong, George?" he asked.

The bodyguard scanned the bushes for several seconds, but didn't draw his pistol. The driver went into a crouch of his own and crept along the edge of the driveway, looking for any sign of movement in the hedgerow separating Rinaldi's property from his nearest neighbor 50 yards away. The guard watched him impassively from his post next to the gate. "The perimeter is secure," he called out. "I checked it myself not five minutes ago!"

Returning to the car, the driver shook his head.

"I heard it too," Pauli said. "But if anyone's hiding in there, it would be more trouble than it's worth to chase him out."

Pauli shrugged expressively.

"Besides, we'd be dead by now if he had a gun and wanted to kill us."

Valenti nodded and rose from his crouch. "He's right George. Come on, let's go inside."

George Stephanos dropped his hand, squared his shoulders and followed Valenti up four steps to the portal of Berto Rinaldi's spacious Bryn Mawr home. While Pauli wrestled their bags from the trunk, Stephanos rang the doorbell, whose musical chime sounded out Ave Maria.

The door was opened after only a moment or two, by a pretty young woman, wearing a white cap and a starched blue pinafore over a collared white blouse. "Good evening, gentlemen," Maria Ginoble said, curtsying. "Mr. Rinaldi and his other guests are waiting for you in the library."

Ginoble took their coats from Pauli. "Leave the bags here," she told them. "Jules will carry them to your rooms." The maid ushered them through an ample center hall to the library, a magnificent panel-lined room with a vaulted ceiling which occupied a wing of its own at the back of the house.

There, ensconced in wing chairs arranged before a genteel fire sat three men. Berto Rinaldi was sprawled elegantly in the chair closest to the fire. His long legs, clad in British tan, were crossed ankle on thigh. He cradled a snifter of brandy carelessly in his left hand, while his right hand was caressing an unlit Cuban cigar as if he were coaxing a reluctant lover to arousal.

Rinaldi didn't deign to rise from his chair as Valenti, Stephanos and Pauli entered the library. He waved his cigar at them like a magician's wand. "Martin, how about fixing our guests a drink, a Dewar's and soda for Mr. Valenti and a Budweiser for Mr. Stephanos."

The newcomers nodded, impressed by Rinaldi's gift of recall.

"Have a seat gentlemen," their host said. "Martin has just rejoined us from a special assignment with news that has altered my opinion of Giovanni's plan to neutralize a considerable threat to our mutual well-being."

The occupants of the other two chairs were not as aloof as their host. Frederico Scarlata, who represented the Chicago mob's interests in Las Vegas and Hollywood, and Luigi Amato, a Louisiana based mobster, jumped to their feet and took turns embracing Valenti. Rinaldi waited impatiently while the requisite round of cheek kissing and shoulder slapping was accomplished and his visitors had returned to their seats.

"Now that you've paid homage to homo erotica do you think we can get on with the meeting?" Rinaldi asked. "There have been important developments and we have much to discuss."

Valenti grinned at his friend Amato. "I think we've just been insulted, Luigi," he said.

"Take no offense, old friend. Our ivy league colleague is miffed because as it turns out we were right and he was wrong," Amato replied.

"Recent developments have strengthened your position," Rinaldi said.

He set his brandy sifter down on a table, uncrossed his legs and leaned forward supporting his chin with his hand like the thinking man.

"What developments are those?" Valenti asked.

"Our assets in Cuba tell us that one of Castro's whores has been executed, rather spectacularly for her role in a conspiracy to assassinate el presidente."

There was a crash from the bar where Martin Pauli was pouring Valenti's drink.

"I'm sorry, Mr. Rinaldi," Pauli said. "The tumbler slipped out of my hand."

"Obviously," Rinaldi said.

Pauli stooped, picked up the glass shards and dropped them in a trashcan. He mopped up the liquid with a bar rag and built another drink, which he delivered to Valenti.

Valenti took a sip and smiled in appreciation.

"What about my beer?" Stephanos asked.

Pauli gritted his teeth. "On its way."

Valenti swirled his Scotch while Pauli delivered Stephanos's Budweiser.

Leaning back in his chair, Valenti said: "Before we go any further, Berto, are you certain we can speak candidly? George noted a disturbance as we arrived."

"I think there may have been a guy hiding in the bushes watching the house," Stephanos said.

"There was, without a doubt," Rinaldi replied. "The local gendarmes keep a careful watch on comings and goings here. Your picture probably was taken as well, I trust that you smiled."

"Why don't you chase them off?" Stephanos asked.

"That would make them even more vigilant," Rinaldi observed.

His teeth gleamed in the firelight. "What's outside is outside. Your words will not escape this place, I assure you. Now, getting back to Castro's whore. It seems her offense was tipping off the Kennedys to Fidel's exact whereabouts. This facilitated a cruise missile attack on a villa at Cojimar that killed one of several imposters Castro employs for security purposes and not the great man himself."

"How does that affect my plan?" Valenti wanted to know.

Before answering, Rinaldi took up his cigar and made a production of lighting it. He tossed the spent match in the fireplace and blew a smoke ring. "The Cubans certainly know their way around a good cigar."

"Martin tells me that Kennedy personally ordered the attack," Rinaldi continued. "So it would seem only natural that Castro would return fire."

"Which gives us perfect cover for my plan to kill the bastard," Valenti interjected.

"Precisely," Rinaldi said. "So my advice now is that you proceed with the plan. Are your assets still in place?"

Amato rubbed his hands in anticipation.

"We've got the perfect guy for the job. He's a former Marine sharpshooter and he loves Castro's ass," he said. "Tell him about the attack on Castro and he'll be locked and loaded. All we have to do is point him at the president. He'll be willing . . . and expendable."

"How about contingency planning if our friend survives his mission but is collared by the long arm of the law?" Rinaldi asked.

"Also taken care of. We've got a willing soldier with a plausible back story—his abiding love of our American pope," Valenti said.

"You've certainly changed your tune, Berto," Scarlata said. His voice was gravelly and thick with phlegm. "It was just last week that you were professing your love for the pope of Pennsylvania Avenue and now you're eager to excommunicate him. It wouldn't have anything to do with the death of your daughter, would it?"

The room fell silent under the weight of the thousand-pound gorilla Scarlata had just set free of its cage.

"You're a hard man Fredrico," Amato said.

"Jesus Scarlata. Talk about farting in church," Valenti added.

Scarlata wasn't through by a long shot. "At our last meeting you threatened to expose our plot to the feds should we carry it out. Could this change of heart have something to do with the life-threatening injury recently sustained by your estranged grandson?" he asked.

"You have any idea of what he's talking about, Giovanni," Luigi Amato asked.

Valenti shook his head.

Rinaldi rose stiffly to his feet and approached Scarlata a threat implicit in his posture and demeanor. He was standing in front of Scarlata with his fists clenched when Maria Ginoble entered the room.

"Mr. Rinaldi," she said. "I know you told me not to disturb you, but Le . . ."

She stopped talking abruptly as Lenny Davenport, the famous crooner and MGM star, swept into the room behind her.

"Berto is this any way to greet an old friend, to keep him waiting in the vestibule while there are Cuban cigars, good brandy and good company to be had in the library?"

"Lenny?" Rinaldi said, in wonder. "I wasn't expecting you until tomorrow."

"Let's just say that I was lured to Philadelphia a day early on false pretenses," Davenport said.

"False pretenses?" Rinaldi asked.

"I was able and I thought she was willing," Davenport replied. "I was wrong."

Scarlata, welcoming the interruption, rose to his feet. "That's our Lenny always thinking with his dick."

31

WEDNESDAY, NOVEMBER 20, 1963

MIAMI, FLORIDA — It was a nondescript house on a nondescript street. The neighbors were wage slaves all. They worked for banks, real estate offices, hotels, rent-a-car agencies, restaurants, taverns and various other enterprises attendant to tourism, the lifeblood of south Florida. Nestled among the cookie-cutter ranches was the current abode of Robert Cabot, who was living a quiet life on a quiet street. Cabot prided himself on being a chameleon, on being able to disappear into whatever environment his service to the United States demanded. His neighbors thought, variously, that he was an accountant, a banker or, perhaps, a lawyer. They would never have guessed, spy.

That's why Cabot wasn't particularly pleased to see Martin Pauli pull a cherry red 1963 Chevrolet Impala convertible into his driveway. Pauli had called from the airport, so Cabot was expecting his arrival. He opened his front door before his visitor could ring the bell.

"Jesus, Martin. Couldn't you have picked a subtler car? My neighbors will be talking about this for a week," Cabot said.

He stepped back so Pauli could come inside.

"Avis was tapped out and this is the only car Hertz had left," Pauli said.

His face was haggard, his suit rumpled and his eyes bloodshot. He smelled of stale smoke, sweat and something more, what was it? Cabot prided himself on his powers of observation.

"How many rum and cokes did you have on the flight?" he asked as he ushered Pauli to the back of the house, where the two men took up chairs aligned on either side of Cabot's kitchen table.

Pauli scratched his jaw with the nails of his left hand. "Thanks for asking. I'll have a martini," he said, dryly.

"You're not going to be staying long enough to have a drink. Do you know what a risk I took bringing this home with me?" he asked.

He motioned to a forest green file folder with the words Top Secret stamped to its cover in red capital letters.

"I've been taking far more dangerous risks for the agency for the past two years," Pauli replied. "You owe me this much."

Cabot studied the younger man's face, revising his estimate of the number of rum and cokes Pauli had consumed in flight from four to five. "You sure you're ready for this?"

Pauli struggled to swallow his own spit and glanced longingly at Cabot's refrigerator. "Sure you don't have a beer or something in there?"

Cabot rose to his feet. He fetched a longneck Budweiser from the refrigerator and popped the top with a church key. He sat the beer down in front of Pauli and took his seat again. "It's your funeral." He pushed the file folder toward Pauli.

Pauli opened the folder as if he were defusing a bomb. He drew in his breath sharply as the image on the 8-by 10-inch glossy black-and-white photograph registered on the back of his retinas. He bit his lip so hard that it bled.

"So it's true," he said. "Castro killed her.

"Yes. Rumor has it that he shot her himself. There were three other images, but I thought this one was sufficient. Dig a little deeper in the file and you'll find a letter that arrived yesterday at the letter drop in Washington, D.C.

Pauli extracted the note from the envelope, which already had been slit open. He drew in his breath sharply as he realized that it was written on the letterhead of the Havana Hilton.

He read the letter, which was clearly written in Spanish in Bonita's slanted handwriting.

Dear Emilio,

Do not be dismayed if terrible pictures of me make it into the official dispatches. The injuries, I am assured, will have been inflicted post mortem. Fidel for all his faults has been my patron in a lot of ways and while my fate is sealed, he assures me that my death will be painless.

If I try to reveal the details of how I came to be in his custody, he will refuse to deliver this letter. He has, however, offered this final kindness.

He's letting me tell you how much I love you and how I will always treasure our brief time together. I have loved many men, but you are the only man I have ever loved truly.

I pray that someday you will understand that distinction and when you think of me, I hope you will smile.

Pauli finished reading the note and threw it on the table. He slapped his right hand down violently on the tabletop and wiped his mouth with the back of his left hand. He stared at Cabot like a sniper peering through the sights of a rifle.

He waved his hand at the letter. "Is that her blood," he asked.

Cabot shrugged. "There's not enough of a sample to type it but we have confirmed that it's human blood."

"God I want to kill that bastard!" Pauli said. He clenched and unclenched his fists.

"So do we all," Cabot agreed. "But the word is out. The Kennedys are pulling the plug on the operation. With an election coming up they can't afford another Bay of Pigs. They're going to wait now and settle Castro's hash in a second administration."

"What about the units training in Nicaragua," Pauli asked, bitterly. "You said that I could join them there."

"That of course, won't be necessary, at least not now. But believe me, there will be plenty of work for you with the agency. Bonita did well; we missed the bastard by a whisker."

"Send me in! Send me in now! I'll kill the son of a bitch myself!"

Cabot laid a hand on Pauli's arm.

"I can't do that and you know it. Castro is off limits. Period. At least until Kennedy gets re-elected. The word has come down from on high."

"The longer we wait, the more difficult it will be," Pauli said. "Waiting just gives Castro more time to consolidate his power."

"You know that and I know that, but the politicians don't care. The name of the game now is to get Kennedy re-elected. And the suits have changed their minds. They don't think invading Cuba is the way to do it."

He narrowed his eyes and considered Pauli like a swimmer trying to decide if the water was warm enough.

"There are those in the intelligence community and in industry who would prefer a more vigorous pursuit of the bad guys in Cuba and Vietnam. And there are those who fear that will never happen under the namby pamby Kennedys. They're micromanaging wet ops far too much for my liking," Cabot said.

"Do you think the Republicans have a better answer?" Pauli asked.

He took a long swallow of beer and considering his mentor through half-closed eyes.

"I think Richard Nixon has the stones for the job," Cabot replied. "More than that, I think he's the rightful king. That bastard Richard Daley stole the election for Kennedy it's as simple as that. Kennedy carried Illinois by 9,000 votes. Without Daley's influence, Nixon would be our president, Castro would be dead . . ."

"And Bonita would still be alive," Pauli said.

Cabot shrugged. "You intimated in your last message that you had some intelligence for me from our Italian friends. What is it you need to tell me?"

Pauli took another pull of beer. "Would you believe me if I reported that Berto Rinaldi continues to be a voice of reason among his colleagues and is steadfast in his promise to implicate them in the event of the president's untimely demise."

"Is there good reason for me not to believe you?" Cabot asked.

"Let's just say that Berto must be an imminently reasonable man," Pauli said.

He winked at Cabot.

"How reasonable is he? Is he reasonable enough, for instance, to overlook Kennedy's role in the suicide of his daughter?" Cabot asked.

"More than that, he's willing to overlook the crippling of his grandson who was thrown down a flight of stairs by Kennedy's secret service agents," Pauli added.

"So it is as we feared, or hoped? Cabot said.

Pauli nodded.

"What you do with that information is up to you," he said. "Do you want details for the file? Or do you want deniability?"

Cabot puffed out his cheeks.

"I think I know enough already, don't you?" Cabot said.

"You're the smartest person I know," Pauli agreed, sealing the fate of a president.

32

PHILADELPHIA, PENNSYLVANIA — William Berde heeded a thump he thought portended the arrival of The Daily News. His front door flew open as if propelled by a gale, and Maria Ginoble's head struck his hardwood floor with the resonance of a watermelon dropped from the back of a pickup truck.

She stared at him through dead eyes.

Berde ducked, and then straightened, feeling stupid. If killing him was the object of this exercise, he would be dead already. He was a perfect target framed in his doorway with Maria Ginoble sprawled dead at his feet.

Maria had been tortured and killed elsewhere. That much was obvious. So there was no need to protect his front stoop as a crime scene; there was no harm in bringing her inside away from the prying eyes of his neighbors. Glancing about, he noticed no commotion of blinds being drawn too quickly or of doors shutting too suddenly among the houses to his left and right and across the street.

Berde dragged Maria's corpse into his narrow little foyer and shut the door. He winced at the trail of blood she left on his pristine hardwood. Berde had spent a lot of time restoring his narrow three-story row house one block off Broad Street. Part of him resented Maria's defiling his space. He knelt on one knee beside her. She was not a pretty sight.

Her nose veered sharply to the left. The cartilage bunched under the surface of the skin looked like the folds in a lizard's neck. Cigarette burns cratered her cheeks; her tongue lolled; her eyes protruded. A wire garrote twisted tightly about her neck created an obscene crescent of puffy flesh resembling a toothless smile stretching from ear to ear.

This was not Maria, he told himself. This was not the pretty young Puerto Rican girl he had sought out and seduced because she was a servant in the household of Berto Rinaldi, consiglere to the Philadelphia mob. This obscene caricature of beautiful young Maria had been sent by the devil to torment him for the sins of hubris and of lust.

Berde wasn't a Catholic, but he had taken Maria to church at venues far from the prying eyes of the Rinaldis. Now, in tribute, he made the sign of the cross as he had seen Maria do, touching his forehead and chest. Then, overcoming his revulsion at last, he swept her up and brought her close to him, whispering in her ear:

"Maria, Maria. What have they done to you? What have I done to you?"

She was unyielding and unforgiving in his embrace. As he lowered her gently to the floor, he noticed an envelope pinned to her skirt. He extracted the note inside and held it up in the morning light streaming through the rectangular window of his front door.

"Unless you want the same thing to happen to Sarah, bring the tape to the Pink Cat, tonight at 9."

Oh God, not Sarah, too. He couldn't abide a similar fate befalling Maria's 16-year-old sister. He had done the Ginoble family enough harm already.

Berde stood, wiped his hands on the back of his pants and stared at Maria, unsure of what to do next. He turned, climbed the stairs to his bedroom, and collected a film canister and the tape Maria had delivered to him the night before.

"Whad-ya get?" he had asked as she pressed the tape into his hand during their furtive rendezvous on the Bryn Mawr College campus near the Thomas Cloisters Fountain in which Katherine Hepburn had so famously skinny-dipped.

"I'm not sure," she said. "I was busy in the kitchen preparing food for his guests. Mr. Rinaldi hadn't entertained that many people since the memorial service for his daughter two weeks ago."

"Who were his guests?"

"Lenny Davenport, for one."

Her eyes were aglow in the darkness.

"He joined the men for cigars and brandy. You should have seen those greaseballs fawning on him."

Berde smiled at her choice of words. Apparently she paid attention when he slipped into cop speak.

"Doesn't surprise me Davenport showed up. His ties to the mob are common knowledge. Did you recognize any of the greaseballs?"

"You should know. Mr. Rinaldi warned his guests that someone was outside in the bushes taking pictures. My guess is that someone was you."

"That's the price of infamy. One of them may have been Giovanni Valenti from Miami. I'll have to develop the film to be sure, but if it's Valenti, we're talking some high octane juice."

Berde was talking fast. His skin was flushed and hot like that of a junkie riding the crest of a heroin high. Maria was amused by his ardor.

"You really love this stuff, don't you?" she asked.

They both tensed as they were suddenly silhouetted against the M. Carey Thomas Library in the headlights of an approaching automobile. The driver bumped off his high beams and eased by slowly.

"Listen, I have to get back. Mr. Rinaldi doesn't like it if I'm out late when I have to work the next morning."

"You don't think he knows what you're up to? I couldn't stand it if something were to happen to you. Damn it. I should never have gotten you involved in this."

Maria stepped forward straining on her tiptoes to give him a quick kiss on the lips. "I'm doing this because I love you, and because Mr. Rinaldi shouldn't be helping those bad men."

Her innocence was sublime. Berde's heart hurt. "I love you, too," he replied.

He surprised himself with the admission. "I really do."

"I know that, silly."

She kissed him again and walked away. She looked over her shoulder and smiled at him one last time. Then the darkness swallowed her whole.

Berde put the tape and film canister down on a table in the foyer and picked up the phone. He stared for a few moments more at the corpse that had been Maria Ginoble before dialing a number that rang on the desk of Police Lieutenant Johnny Cole.

"Johnny? It's Bill. Don't talk. Just listen."

"Where have you been, asshole. I don't care how deep your cover is; you're supposed to check in with me twice a week."

"Maria's dead! They dumped her at my front door this morning."

"Who's Maria?"

"My cover's blown to smithereens and I've got to lay low until I figure out what to do next."

"Who's Maria," Cole asked again.

"Was. She was a maid in Berto Rinaldi's household. There was a big powwow at his place last night and she taped it for me. Johnny, I was outside in the bushes when they arrived and I think I may have spotted Giovanni Valenti!"

"Valenti? The Miami mobster? Sweet Jesus."

"Berde back pedaled. "I don't know for sure. I haven't had time to develop the film or listen to the tape. But this must be hot because Maria's dead. Goddamn it Johnny. They broke her nose and burned her face with cigarettes before they garroted her!"

Berde was crying now and Cole was smart enough to keep his mouth shut and let the emotional firestorm burn itself out.

Berde set down the phone and wrestled his handkerchief from his back pocket. He blew his nose and picked up the handset again.

"Can you send a couple of uniforms to my house to take care of Maria? She's in the foyer. I'll leave the key under the flower pot on my back porch."

"Pluck that wild hair from your ass and listen to me. I want you to stay put until the uniforms show up. They're already on their way. I want you to have an armed escort when you bring that tape in to headquarters. And you'd better tell me that Judge Schaeffer signed off on the tap. God I'd love to nail Valenti."

Berde slammed down the phone without answering. He picked up the tape and film canister and headed to the kitchen to collect his car keys and navy pea coat.

Berde left his house with no clear idea of what to do next other than to put as much distance as possible between him and the late Maria Ginoble. Inspiration struck as he settled in behind the wheel of his 1959 Studebaker Lark. His buddy Dave Mahaffey was just coming off a third-shift weekend . . . and he had a darkroom in his basement. Mahaffey wouldn't be happy to see Berde at 8:30 a.m. on a Monday morning on his day off, but Berde had no other options. He had to identify all of the guests at Berto Rinaldi's home on the evening of Sunday, Nov. 17, 1963.

If he didn't survive his encounter with the mob minions that, anyway, could be his legacy.

33

MONDAY, NOVEMBER 18, 1963

FAIRVIEW, NEW JERSEY — Jacob Manley was stocking beer in a cooler at the Pink Cat when his high school chum Bill Berde took a seat at the bar. Like Manley, Berde had grown up in Fairview. They were in the same class at Camden High. Berde was a sergeant in the Philadelphia Police Department. Jacob had heard through the FOP grapevine that his friend was working undercover.

The hands of the Budweiser clock were aimed at 4:35 and Jacob was using the lull to prepare for the storm of beer drinkers who would descend upon the Pink Cat when happy hour started at 5.

"Hey Jacob, what's new?" Berde asked.

Jacob looked up from his task.

Berde's face was pasty white; his eyes were bloodshot; there was a smear of snot on his right cheek and the corners of his mouth were caked with chalky dried spit.

"Jesus Bill you look like shit."

"That's right Jacob never pull your punches."

Jacob threw a fake jab at Berde's jaw. Berde didn't flinch. It was as if his synapses had short-circuited.

"Sorry. I've just had a real shock." Berde rubbed his mouth with the back of his hand and tried to swallow. His halitosis was palpable. Jacob stepped back in disbelief.

"Jesus. I'm as dry as the Sahara. Gimme a beer will ya? And keep em coming until I'm drunk enough to tell you all about Maria."

"Who's Maria?"

"The girl I just killed . . . or might as well have."

"What!"

Berde folded his hands like a supplicant. "She was an informant and they got to her."

"Who's they? The mob?"

Berde pointed a forefinger at Manley's chest. "Give that man a kewpie doll. And give me a shot of Old Crow while you're at it. I've got some forgetting to do."

Manley pulled an ice-cold Camden from the cooler, opened it with a church key, and set it down in front of Berde. He picked up a shot glass and studied Berde for a long moment over its rim. He swiped the shot glass with a bar rag and set it down in front of Berde, too. "I'll pour you a shot, but when I decide you've had too many you'll hand over your car keys without a whimper."

Berde licked his lips and nodded.

Manley studied his face for a long moment. "No bullshit!"

"No bullshit. Now set it up Jacob, please?"

Jacob filled Berde's shot glass to the rim. "Anything I can do to help?"

Berde shook his head. "Nope. It's out of your jurisdiction old buddy. Besides, the boys must be all over it by now, not that anyone will ever be able to prove it was the mob."

Berde seized the shot glass with the desperation of a drowning man grabbing a life preserver. He tipped his head back and swallowed the whiskey in one gulp. He chased it with a long pull of Camden. "Thanks. I needed that."

Berde sucked down the rest of his Camden in four or five long swallows and slid a key ring across the bar.

"Set me up again while I take a piss."

He pushed back his bar stool and climbed to his feet, without a wobble. He held his arms up at shoulder height and stood on one leg. His double-breasted pea coat was buttoned all the way to the collar. He looked like a kid dressed to play in the snow.

Berde flapped his arms like a goony bird cleared for takeoff. "Look ma, no hands!" he said. A thick 5- by 8-inch manila envelope fell from his coat pocket. Berde stooped, retrieved the envelope and shoved it back into his pocket.

Manley waved at him dismissively. "Take care of your business and the drinks will be waiting for you when you come back. And Bill?"

"Yes."

"Wash your face and gargle with some tap water while you're at it. It will do wonders for your sex life."

Berde laughed. "I just want to get drunk. I'm not out to get laid, because, hell, I'm screwed already."

Berde was carrying his heavy pea coat over his left arm when he emerged from the bathroom and joined three early birds watching the minutes tick away until happy hour. Berde sat down, draped the pea coat over his knees, and quickly finished off the shot and beer Manley had waiting for him.

"How 'bout another round," he yelled at Manley who was busy with another customer.

Glancing up from a cooler, Manley noticed that Berde had washed his face and combed his hair. His face had an alcoholic glow and his eyes gleamed as if they were backlit by a bonfire.

"I'll take care of it Jacob," said Sylvia Hanrahan who had arrived to start her shift while Berde was in the men's room.

"Thanks Sylvia."

Manley set up a beer for another customer, but before he made change, he paused and patted his left pants' pocket where he'd stored Bill Berde's car keys . . . just to be sure.

34

FAIRVIEW, NEW JERSEY — In the inevitable progression of happy hour, kidneys distilled Camden beer to its essential element and the graffiti over the urinals reminded patrons of the obvious:

"You don't buy beer, you rent it."

The babble of drunken voices, clinking of glasses, and the lilt of alcohol-induced mating rituals built to a crescendo that was impossible to sustain. As seven o'clock approached, the happy hour drinkers staggered off to face the music of neglected spouses and restless children over a late dinner.

The pace for Jacob and Sylvia slowed, offering a bit of respite before a second wave of revelers washed up like flotsam on the shoals of the Pink Cat. These were serious drinkers, who had no regard for the cost of beers and shots and were driven by their need to recapture the glow of the last night's drunk, or perhaps to chase away the last vestiges of a lunchtime hangover with another hair of the dog.

At 9 o'clock, Jacob realized that it had been some time since he'd seen Bill Berde. By his recollection, he'd served Bill five beers and four shots. He conferred with Sylvia, who said she had served him four beers and two glasses of rose.

Hearing that news, Jacob shuddered.

"I wouldn't give you a plug nickel for his head tomorrow morning, unless he bought the wine for a lady."

He patted his pocket, confirming anew that Berde's car keys resided there still. "Oh well," he said to Sylvia. "I have his keys. If he wants his car back, he'll show up . . . eventually."

Their conversation was interrupted by the arrival of Lenny Davenport.

Sylvia spotted him first.

"Jesus Christ Jacob. That guy looks for all the world like, like . . .

"Jules Tripoli?" Manley said.

He glared at the fat man stationed on the entertainer's right flank like a fighter guarding a B-29.

"No, Lenny Davenport, silly!" Sylvia said. "I just love his records."

Davenport was trim, manicured and confident and made no attempt to be inconspicuous. He raised his right arm in greeting as he walked into the bar, and then began shaking hands like a politician working the crowd at a pig roast.

While Hanrahan rushed forward to greet the singer, Manley hung back and observed Davenport's entourage through cop eyes. In addition to Jules Tripoli, a mob enforcer with an evil reputation, he recognized the suave attorney, Berto Rinaldi, who was wearing an Italian cut suit of a quality rivaling the one worn by his more famous companion. Jacob was pretty sure one of the men in Davenport's entourage was Frederico Scarlata, a mobster with a national reputation.

He wondered if their presence had anything to do with Bill Berde's showing up at the bar with his tale of woe. Manley scanned the crowd anew, searching for his friend among the people crowding about Davenport. He noticed that Tripoli was pushing his way through the crowd and studying the customers as if to assess any security risks among them.

Satisfied, he nodded at Rinaldi who smiled and escorted his friends to a table, which Sylvia Hanrahan had no trouble clearing of customers eager to defer to a celebrity. Davenport shook a few more hands before joining the others at the table. As Sylvia hurried to the bar with their drink orders, Manley noticed Tripoli slipping quietly out the front door, probably to establish security on the perimeter.

"Lenny would like a Jack Daniels on the rocks. Make it a double and put it on my tab," Sylvia said.

She was out of breath and her eyes sparkled with excitement. "How 'bout the other guys," Jacob asked.

Sylvia was so flustered she had to concentrate to remember the rest of the order.

"Let me think. Oh yeah. I need a glass of Merlot, a Budweiser and a whiskey and soda."

"Merlot? What kind of wine cellar do they think we have here? Closest I can come is a Gallo Burgundy. Ask 'em if that's OK while I build the other drinks."

Manley had the order set up when Sylvia made her way back to the waitress station. "The wine drinker will have a Dewar's scotch instead. Neat, whatever that means."

Manley nodded. As he poured the Dewar's, he noticed Bill Berde emerging from the bathroom. Berde skirted the crowd around Davenport's table and made his way to the front door. Either he didn't recognize Davenport or he didn't care. Catching Jacob's eye, Berde smiled, winked, and made the OK sign with his thumb and forefinger. Manley set the Dewar's on the tray next to Davenport's Jack Daniels as Berde opened the door and stepped outside.

Manley didn't see his friend again until early the next morning under appallingly different circumstances. Phone calls at 3:30 a.m. seldom portend good news and this call from the watch superintendent at his precinct spelled disaster for Bill Berde.

"Jacob," Carlton Smith said. "A patrol in the 200 block of Kansas Road in Fairview came across a man slumped over the wheel of a Studebaker. It's pretty clear the guy is dead. I know this is your day off but could you go over and check it out? We're really short staffed right now."

Manley eased Bill's head off the steering wheel and stared into his friend's dead face. He looked ghastly in the glow of the patrol officer's big flashlight. The car stunk of piss and shit. Berde had lost control of his bladder and his sphincter in extremis.

"What an awful epitaph for a good cop," Manley said.

The patrol officer turned the flashlight blinding him. "What?"

"Point that thing somewhere else," Manley said.

"Sorry."

Manley crouched beside the pile of bones and clothes and stink that had been Bill Berde. His cheeks burned with shame. Berde had never stopped by the bar to pick up his car keys and Jacob had been lazy. It was simpler to conclude that Berde had caught a cab home than to raise the alarm and beat the bushes for his friend.

He stood, making room for the forensics techs. After the body was bagged and removed, Manley went home and burned the bar napkin inscribed with the words:

"To Jacob Manley, who pours a mean JD. Warmest regards, Lenny Davenport."

35

FRIDAY, OCTOBER 17, 2003

FORT EUSTIS, VIRGINIA — Mike Kincaid awoke to banging and clanging and men's voices calling to one another. His first thought, having been dragged from a dream that had stiffened his manhood with the remote hope of morning sex, was that garbage men have no regard for the sanctity of sleep.

"It's OK, honey. I took out the trash last night."

"I love it when you call me honey," Emilio Sanchez said.

"What!" Kincaid sat up abruptly, banging his head on the underside of a chart table. "Ouch. Son of a bitch."

"Quiet you guys," said a sleepy female.

In Kincaid's semi-somnolent stupor, he mistook the voice for that of his dead wife. Hope and regret collided creating a violent updraft that subsided suddenly leaving him in a dizzying emotional freefall when he realized the voice belonged to Sharon Albright.

He lay down and curled into the fetal position, aware now that he and his companions were uncomfortably ensconced in sleeping bags atop air mattresses on the bridge of the former USS *Compass Island*, which years of neglect had reduced to a rust-flecked bucket held together tenuously by fifty-year-old rivets and bolts. It was a crime that time had obscured the hard work of the thousands of sailors who over the years had invested so much sweat equity in chipping and sanding and painting in the inexorable and, as it turned out, futile, war against the elements.

As he lay there, remorseful once again for prolonging Alice's life and then ending it, Kincaid sorted through the events leading to his present circumstances. William Fetrow and Bill Grisham had organized his defense as Sanchez had described. Fetrow would handle the alibi documentation in New Bloomfield and

Grisham would backtrack the planted evidence that led to Kincaid's arrest in the first place. Fetrow was collecting the sworn affidavits of two waitresses and six customers who could attest to Kincaid's presence at 7 p.m. on Sept. 19 and again at 8 a.m. on Sept. 20, at the County Seat restaurant in New Bloomfield.

The customers included two lawyers, the district attorney and the president judge of the Perry County Court of Common Pleas. Both lawyers were fairly confident that the charges against Kincaid would be dropped at the preliminary hearing. Grisham had cultivated a spy in the medical examiner's office who told him the time of death was somewhere between 9 p.m. on Friday, Sept. 19, and 3 a.m. on Saturday, Sept. 20.

"I've seldom seen such sloppy police work," Grisham told Kincaid. "I know Fronk and Harriott. They are usually much more thorough. The ballistics are irrefutable, but given what we know they should be looking for the person who planted the gun in your trunk and the letter from the insurance company in your suitcase, rather than wasting their time and ours trying to hang what's obviously a bum rap on you."

"So what do you make of that?" Kincaid wanted to know.

"I'd say that they were crowded off their game. Someone important wanted you to cool your ass in jail for a while, and probably was dismayed that you made bail," Grisham said. "You got lucky when you pulled Evan Steven as the district magistrate. He pretty much lives up to his name."

"Any idea who might have wanted me to be arrested so badly?"

"I'm working on that. I've put out some feelers; we'll see what pops up."

"So there's really no need for me to stick around Fairview?" Kincaid asked.

"Nope. Just make sure you show up for your preliminary hearing. Meanwhile I'll keep working to get the charges dismissed altogether."

Thus reassured, Kincaid felt better about allowing Sanchez to pressure him into stowing away aboard the *Compass Island*. He rationalized his capitulation by harboring a secret ambition. He knew his way around a computer keyboard more intimately than that whelp Gale Johnston. His first-person account of how the CIA stomped on his civil rights to hide the truth about JFK's assassination would be a compelling story. Of that, he was certain.

Sanchez staged their expedition aboard the *Compass Island* from the luxurious Kingsmill Resort and Spa at Williamsburg, Virginia. It was just a mile and a half, upstream of the cluster of ships the *Compass Island* occupied in the James River Reserve Fleet.

Their accommodations were expensive, but Sanchez had insisted on picking up the tab. Kincaid concluded that he was merely offering the condemned the equivalent of their final meal. The women accepted his largesse eagerly, signing up for what the brochure called a Classic Spa Experience. Johnston who had toured several of the ghost ships for her stories in the Virginia Pilot knew what was in store. The amenities aboard the *Compass Island* would be primitive, so why not enjoy a bit of comfort now, she told Albright.

While the women were being rubbed and buffed, Kincaid buried his nose in a book and in frequent draughts of expensive bourbon while Sanchez busied himself with the preparations. To facilitate its passage from Fort Eustis to Hartlepool, England, the *Compass Island* was to be equipped with modern, diesel-powered bilge pumps to combat the insipid infiltration of sea water through her leaky hull.

Sanchez bribed the civilian contractor hired to install the bilge pumps and stocked the *Compass Island* with a boatload of provisions which he apparently had assembled well in advance. Under the pretense that Kincaid was Commander Clinton Pierce, USN retired, a former captain of the old ship, the Maritime Administration authorized the four of them to board the USS *Compass Island* the day before it was to embark. Their cover story was that Johnston was a freelance reporter commissioned by All Hands Magazine to do a story on a former captain's fond farewell as his old command began its final voyage.

Sanchez was billed as the photographer, while Sharon Albright pretended to be Commander Pierce's daughter. They arrived at the old ship in a boat piloted by the contractor whose mission was a final inspection of the bilge pumps. When the contractor left, a bribe ensured that they stayed behind.

Kincaid was impressed with Sanchez's organizational skills. The provisions he accumulated included a Sterno stove, a small copper-bottomed pot, tins of soup and meats, four cases of bottled water, three bags of apples, two bed pans, one for the men and one for the women, moist toweletts, tampons, toilet paper, sleeping bags, air mattresses, a portable torch and two sets of replacement bottles, and an air tester to ensure it was safe to enter closed off spaces of the ship.

The plan was to lay low aboard the *Compass Island* until they were well out to sea, on the offside chance that they might be spotted and removed from the ship before they had recovered the documents.

They had spent a restless night, lying on the dusty green tile of the bridge waiting for the ship to disembark, which apparently it now was prepared to do, with the assistance of the ocean-going tugboat, now positioning itself, noisily, off the bow of the *Compass Island*.

Being careful not to bang his head on the chart table a second time, Kincaid arose to a crouch and peeked out the bridge window. He caught a glimpse of the stern of the tugboat and of two men clad in work clothes and hard hats waiting on the forecastle to ensure that the heavy wire tether was positioned properly in the chocks and securely attached to its stanchion for the final voyage ahead.

The name of the tugboat was emblazoned in large letters across the stern. Daddy's Little Princess. An unusual name that.

Just then Sanchez pulled him back sharply by his belt. "Keep your head down, stupid. We don't want to be noticed. Not yet, anyway."

Kincaid plopped down on his butt and grabbed his right knee, which didn't take kindly to sudden movements. He rubbed his knee and glared at Sanchez.

"You didn't have to do that, asshole. I would have dropped down if you'd asked me to."

"I've got a lot invested in this operation. I can't risk having you fuck it up at the last minute."

"Now boys," Albright said. "Play nice."

36

WASHINGTON, D.C. — U.S. Senator Wiley Patterson slid behind his desk in the Senate office building early on a clear Friday morning, eager to tackle the new day. His meeting with George W. Bush the day before still had his corpuscles coursing. Cheney's heart was weak and George had lost confidence in him as the war in Iraq dragged on, and on.

"The Democrats occupy the moral high ground here, or at least they think they do," George W. Bush said. "They take pot shots every time Rummy or Dick break cover. I'm tired of it. Would you consider replacing Cheney on the Republican ticket should his health suddenly fail him?"

Does a cat have an ass?

Senator Patterson's first order of business this day was to touch base with his younger brother, who was spearheading the effort to contain the danger posed by Emilio Sanchez. He punched the numbers for his brother's private line. Albert Patterson answered on the second ring.

"Is everything copasetic, brother?" Wiley asked.

"Sanchez wants a helicopter to pick him up tomorrow afternoon off the coast of New Jersey. He hid grandma's diary aboard Dad's old ship, the *Compass Island*, which is being towed across the ocean to be demolished somewhere in England. Robert Cabot is so hyped he's gonna join Pepitone aboard that helicopter. Says he wants to see this thing through, personally."

"Are you sure we're not overreacting? Great grandpa was dirty, but we're as clean as a whistle . . . at least until now. That's what Dad says, anyway," Wiley said.

"Dad's lost the fire in his belly," Al replied. "Don't go getting cold feet on me. Cabot agrees. This is the thing to do. Keep your eye on the prize Mr. Vice President."

Wiley Patterson's balls tingled when his brother said that. Yes, the prize was within his grasp if he had the courage to take hold of it.

"OK Al. I'll follow your lead, but this had better not bite me in the ass."

"Relax, big bro. I've got your back on this one."

"Yeah, but who has your back?"

"Cabot. He and Pepitone will neutralize Sanchez."

"I can't countenance murder."

"Don't lose any sleep over Sanchez. He's already killed two people," Al Patterson said.

"Who? No don't answer that I need deniability."

"Then deny you know this. Cabot's pretty sure Sanchez killed a U.S. Navy SEAL named Cloyd Murphy."

"Slow down. You're losing me," Senator Patterson said. "Cabot says that the serial number on the Sig 9 that the Camden police recovered from Kincaid's trunk matches a weapon issued to a petty officer who was murdered during a training exercise aboard an abandoned ship in the James River Reserve Fleet back in March. Care to guess the name of that ship?"

"The *Compass Island*?"

"Bingo."

"God damn it. That means Sanchez killed Jacob Manley as well," Senator Patterson said.

"Probably," his brother agreed.

"Has the CIA reported in with the Camden police?" the senator asked.

"Nope. Cabot asked them not to. He figures that Sanchez tried to recover the documents back in March, but he stumbled into a SEALs training mission and had to kill Murphy. He used Murphy's Sig 9 to kill Jacob Manley and then planted it in Kincaid's trunk."

"Why would he do that?"

"To facilitate Kincaid's cooperation. Cabot expedited Kincaid's arrest in an attempt to contain that situation, but the plan backfired. Kincaid caught a DJ with a brain and Sanchez was able to spring him on bail."

"Why would Sanchez want to murder Kincaid's stepfather?"

"Think about that one for a moment?" Al Patterson said.

"Shit! I'd be the obvious suspect if the police find out Manley was blackmailing me."

"Bingo. What's more, I'm betting that Cabot told Sanchez that Manley was blackmailing you . . . knowing full well how Sanchez would react."

"How would Manley's death be in Sanchez's self-interest?"

"It wouldn't surprise me if both Cabot and Sanchez have a stake in securing the record of great grandpa's meeting with his mob minions back in 1963."

"What can that be?"

"I don't know for sure. I've got Pepitone sniffing around that issue, but I don't know whether he's working for us or for Cabot. His loyalties lie with whoever is paying him the most and Cabot has deep pockets."

"So why did Sanchez draw Kincaid, Johnston and Albright into his snare?" the senator asked.

"For leverage. To pry even more money from us. Think about it. Gale Johnston worked for one of our papers for Christ's sake. How better to get our attention? Kincaid is the only surviving witness to dad's accident on the bridge of the *Compass Island* . . ."

"And Johnston backs up his threat to publish a book," Wiley Patterson said. "But what about Albright? Why did he involve her?"

"Two reasons. First, Sanchez needed her to unlock Kincaid's memory of Dad's attack on Kennedy aboard the *Compass Island*. Cabot wanted Kincaid killed back in 1963. Sanchez intervened. Suggested they turn Kincaid over to the psych types instead."

"Brain washing?"

"Yeah. Something like that, but Cabot thinks Sanchez had another reason to reel the good doctor in," Al Patterson said.

"What was that?"

"Albright was Sanchez's therapist. Cabot suspects that maybe he let something dangerous slip during a therapy session and now he wants to silence her. This little expedition he's organized lets him gather all his liabilities together in one spot and then dispose of them beyond the prying eyes of law enforcement."

"Jesus, Al. The bodies are piling up like cordwood. Dad's right. We shouldn't have anything to do with this. I think we should tell Cabot that we're not interested in his final solution. I need to wash my hands of this and now!"

"Not an option, big bro. The train's left the station and is traveling at full speed. We can't jump off now. The impact would kill us all. Now go back to being a United States senator and a candidate for vice president and let me and Cabot handle the details. And Wiley . . .

"Yes."

"We never had this conversation. Right?"

Wiley Patterson squeezed the phone to his ear so tightly that it hurt. "What conversation?" He hung up the phone.

37

FRIDAY, OCTOBER 17, 2003

OFF THE COAST OF DELAWARE — Marcie McDermott brushed her teeth in the small stainless steel washbasin in the captain's cabin aboard Daddy's Little Princess. She hated the name her father had selected for the powerful oceangoing tug. It belittled the boat's formidable attributes. Daddy's Little Princess was well-suited for its current enterprise, towing a 17,000-ton ship across the Atlantic Ocean.

Marcie's father, Edmund McDermott, founder of McDermott Towing Service Inc. of Hampton Roads, Virginia, had done the best he could, raising a daughter in a man's world. His wife, Marcie's mother, Shirley, was killed in an automobile accident when Marcie was 2. A drunk driver in a 1969 Ford Econoliner bounced over the medial strip and struck Shirley's little 1966 Volkswagen head on.

Daddy's Little Princess was finished three years later when Marcie was a pigtailed five-year-old, cast by inclination as well as circumstance in the mold of Pippy Longstockings. Edmund McDermott's business flourished, but his daughter grew up on the docks. That was the compromise Edmund reached, balancing the exigency of building a business with the imperative of nurturing a small child and a girl at that.

Marcie didn't see growing up on the docks (and aboard a tugboat) as a compromise, even if her father did. She saw it as a glorious adventure and had grown up to be a bawdy, hardworking woman who was in touch with her feminine side but was aggressive in the pursuit of what she wanted, professionally . . . and romantically, which was the source off her present discomfort.

Marcie was the titular captain of Daddy's Little Princess, but Kirk Cramer was in charge (unless he really screwed up) on this, his shakedown cruise to earn his master's papers. Kirk, 35, was a furry bear of a man. He stood six-foot three-inches tall, weighed 220 pounds and bore the scars of one who had learned the business from the bottom up. At this stage in his career, he knew his way around an oceangoing tugboat as intimately as he knew his way around Marcie McDermott.

They had been lovers until six months ago when Marcie learned that Kirk had consummated a flirtation with the pretty little chippie Edmund McDermott hired to be his personal secretary. Cheryl Miller came on board after Ethel, Edmund's longtime girl Friday, finally gave up trying to lure the boss into a romantic relationship and moved on to greener pastures. Tongues wagged when petite, short-skirted, scoop-bloused Cheryl Miller, all 5 voluptuous feet of her, moved into Ethel's old desk.

Everyone assumed that the old man had finally succumbed to a mid-life crisis. Everyone was wrong. Edmund was oblivious to Cheryl's charms. The only thing he cared about was that she could type 70 words per minute.

Kirk had other interests. He slept with both women until Marcie found out and banished him from her bed. Kirk responded by proposing marriage. Marcie turned him down. So Kirk moved down the list. Now, Cheryl was wearing a large diamond (Marcie figured it at two-thirds of a karat) on the ring finger of her right hand.

Marcie spit, spotting the stainless steel with white froth. She ran just enough water to fill a Dixie cup. She swished the water about in her mouth and spit just so to rinse the froth down the drain. Water conservation came as second nature to her. The tugboat's evaporators, which distilled seawater, were old and balky. It was best not to over stress them.

Marcie sniffed her pits and decided she could do without a sponge bath. She studied herself in the mirror above the sink. She liked what she saw. Hers was a wind-burnt face, with a swatch of freckles across the nose. She was 36, but her neck, jaw line, and chin were chiseled still. No wattles or jowls on board.

Her breasts weren't overly generous, but Marcie was glad she didn't have big boobs. They'd have gotten in her way when she was working. Unlike some of her more generously endowed friends there was no sag. Marcie hummed a little tune and laughed, thinking of the words: "Do your boobs hang low? Do they wobble to and fro? Can you tie them in a knot? Can you tie them in a bow?"

She slipped on the long-sleeved denim shirt she wore instead of pajamas or a nightgown. She had borrowed the shirt from Kirk back when they were still dating and had never returned it. She considered it her due under community property rules. She'd sleep with it unbuttoned tonight, because autumn hadn't arrived off the coast of Delaware and the daytime highs were in the mid-70s. It was stuffy in the captain's stateroom, which she had claimed as her own despite Kirk's growing status with McDermott Towing Inc.

She turned back the bedclothes and crawled in her double-wide bunk wearing just her panties and Kirk's old shirt. She fluffed up the pillow, kicked around until she had the bed clothes loosened enough to accommodate her feet (she had big feet, size 10—Kirk had always teased her about her feet) and she flipped off the wall switch. Sometime during the night she stirred in the languid embrace of an erotic dream. She was sleeping on her side with her back to the door and someone was lying spoon like behind her. Rough fingers teased the nipple of her right breast. A hardness pressed upward between her legs from behind. Ummm! That felt nice, she thought, snuggling backward and grinding her bottom. Suddenly she sat bolt upright. This was no dream. That was a for real hard-on.

"God damn it Kirk. Get out of my bed this instant. You hairy pervert!"

"Now why would you want me to do that when you seem to be enjoying yourself so?" he asked.

"Piss off Kirk. You've made your choice in women. Now pack up your gear and get out of here."

"Oh come on Marcie. What will it hurt? I know you want to."

"What I want is irrelevant," Marcie replied. "What I need, you can't give me anymore."

"And what's that?"

"Monogamy!"

She elbowed him in the ribs "Out."

Grumbling, he swung his legs over the bed and kicked around on the floor trying to find his boxer shorts in the scant starlight eking through the cabin's lone, spray-flecked porthole.

He got one foot in his shorts and stumbled heavily into the bulkhead while trying to put the other foot in.

"Shit!"

Marcie laughed. "Lose about 20 pounds big guy and you'll be able to see your feet."

"Not in this light," he replied.

He pulled up his shorts and took a couple steps toward the door.

"Last chance."

"Out!" Marcie said, with false force to obscure her growing indecision. It would be nice . . . she thought to herself. And what would it hurt? But then her resolve stiffened. It was even harder than his manhood, which was poking up a tent in the front of his boxer shorts.

"Out," she said, again.

He left, mumbling something about a cold shower. Marcie rolled over and went back to sleep. This time her erotic dreams really were dreams and the bonus was, she didn't have to sleep in the wet spot. Men, who needs them?

Marcie slept to the thrum, thrum, thrumming of the tug's powerful twin diesels. The single screw drove Daddy's Little Princess forward at a stately 6 knots past Delaware's Delmarva Peninsula. Behind it 200 yards or so, the USS *Compass Island* rose and fell at the end of its tether, at sea again after years at moorage in the James River Reserve Fleet.

Marcie awoke at 5 a.m. and took a quick shower in the head down the passageway. She flipped a sign on the door handle to warn the otherwise all male crew of seven to keep out. Dressed in her work uniform of dungarees, a short-sleeved denim shirt, and steel-toed work boots, she clomped into the galley and poured a cup of coffee, which she drank black, although she would have preferred cream and sugar, to prove to her crew that she was tough.

She wandered aft to the fantail to check the dual-drum towing assembly then watched as the *Compass Island* rose and fell at the end of the heavy wire rope. She felt a mariner's regret at the fate that awaited the old girl. Rust-blotched though she was, she had an elegance born of superior design. The ocean embraced the old ship like a lover as her bow cut through the gentle swells.

A flash of light from the forecastle of the old ship caught her attention. She was visited with an uneasy feeling that someone was watching her through binoculars, but whom? The *Compass Island* was a Ghost Ship; at least that was what the newspapers were calling her.

She shielded her eyes with her hand and leaned forward studying the forecastle of the *Compass Island*. What was that? Was that a man ducking for cover behind the bulwark or was it a shadow cast by a cloud before the sun?

"Son of a bitch, there's someone on that ship!" she said to herself. As she headed back toward the pilothouse, she felt a tingling between her shoulder blades as if she'd just turned her back on the devil.

38

OFF THE COAST OF NEW JERSEY — The tugboat churned the ocean like a Cuisinart on steroids. As he watched through 7x binoculars from the forecastle deck of the former USS *Compass Island*, Mike Kincaid saw a sailor make his way along the port side of the tugboat.

Kincaid noticed a fullness to the sailor's denim work shirt and realized that he was a she, with honey blonde hair chopped short in the pageboy style. Suddenly, she stared his way and Kincaid, instinctively ducked behind the bulwark, even though he knew it was unlikely he had been spotted.

Kincaid heard footsteps and turned to see Emilio Sanchez coming toward him across the forecastle deck. Sanchez crouched even though the difference in the size of the two vessels made it unlikely that anybody aboard the tugboat might spot him.

"Jesus Mike, why don't you let me do all the hard work I've already lugged the cutting torch all the way from the quarterdeck. I could have used an extra set of hands."

Kincaid rose to a crouch on creaky knees and lurched forward to join Sanchez at the V-shaped baffle welded to the forecastle deck to keep seawater from overflowing the forward hatch during heavy seas.

"Sorry Skeeter, I just couldn't resist doing some exploring. It's a crying shame what's become of our old ship. She deserves a better fate."

"She served her purpose. She'd have been demolished long ago if it weren't for the *Observation Island*."

"Her sister ship?"

Sanchez nodded. "Yep. They kept the CI for spare parts for The *Observation Island*. She's still in service as a platform for a COBRA radar array. She's still on station in the Far East as a forward listening post to detect missile launches. She's the oldest ship in active service for the U.S. Navy, although the plan is to retire her in 2008."

"How do you know that?" Kincaid asked.

"The Internet, mostly." Sanchez exuded impatience. "Let's get busy; we've got work to do."

The two men made their way down the starboard side stairs leading from the forecastle to the main deck where they found the two women waiting for them next to the door leading to the spaces below the forecastle. Johnston sprawled on the deck with her back against the bulwark. She had the desperate look of a woman at the end of a line waiting to use the bathroom.

"How could you possibly be sea sick?" Sanchez asked her. "The sea is about as calm as you're going to ever see it."

"Just shut up and get on with it before I throw up on your shoes," Johnston said.

Kincaid yanked on the door handle. The dogs screeched and moved an inch or so. He yanked harder. The dogs lost their bite on the frame and the door swung open on rusty hinges.

Sanchez pulled a large police-style flashlight from its holster on his belt, clicked it on and shone it into the compartment. He stuck his head inside and sniffed tentatively.

"Whew, smells like the shower room at a reform school, but I don't think we'll have to break out the air-tester," he announced. "Still we'd better wait a few minutes before we go inside, just to let things air out a bit."

He pulled the door all the way open and secured it to the bulkhead, with the hook welded to the door for that purpose.

Clicking off the flashlight he sat down, propping himself against the bulwark.

"This is one of those times when I regret having stopped smoking cigarettes," he said. "Remember sea store cigarettes, Mike?"

Kincaid leaned against the rail, but didn't sit down, in deference to his knees. He smiled. "You bet. As soon as the ship cleared the harbor, the ship store could sell cigarettes tax-free. As I recall they were fifteen cents a pack. It was a lot easier to be a smoker back then before the surgeon general weighed in. Cheaper, too."

He looked over his right shoulder at the sea, which, at the moment was behaving itself beneath a brisk wind that stirred just an occasional whitecap. The sun was standing at port arms radiantly conspicuous above the ranks of puffy cirrus clouds as daytime followed its course west.

It was shaping up to be a pretty spectacular October day and Kincaid allowed himself the luxury of a smile. Sharon Albright glanced at him just as the smile materialized on his face. In that moment, she caught a glimpse of the young sailor who had trod these very decks forty years ago.

The moment was ruined by the sudden arrival of Gale Johnston at the ship's rail, fortunately downwind of Kincaid. Leaning over the rail, Johnston offered up the contents of her stomach like a cruise ship diva with three martinis on board.

Kincaid reached into his back pocket and pulled out a clean handkerchief.

"Here, take this. And, by the way, Gale?"

Johnston wiped the dribble from her chin and the pasty residue from the corners of her mouth. "Yes."

"Thanks for puking downwind. It's a bit of nautical protocol that is much appreciated among shipmates. And before you ask . . . I don't want my handkerchief back."

Albright laughed. Johnston scowled. And the status quo was restored.

"I think we can go inside now," Sanchez said.

He clicked on his big flashlight, stepped over the raised threshold of the watertight door, and disappeared into the darkness beyond. After a moment, he leaned back through the door and picked up the torch cart caddy.

"Come on Mike," he said, "let's have a look inside."

This was the moment Kincaid had been quietly dreading. The last time he had set foot in the forecastle was forty years ago to fight a fire in the sail locker. The ghostly image of the tall man in dungarees who had materialized in swirling smoke haunted him still.

Kincaid recalled the apparition's final words still:

"Mike me boy, is this world for real or for pretend? Come see me again and I'll answer you that."

Kincaid deferred to the women, but not for gallantry's sake. "After you, ladies. And I'd stay close to Sanchez if I were you. It's bound to be as dark as the ace of spades in there."

The women stepped through the door and Kincaid followed, clicking on his own flashlight to back light the enterprise. The space below the forecastle deck was full of dark corners that couldn't be reached by the sunlight streaming through the open door or by the beams of their flashlights. Tentative strands of light leaked through rust holes in the deck above, but added to rather than subtracted from the pervasive feeling of gloom, foreboding and neglect.

Kincaid struggled to remember the layout of the forecastle while keeping his eyes peeled for ghosts. The steel deck of the forecastle covered what had been the hatch to hold number one, which housed the ship's 300-kilowatt emergency generator. To his right as he stepped through the door was the fan room, which contained the blowers and conduit for the forward ventilation system.

To his left was the battery locker and moving forward on the port side was the sail locker where years ago Kincaid and BM2 McBride had extinguished a fire while the ship was in port at the Brooklyn Navy Yard. Next came a wire-meshed enclosure that had been the ship's brig. Forward of the brig and amidships was the decking that covered the chain locker where the anchor chains were stored when the ship was underway. Forward of the brig on either side of the bow were the two hawser pipes which channeled the anchor chains down to their locker below. And forward of the hawser pipes was a compartment at the very apex of the ship which had contained the emergency radio room.

The air in the forecastle was dusty and stuffy and smelled of mildew, ancient diesel oil and grease. The deck underfoot as they approached the door to the emergency radio room was slippery with a thin layer of slime created from the dust by rainwater that had infiltrated through rust holes in the deck above.

"Hold the light for me will you?" Sanchez asked.

He handed his heavy police flashlight to Albright, who without being instructed directed the beam over his shoulder as he worked. Sanchez opened the valves to the oxygen and acetylene tanks, powering up the system. He pulled on a pair of heavy work gloves to protect his hands and handed Kincaid a flint and metal striker.

He opened a valve at the base of the nozzle starting the gases flowing.

"Light me."

Kincaid clicked the striker twice before the sparks ignited the gas with a whoosh.

"Step back folks," Sanchez said.

Settling a pair of safety goggles over his eyes he went to work cutting through the door latch, which had been welded to a plate on the doorframe. The interior door was not watertight. In 1963, it had been secured with a security lock that required the proper sequence of numbered buttons to be depressed to unlatch the door. The latch assembly had been yanked from the door, so the only combination Sanchez needed to open it was that of oxygen and acetylene.

The blue tip of the torch turned the metal red hot and soon the weld was severed. Sanchez closed the valve, extinguishing the torch. He took a deep breath. "OK," he said, more to himself than to his companions. "This is it. Are we wasting our time, or not?"

He pulled on the knob and door opened with a screech that made Kincaid's skin crawl. Without meaning to, he looked over his shoulder to see if any apparitions lurked. The coast was clear.

"Don't you think you should wait a minute to make sure the air's OK?" Kincaid asked.

"Can't be any worse than it is right here," Sanchez replied.

He directed the beam of the flashlight into the emergency radio room and stepped inside.

"That explains it," Sanchez exclaimed.

"Explains what?" Johnston asked.

"Why they welded this space shut."

"Well, why did they?" Kincaid asked.

Curious now, Kincaid shouldered the women out of the way and stepped into the compartment.

Sanchez shone his flashlight at an object on the deck to Kincaid's left. "Look right here."

"What is it?" Kincaid asked, just as recognition dawned.

"It's an old 20 millimeter cannon, an Okeliron if I'm not mistaken. And look, they've left a couple of the ammunition drums as well. There are probably some live rounds in there. That's why they welded this space shut. Some yard bird got lazy and didn't feel like disposing of the cannon and ammo as surplus ordnance. Probably too much paperwork involved. So he shoved it in here, welded the door shut and decided to let the ship salvagers deal with it."

Sanchez's interest in the cannon quickly waned and he took six quick steps forward, shining his flashlight on the bulkhead.

"Let's see; they've pulled all the radio gear out of here, but as I recall, the transmitter was right about here."

He shone his flashlight on a section of the bulkhead. "Good. The insulation still is intact. Mike, keep the flashlight trained right here."

As Sanchez handed off his big flashlight, Kincaid was aware of the women entering the compartment behind them. Ignoring them, he kept both flashlights trained on the spot Sanchez had indicated. Sanchez pulled off his work gloves and dropped them on the deck. He took a folding knife from his pocket and knelt on one knee.

"A little to the left Mike," he said. "That's right. I sealed off the cut in the insulation with duct tape, but I can't tell the original from the new tape after all these years."

Sanchez made a foot-long vertical cut through the tape holding the insulation to a hull frame, stopping at the deck. He turned the blade and made another long cut along the deck, creating an L-shaped flap. He peeled back the insulation and snaked an arm inside along the hull plates.

"It's not here, damn it! Maybe I need to be one frame over."

Sanchez repeated the process about a foot to the right of his initial cut and groped around between the bulkhead and the insulation for several seconds.

"By God, here it is!" he bellowed. Sanchez pulled out a 12-inch by 24-inch envelope and waved it about like a kid showing off his first trout.

39

OFF THE COAST OF NEW JERSEY — Sharon Albright noticed the sound as soon as she stepped into the compartment. It was a gaspy wheezing death rattle—the sort of sound a sucking chest wound makes.

How that particular association leapt to her mind was a mystery because she couldn't recall having ever experienced a sucking chest wound. Not in this lifetime, anyway. The compartment under the forecastle deck of the USS *Compass Island* was dark and mildewy. She would rather have been anyplace else in the world.

The awful sound was so pervasive that she wondered why the others didn't notice it. But they were oblivious, too caught up in the drama of digging for buried treasure to notice the oppressive pressure gathering around them.

The wheezing became a strangled gurgle and in that awful, fetid wetness was a subtext that only she could hear. The words slithered sibilantly across the face of her consciousness, leaving a vile slime trail that threatened to defile her soul.

"Come rot with me me darlin'. I've misssssed you so. I'm right here, right now, right below. Who am I? I think you know." God! The others had to hear it. Why couldn't they hear it?

Was she crazy, or were they?

"No, don't even go there," she told herself. "You can handle this. You've handled worse."

Albright had long ago constructed a stout rampart to defend herself against the hordes of barbarian memories that were forever massed on the borders of her psyche. She took cover behind it now.

Mustering her resolve she drowned out the voice in the white noise of a litany of quasi-religious import that had enabled her to survive, even thrive, amid the cacophony of voices calling to her from the past, exhorting her to do this, or that. To take heed! Hark! Or, beware!

"My name is Sharon Albright and I have nothing to fear. My name is Sharon Albright and I am not afraid."

And then there was nothing but the white noise. The gurgling, muttering sibilance ceased and the pressure building around her dissipated. She noticed its passing as a puff of foul air against her cheek and as lingering whiff of decadence and decay.

Emilio Sanchez, captured still in the beam of Kincaid's flashlight, was grinning and waving his manila envelope about as if he were Lancelot in possession of the Holy Grail at long last.

A scream rent the air with the stridence of a fire siren. Kincaid and Sanchez instinctively turned toward the sound, skewering Gale Johnston to the shadows behind her like an insect pinned to a wax board.

Johnston's face was a study in contrast. She bore the shocked look of someone both terrified and mesmerized at the same time. She was a deer frozen in the headlights of an oncoming tractor-trailer, but her voice still worked, and how.

"Get away from me!" she screamed.

Her eyes darted back and forth across the compartment as if she were following the flight of a colony of bats suddenly roused from the sanctuary of their dank, dark cave.

Kincaid turned off his flashlight and went to her, but she shied from his approach, cowering as if she thought Kincaid meant her harm. She collapsed abruptly onto the deck. She flailed her arms as if bats had descended upon her and were nesting in her hair.

"Get away! Get away!" she screamed.

"Gale! What's wrong?" Kincaid yelled, alarmed by the strident urgency of this woman who heretofore had exuded a masculine sort of self-confidence and self-sufficiency that warned all others and men in particular to stay away, to keep their distance.

Bending, he grasped her shoulders and drew her toward him in a bear-like embrace. A flailing fist caught him on the jaw, but the blow did little more than startle him because he had moved toward her shortening the arc of her swing.

"God damn it Skeeter. A little help here, please."

Sanchez shoved his precious envelop under an arm and hurried forward, shining the flashlight on the deck ahead to light the path back to daylight.

"Let's get her out of here," he said. "She's probably just claustrophobic. She'll be better once we get her outside."

Stooping, Kincaid threw Johnston over his shoulder in a fireman's carry and followed close behind Sanchez. He nearly tripped over the raised threshold of the watertight door, but he carried her without pause until they were outside once again and a fresh ocean breeze began scrubbing the stench of forgotten spaces from their hair, from their clothes and from their nostrils. His pulse was pounding as he lowered her to the deck just beyond the forecastle. He went down on one knee beside her, as much to catch his breath as to tend to the stricken woman. Albright shouldered him aside.

"I'm a doctor, remember?"

Albright grasped Johnston's right wrist with her left hand and laid her index and middle fingers of her right hand on her patient's wrist.

"Her pulse is slow but steady," she said, after 30 seconds or so. Albright put her hand on Johnston's forehead and stared intently at her chest, watching it rise and fall.

After a minute more, Albright added: "She's not feverish. Her respiration is slow, much slower than normal, actually. It's almost as if she's meditating."

Albright rose and stood for a moment staring at Johnston.

"Prop her in the corner there, so she'll be comfortable while I think."

Albright pointed to the spot where the bulwark met the bulkhead of the forecastle.

Kincaid did as she instructed.

Albright knelt down beside Johnston again and stared intently into her face as if she were trying to peel away her skin to see what was underneath. Meanwhile, Sanchez unwound the string fastener of his precious envelope and carefully pulled out the contents. The envelope contained two motley covered blue books, the kind college students use for essay exams; a yellowed envelope, with the words "Hugh Patterson, USS *Compass Island* EAG 153, FPO 46173, Brooklyn, N.Y., written on the outside in cramped cursive; and several yellow sheets of teletype paper, torn ragged at the ends and held together with a rusty paper clip.

"They are all here!" Sanchez exclaimed. "The bastards are finally going to pay."

40

SATURDAY, OCTOBER 18, 2003

OFF THE COAST OF NEW JERSEY — John Franklin Kincaid awoke with a start from his long slumber, aroused by the sense that an old nemesis was near. It was she. He was certain of it. His rage built quickly to a boil.

He could tell that she felt his presence as well and that he terrified her still. Her fear aroused him in the old familiar sexual way.

"Come rot with me, me darlin'," he whispered. *"I've missssed you so. I'm right here, right now, right below. Who am I? I think you know."*

Her fear built and he was in his glory, in command again as this weak woman cowered before his rage. But then the connection was lost, her fear dissipated.

"Get away! Get away!

The words came to him as if they'd been transmitted directly to his aural nerve endings and in a startling epiphany; he realized that they were his own. He could hear the sound of his breathing and feel his heart constrict and relax.

There was hard metal behind his spine, just as there had been all those years ago, as he had died in agonizing increments alone and sobbing in a 20-square-foot steel prison. It was all her fault damn it. Kathleen had been unfaithful, but worse than that she and her lover had taken him off his game at the precise moment that being sharp was essential to his survival.

Kathleen hadn't killed him of course, but she might as well have and Jacob could have saved him, but didn't. Instead he'd sealed him alone and dying inside a steel tomb. They did this to him. They would have to pay.

But something was wrong. Something was amiss. He was expecting a powerful swell of shoulder muscles as he pushed himself up to a sitting position. Instead, he felt a weak spindly response as his brain told his forearms to tense and his biceps to contract and his deltoids to push.

He was not alone inside this skin. The other presence reasserted itself, countermanding his best intention to arise, to stand, to confront whatever obstacles this new day arrayed before him.

"No," said a tiny voice in his inner ear. "I must rest. I've had a shock. My name is Gale Johnston and I'm so afraid."

He felt a slap on his cheek. His eyes leapt open and he was staring into the face of his enemy. Her form was different. She was taller, leaner and more angular, than he remembered, but he recognized her for whom she had been.

He seized control again from the terrified Gale Johnston, commandeering the nerves, fibers and muscles of her speech as his own.

"You're a fucking bitch, Kathleen," he said.

God damn it! What was wrong? He sounded like a Goddamn woman, and he hated women. They were good for nothing more than cleaning, cooking and fucking. It was as simple as that.

"Shut up you pig," said his womanly voice now under control of his other.

This couldn't be happening to him. The crazy gods had resurrected him in female form. It was bad theatre and he would have nothing more to do with it. He'd bide his time until he was stronger. Until he could claim this body as his own, he'd bide his time.

"What did she just say?" Mike Kincaid asked, staring aghast at the contorted countenance of Gale Johnston.

"I think she said: 'You're a fucking bitch Kathleen,' and "Shut up you pig,'" Sharon Albright said.

"That mean anything to you?" Kincaid asked.

"Nope," Sharon Albright lied. In that moment, the certainty that she had been Kathleen Jablonski descended upon Sharon Albright. She knew that the bastard John Kincaid now lay before her in another guise.

She looked over her shoulder at her son. Mike Kincaid had been a hulking 17-year-old the last time Kathleen Manley clapped eyes on him. He had grown into a lumbering bear of a man who had endured much but was on the cusp of a revelation that would change the course of his life. She smiled a mother's smile at Mike Kincaid, who smiled back not just with his mouth and his eyes but with his soul as well.

She turned to John Kincaid lying before her in the body that now belonged to Gale Johnston and she said:

"Welcome home John you son of a bitch. Nobody has missed you."

Sharon Albright slapped John Kincaid across the face. Hard. And then Albright scooped Gale Johnston up in her arms, drew her close, and whispered fiercely in her ear: "Your name is Gale Johnston and you have nothing to fear. Your name is Gale Johnston and you are not afraid."

The imprint of Albright's hand was still on her cheek, but Johnston suddenly smiled. Her eyes cleared. Albright released her and Johnston rose to her feet while Kincaid and Sanchez stared at her as if she was an alien parasite suddenly escaping the thorax of its human host.

"That's some bedside manner you've got there," Sanchez told Albright. "Glad you didn't use that technique in my treatment, although it seems to have worked."

"Shut up Emilio," the two women said in scary unison.

"I think we have some more work to do. Don't we Sharon?" Johnston asked.

Albright smiled and nodded her head.

"What's directly below the emergency radio room?" Albright asked.

The two men looked at each other and shrugged.

"Nothing, as far as I can recall," Kincaid replied, answering for both men. "The Compass Island, like most ships has some empty compartments in her holds."

Sanchez nodded. "They call them voids," he said. "But you've got to be careful opening them up. Sometimes they're full of noxious or even explosive fumes."

"There's a hatch on the floor of the emergency radio room," Johnston said. "Think we can open it?"

"Why would we want to do that?" Sanchez said. "We've already got what we came for."

He waved the documents in his right hand.

"This ship holds some other secrets as well," Albright said. "Such as?" Sanchez asked.

"Such as the answer to the question: "Whatever became of JFK?"

"I thought we'd already answered that question," Sanchez said.

"You're only half right," Johnston replied.

41

FAIRVIEW, NEW JERSEY — John Kincaid was pissed and primed for trouble as he elbowed his way to the bar at the Pink Cat at 5:30 on a hot August afternoon. Kathleen, was cheating on him. He knew it for a fact. He just hadn't caught them in the act, yet. But he would. He would.

The barmaid, Sylvia Hanrahan, was hard-pressed to keep up with the happy hour rush, but she came a running when Kincaid gestured impatiently that he wanted a drink. Kincaid was not a man to get on the wrong side of. Pandered to, he was a good tipper. Neglected, he was a dangerous bastard who would think nothing of using his influence with his friend, Frank Simkins, the bar owner, to have a barmaid fired.

Kincaid smacked a five dollar bill on the bar top. "Gimmie a Camden and a shot, Sylvia. Shake that cute little ass while you're getting it and I'll pay double."

Sylvia hated herself for doing it, but she made a production of bending over the beer cooler to grab a can of Camden. She gave him an eyeful of her other attributes as she bent forward to pour the shot glass full to the rim with Old Forester bourbon, his favorite.

Kincaid winked and said: "Keep the change, baby, and pay attention. I'm real thirsty."

Kincaid tossed the bourbon back in one gulp. He took a long pull on his beer and drew a circle in the air with his right index finger to signal Sylvia that he was ready for another shot.

It was a clear evening and even though the temperature had moderated slightly from a high of 92 degrees, it still was steamy inside the Pink Cat. The electric fans did little more than move the heat and cigarette smoke from one end of the bar to the other. Kincaid had punched out at 5 p.m. and made straight for the Pink Cat to drown his growing resentment for his old buddy Jacob Manley.

Jake was fucking Kathleen. Kincaid was certain of it. What should he do? The shots and beers should help him sort things out. He always thought more clearly when he had a buzz on.

While Kincaid was saluting his second round, a short heavy-set man parallel parked his car outside, grinding the Ford's tires hard against the curb in his haste to be done with the task and join the happy hour crowd inside the Pink Cat. The moon was one day past full and hung like a fiery ornament ablaze in the waning sunlight that glittered off the heavy machinery assembled on a hillside nearby for the construction of the Walt Whitman Bridge. Another man might have paused to enjoy the spectacle afforded by the rising moon and setting sun, but Jack Sponsler paid it no heed. He threw open the door of the Pink Cat and stalked to the bar.

Sponsler, a bulldog of a man with sagging jowls and the florid complexion of a heavy drinker, was shop steward for the Industrial Union of Marine and Shipworkers of America (IUM-SA). His bad mood was palpable and Sylvia Hanrahan, ignoring several other customers who were clamoring for her attention, quickly made her way to Sponsler who had taken up station on Kincaid's left shoulder.

"Whatlitbe Jack?" she asked.

"Two Ballentines and a double Granddad," Sponsler said, doubling up on his order because the clock was ticking on happy hour.

"Sure thing."

Sylvia hurried off to fill Sponsler's order.

"Goddamn Maritime Administration," Sponsler said.

He bumped a shoulder into Kincaid's arm to get his attention.

Kincaid swallowed a long pull of beer and wiped his mouth with the back of his hand. "What's got your hemorrhoids so inflamed?"

"We were supposed to get 20 contracts for break-bulk cargo ships," Sponsler said. "Now it looks like we're only going to get five."

"You mean the Mariner Class C4-S-1As," Kincaid said. "I bent the bow plates for Hull 492 a couple weeks ago. Last I heard they were just about ready to move the forecastle to the ways."

Contracts 492 through 496 aren't the problem. We've got them under way. But now it looks like we're losing the rest to Bath Ironworks."

"Bath's a nonunion shop," Kincaid observed. "Is someone busting our balls, or what?"

"There's no doubt our balls are being busted. Question is. Who's doing the busting and what are we going to do about it?" Sponsler took a slug of Ballentine.

"Seems to me that's management's problem."

Sponsler wiped his mouth and nodded vigorously. "Normally, I'd agree with you, big guy, but in this case their problem is our problem and the ball less bastards in management won't bend the rules even to save their own ass."

Sponsler drained his Grand Dad and burped. "You still friends with that maritime commissioner?"

"Bought him fair and square."

"Well it don't look like he's stayin' bought."

"He's on the installment plan," Kincaid replied.

"Must be time for another payment. Think you could divert a little more money from the pension fund—for a worthy cause?"

"Keeping our jobs seems worthy enough. Think 10 Gs will be enough?"

"Better make it 12," Sponsler said. "Betty's got her eye on this diamond broach and Kathleen probably could use a bauble for herself as well."

Kincaid's snarl rose above the happy hour hubbub. "She ain't getting shit from me, 'cept maybe the back of my hand."

Sponsler backpedaled.

"Easy big guy."

Kincaid twirled an index finger and nodded at Sylvia, who got busy assembling the next round. As Sylvia delivered Kincaid's third beer and attendant shot, she leaned forward, affording the two union men another spectacular view of her cleavage. "Two guys down at the end of the bar bought this round. Wanted to know if it was all right if they came over to talk to you."

"What about me?" Sponsler asked. His voice was thick with liquor. "Don't they want to talk to me, too?"

"Sure they do Jack," Sylvia said. "Bought you a round, too. Just couldn't carry it all in one trip."

"Tell 'em to come on over," Kincaid said.

Sylvia motioned to a tall, skinny, beak-nosed man of dangerous demeanor who was slouched over his drink like a vulture considering a cow's carcass. A short man with no neck, thick shoulders and stubby arms stood, almost at attention on the taller man's starboard side. Both men picked up their drinks and started across the room.

"I'm betting the tall guy's the brains and the short one's the muscle," Sponsler said.

Kincaid took a long pull on his free beer and watched their approach warily.

The newcomers carved out some space along the bar next to the two union men.

Sure enough, the tall guy did the talking. "You Kincaid?" he asked.

"Yep." He raised his glass. "Thanks for the suds."

"Think of it as a professional courtesy. I'm told you are a fellow who can get things done, or undone, at New York Ship."

"Maybe so," Kincaid said. "But we're going nowhere with this until I know who you are and who pulls your strings."

The short guy grabbed the tall one by the arm and whispered something in his ear as the two men strained in opposite directions, one up and the other down, for a private consultation. The tall guy shook his head, in agreement or dissent, Kincaid couldn't be sure.

"Name's Burt. Burt Lancaster," the tall guy said.

Kincaid couldn't tell if he was joking.

"My friend here don't think we owe you nothing, other than a warning."

"What's his name?" Sponsler asked. He waggled a thumb at the shorter man. "Kirk Douglas?"

The beefy guy glared. "Wise guy, eh?" His voice had a girlish lisp. It was menacing for reasons Sponsler couldn't fathom.

"But since you asked, it's Jules Tripoli. You'd best take note of that and consider carefully who I am and what I have to say."

"What's that supposed to mean?" Kincaid asked.

The shots and beer had him feeling loose-jointed and fearless.

"It means that you better not try to prevent those Maritime Administration contracts from being shifted to Bath Ironworks," Lancaster said. "Mr. Rin. . . ."

"Shut up, shit for brains!"

Tripoli glared at his companion, cutting him off in mid sentence.

"Keep the boss's name out of it!"

He shook his head in disgust. "What dumb fuck is trying to impress upon you is this. A certain influential man, whom we represent, would appreciate it if you'd back the fuck off any attempt to regain certain contracts you may be losing to build fifteen merchant ships. Capeesh?"

"No. I don't capeesh. I don't fucking speak Italian," Kincaid said. "And I'm going to throw your greasy ass out of my bar."

Kincaid grabbed a beer mug off the bar and smashed it against the side of the fat man's head.

Tripoli was fat-man quick and slipped some of the impact, but the glass shattered and the heavy man's eyes flicked shut, for just an instant. Kincaid, a powerful man, almost six feet five inches tall in his stocking feet, grabbed Tripoli's belt at the small of his back in one hand and the collar of his shirt in the other. He bent at the knees, straightened and lifted Tripoli off his feet. It was a remarkable feat of strength fueled by alcohol and rage at an unfaithful wife.

Tripoli's companion surged forward to help his friend, but Jack Sponsler poked a .32 caliber belly gun in the tall man's stomach. "Easy buster, unless you want to be gut shot."

The tall man backed off and watched helplessly as Kincaid carried Tripoli to the front door of the Pink Cat. Jerry Greg and Brad Conroy, two IUMSA stalwarts, had made their way to the entrance. Conroy flung the front door open just in time as Kincaid struggled forward, tiring now with the exertion of carrying the fat man.

Kincaid had just enough juice left to fling Tripoli out onto the sidewalk. He hit the ground and rolled until his cheek collided with the curb. Lancaster helped him to his feet and both men turned to face a phalanx of New York Ship workers who had filed out of the bar in support of Big John Kincaid.

"You've been warned Kincaid." Tripoli shouted. "Come on Burt. Every dog has its day."

The two interlopers left, with Tripoli limping a bit and casting evil looks over his shoulder.

John Kincaid didn't have to pay for any more drinks that night. But the free drinks did nothing to moderate his mood. He was a mean drunk when he left the Pink Cat and headed home to that bitch Kathleen.

42

THURSDAY, AUGUST 27, 1953

CAMDEN, NEW JERSEY — "Hey Big John. Over here."

The words, high-pitched, almost feminine, bounced off the metal bulkheads, deck and overhead like bingo balls in a spinner.

The voice sounded odd, not at all what he was expecting. John Kincaid wrote it off as a distortion caused by the empty metal space he now occupied. Strange things happen when you yell inside a teakettle. Just ask the tin man.

At 5 p.m., reacting like Pavlov's dogs to the bell signaling the end of the workday, the 1,000 or so men fortunate enough to still have jobs in the post-war recession of 1953, put down their tools and abandoned the fabrication shops, drafting lofts and ways of New York Ship's sprawling shipyard in Camden, New Jersey.

Kincaid stuck around until 6, reacting to a note left in his company mailbox.

"If you want to save those Maritime Administration contracts, meet me at 6 o'clock in the forecastle at Fab Shop 3—Harry B.

Harry Brinkley was John Kincaid's "inside" man with the Maritime Administration.

Two days earlier, Brinkley had been noncommittal when Kincaid called him up to offer him a bribe.

"Harry, I'll give you 5,000 reasons why New York Ship should keep a contract I hear is headin' north," Kincaid said.

"What contract is that?"

Brinkley's voice was guarded, setting off Kincaid's finely tuned bullshit detector.

"Come on Harry, quit screwin' around. You know the one I'm talking about. The C4-S-1As."

"I don't think there's anything I can do about that. The fix is in," Brinkley replied.

"Well, unfix it. God damn it, Harry. I'll give you 10,000 reasons. Don't you want to hear 'em?"

"I'll tell you what, Big John. If I can do anything, I'll let you know."

Kincaid found the note in his company cubby at noon and was delighted that Harry Brinkley seemed to have changed his mind. At 3 p.m. he withdrew $10,000 from the union's account at First National Bank of Fairview. The teller frowned when Kincaid asked for twenty, five-hundred-dollar bills.

"We usually require advance notice for bills of that size," she said. "I'll have to ask the manager to get them from the safe."

Kincaid smiled, winked, and leaned forward as if to bestow a kiss on her cheek. Instead, he whispered in her ear: "He'll do it for me, darlin'. He'll do it for Big John Kincaid."

Big John got a hard-on watching her count out the crisp Federal Reserve notes bearing the picture of William McKinley.

The bills were folded in his canvas money belt as he ducked through the starboard side door leading to the forecastle module positioned in the center of Fabrication Shop 3. He blinked in the glare of the spotlight, which normally would have been directed overhead to diffuse light throughout the forecastle but was pointing directly at the door instead.

"Over here, big John," the girlish voice repeated. He shielded his eyes with his right hand.

"Is that you, Harry?"

Something about the figure standing next to the spotlight didn't seem quite right. Harry Brinkley was tall, just an inch or two shorter than Kincaid.

The silhouette confronting him now was much shorter . . . much too short.

Hair bristled on the back of Kincaid's neck. "Hey. You're not Harry."

Kincaid started to turn.

"Not so fast, asshole." A second man stepped from the shadows and jammed the muzzle of a pistol into the small of his back.

Without being asked, Kincaid raised his hands in surrender.

"You're not so brave without your friends backing you up," the short man said. He swiveled the spotlight so it pointed straight up, and when Kincaid's eyes adjusted, he recognized

the man he had thrown out of the Pink Cat three days earlier.
What was his name? Jules Tripoli. That's right. The guys at
Union Hall said he was an enforcer for mobster Berto Rinaldi
and that Kincaid had better be careful because he'd made a
powerful enemy.

Seems they were right.

"So it's payback time," Kincaid said. He motioned the fat guy
forward.

"Come on grease ball. I'm man enough to give a whippin', or
to take one."

"You'll take more than a whipping asshole."

The man standing behind him prodded him forward with
the gun.

"Back up against the wall over there."

"It's not a wall, stupid. It's a bulkhead," Kincaid said.

"A smart ass to the end. Go."

He pressed harder and Kincaid went.

When he turned, Kincaid recognized the man with the gun.
It was Tripoli's companion, Burt Lancaster.

Tripoli moved next to Lancaster.

"You just don't get it, do you?" Tripoli said.

"Get what?"

"When Mr. Rinaldi says back off. He means back off. So
what do you do? You call a mutual friend and ask him to fix a
contract that ain't broke."

"Brinkley sold me out? Damn it. I bought him fair and
square," John Kincaid said.

"You shudda asked for a receipt," Tripoli said.

"Let's get this over with," Lancaster said.

Lancaster wiped sweat from his forehead with the back of
his left hand, but his revolver was squared unwaveringly on the
middle of Kincaid's chest.

Kincaid got it, finally. They meant to kill him.

He leapt forward.

Lancaster yanked the trigger of his .38. Twice. The explo-
sions and their echoes assaulted Kincaid's ears. The bullets
abused his flesh. The first round nicked him in the base of the
neck. Lancaster corrected his aim as Kincaid surged forward
and the second round caught him squarely in the chest. The
impact was a hammer blow that drove Kincaid back against
the bulkhead. His knees collapsed and he slid down, his back
scraping against the sharp edge of a girder.

"Jesus, Burt. You shudda let me handle it. The wire's quieter," Tripoli said.

"Shadup, Jules. There's nobody around, and he's dead ain't he?"

Lancaster pocketed the gun and stepped forward. He grabbed Kincaid under the arms.

"A little help here. This sumbitch is heavy."

The two men muscled Kincaid's inert body to the lip of an unsealed hatch in the deck.

"On three," Tripoli said. "One, two, three."

They dropped Kincaid feet first. He plummeted through a second open hatch on the deck directly below and into a void in the hull that would be well below the water line in the finished Garden State Mariner.

Lancaster knelt beside the open hatch and fished a flashlight from his jacket pocket. Shining the flashlight down through the hatch, he exclaimed:

"Great shot Jules. The body fell two decks down."

Lancaster was aware of Tripoli's changing position behind him, but concluded that his companion was bending closer to inspect their handiwork.

The sudden pressure of a wire garrote about his neck was an excruciating revelation.

Lancaster dropped the flashlight and struggled in vain to secure a purchase with his fingertips under the edge of the wire. He bucked backward, but Jules was a pro. A knee in the back provided more than enough counter pressure as the wire grated through flesh, muscle and sinew and finally the vulnerable jugular vein. Tripoli didn't want Lancaster to die not knowing why. So he told him.

"Mr. Rinaldi says maybe this will teach you to keep your dick in your pants where his daughter is concerned."

Tripoli gave the garrote a final twist and sent Lancaster's dead body tumbling two decks below, where it fell into the same void that had recently had interred the mortal remains of John Franklin Kincaid.

43

SATURDAY, OCTOBER 18, 2003

OFF THE COAST OF NEW JERSEY — As it turned out, the compartment directly beneath the emergency radio room did not contain noxious or explosive gases. It stunk of neglect and nothing more. It was, merely, an empty narrow sliver of space at the bow of the ship just above the waterline.

While Sanchez was off poring over his precious papers, Mike Kincaid, with much trepidation, helped Albright and Johnston, cut through the metal access hatch in the floor of the emergency radio room. They had to use the torch because the heavy nuts holding the hatch to its frame had rusted solid. No amount of WD-40 could free them.

Kincaid signed on for this fools' errand because Sharon Albright and Gale Johnston had an epiphany.

"He's calling to us Mike. We both heard him. That's why Gale freaked out," Albright said.

"Freaked out? Is that a technical description of some sort of mental illness?"

"I was trying to use words you'd understand. Would you feel better if I said that Gale experienced a psychotic episode born of a head-on collision with something that happened to her in a previous lifetime?"

Kincaid laughed. "OK. I'll bite. Who's calling to you?"

"The man who's buried in the bowels of this ship."

Kincaid shivered. Albright noticed.

"What is it Mike?"

He hesitated. "I hope you don't think that I'm crazy, but years ago I encountered a ghost right here in the forecastle forty some years ago," Kincaid said.

"We're all crazy Mike. That's why I have a job," Albright replied. "Tell me about it."

"We had a fire in the sail locker and I was roused from bed to fight it. It must have been October of 1963, right before we left for our rendezvous with President Kennedy. The forecastle was full of swirling smoke. I've thought about this a thousand times. I can't explain it but suddenly a man materialized in the smoke just beneath one of the battle lanterns. He spoke to me, then poof, he was gone. He just disappeared."

"What did he say?"

"I don't remember it all, but I do recall his last words before he disappeared. 'Is this world for real or for pretend? Come visit me again and I'll answer you that.'"

Kincaid peered into Albright's face. "Do you know who the ghost is, or was?"

Albright nodded. "I think so, but I think it's better if you discover the answer
to that question yourself."

"How?"

"By disinterring his body. It's down there somewhere. I know it is."

She pointed at the floor of the emergency radio room.

Gale Johnston hadn't added anything to the conversation. She had adopted a detached, almost otherworldly demeanor, but she nodded her head vigorously now.

"She's right Kincaid," Johnston said. "I feel it too. Probably more powerfully than Sharon. Not much scares me, but this sure as hell does. Look."

She held up the palms of her hands.

She'd clenched her fists so tightly that her fingernails had carved out four half-moon stigmata in the palms of both hands.

It was hot dirty work on the deck of the former emergency radio room. Kincaid wielded the torch while Johnston and Albright knelt nearby ready to direct their flashlights where he needed light. As the sparks danced like fireflies eluding bats at dusk over a millpond, Kincaid wondered at the sight they must make. The crippled Hephaestus bent with his helpers over a forge intent on an enterprise only the crazy gods would undertake.

Damn a classical education, but who would be his Aphrodite now that Alice was gone? There were no candidates among his helpers this day. Although he sensed an eerie connection to both Albright and Johnston, the attraction was Platonic. As he contemplated these things, the metal hatch fell with a bang to the deck below and when Kincaid directed Sanchez's big police flashlight into the compartment, he saw nothing but the curve of the hull plates where the port side of the ship met the starboard at the bow of the ship.

The compartment's only notable features were another hatch cover on the deck below and a metal ladder welded to the hull to afford access to a space that obviously had served no utility other than structural.

"There's nothing here, ladies," he announced, pulling his head and shoulders back through the opening he had just cut through the hatch cover.

"There's got to be," Albright said. "Let me look."

Kincaid handed her the flashlight and moved out of the way. After a moment or two, Albright said: "There's nothing in there."

Her words were muffled by the empty space below.

Retreating from the hole, Albright sat on her haunches and looked up at Johnston and Kincaid. "There is another hatch down there," she said. "Do you think we can lower the torch and cut through it as well?"

"The torch kit isn't that heavy," Kincaid said. "I'm tall enough that you should be able to hand it down to me if I climb down below. But the real problem is I'm not sure there is enough gas left to cut through a second hatch."

"Sanchez didn't leave anything to chance," Johnston said. "I'm positive there are two replacement bottles among our gear on the quarter deck."

"Yeah, I know. I was just looking for an excuse not to do this. But I can tell you two are committed, and for some reason so am I. I'll get the bottles."

Kincaid took his flashlight and made his way beneath the forecastle and then along the main deck to the edge of the superstructure, leaving the two women behind in the emergency radio room to cement their new relationship with whatever small talk occurred to them. It wasn't pure vanity that made him think that just maybe they were talking about him. He was feeling a connection with these two women that he couldn't explain. As he opened the watertight door to the quarterdeck where their supplies were stored, he glanced aft and noticed that Sanchez had climbed the stairs to the helipad where Kennedy had disembarked from Marine I all those years ago. Sanchez was standing with his back to Kincaid, staring out to sea.

"I wonder what he's doing?" Kincaid asked himself.

Sanchez was in the same position when Kincaid, now burdened with the oxygen and acetylene bottles, headed back forward toward the forecastle. Kincaid looked over his shoulder just as Sanchez turned and the two men made eye contact. Sanchez raised his hand in greeting and Kincaid realized that he was talking on a phone. Kincaid concluded that Sanchez had brought a satellite phone on board, which made sense. Now that he had found what he was looking for, he'd need to alert someone to their presence on board the ship. They hadn't brought enough supplies to last for the entire six-week crossing of the Atlantic.

Kincaid thought about putting down the gas bottles and going back to talk with Sanchez, just to see what he had in mind for their immediate future, but he was reluctant to abandon the women to their own devices any longer than necessary. Their relationship to this point had been mercurial and there was no telling how hot or cold they'd be upon his return.

The women as it turned out were getting along famously. He could hear pleasant voices as he ducked through the door to the forecastle and made his way forward to the emergency radio room.

"The important thing," he heard Albright say as he stepped around the 20mm cannon and ammunition drums on the deck "is to be assertive. You've got to separate who you are from who you've been. Accept the memories as your own and realize you can learn from them, but compartmentalize. And be ready to slam a door shut if you have to."

"Wow," he said, setting the bottles down beside the torch caddy. "You gals seem to be getting along famously."

"Let's just say we've found that we have something in common after all," Albright said.

"And what's that?"

"You!" they said in unison.

Johnston giggled.

It was so out of character that Kincaid did a double take. "You're going to have to explain that one to me, sometime, but for now just train the flashlight so I can see what I'm doing."

He shut the valves on the two spent tanks and disconnected them from the caddy. He slid the two fresh bottles in place, tightened the threading securing them to the hose assembly and opened the valves to charge the system. "See if you can pick this up and remember lift with your legs," he instructed.

Albright bent her knees and grabbed the plastic handle of the torch caddy. Straightening, she picked it up, but Kincaid could tell that she was struggling.

"It'll take the two of you to dangle that down the hole far enough for me to reach it," he said, "but that shouldn't be a problem given your new level of cooperation. Now give me some room."

Kincaid stretched out on his belly on the deck of the emergency radio room and directed the flashlight's beam on the metal ladder, looking for any signs that the rungs or the welds holding it to the hull had rusted through.

Satisfied, he handed the flashlight to Albright and said: "Shine this on the ladder while I climb down."

Kincaid crabbed backward, dangling his feet through the hole he had just cut in the hatch until he could settle them on the first rung of the ladder. He sucked in his gut to keep his shirt from snagging on the hot rough edges of the torch cut.

"Don't shine that thing in my eyes, Sharon," he said. "Shine it below me so I can see where I'm putting my feet."

"I would if you'd move your fat ass out of the way," Albright replied.

She laughed, robbing her words of rancor.

The metal ladder held his weight without protest and as soon as his feet gained purchase on the deck below, he turned on his own flashlight and placed it on the deck, directing it off into the empty compartment.

"OK ladies. Pick up the caddy and lower it as far as you can reach down the hole, but be careful not to lose your balance. I don't want to have to catch you."

The women conferred on the best way to share the load.

They ended up standing on either side of the hole with each of them grasping the caddy handle with two hands. Working in unison, they bent, lifted, and then dangled the torch caddy two or so feet into the compartment below. Kincaid, as he had hoped, was tall enough to reach up and grab the caddy and strong enough to lower it to the deck without incident when the two women let go.

Predictably, the nuts and bolts of the hatch below also were rusted shut and Hephaestus and his assistants soon were back at work burrowing in the bowels of the *Compass Island* like moles, blind to the horror that awaited them below. When the hatch caved in, the three of them stretched out on their stomachs on the deck careful to avoid touching the hot edges of the metal. Albright and Kincaid played their flashlights around the compartment beneath them.

The portion of the compartment directly under the hatch was empty, but as Kincaid panned the flashlight beam forward he noticed that the shipbuilders had welded a series of frames to the deck about two feet apart. Attached to the frames were crisscrossing metal struts that were welded to the hull plates.

"Jesus, what a rat's nest," Kincaid said.

"They're called panting frames and struts," Johnston said. "When the ship is underway they keep the hull plates from panting—from bending back and forth under the pressure of the rushing water."

"How do you know that?" Kincaid asked.

He stared at Johnston, whose face had a strange reddish glow in the backlight of the flashlight beam.

She shook her head. "I'll tell you later. Train your flashlights over there."

Kincaid gasped as the flashlight beam caught something recognizable on the deck below. A large bone stuck out from beneath the metal that had fallen when Kincaid completed his incision through the hatch cover.

He panned the flashlight beam another two or three feet forward until it illuminated what quite obviously was a human skull resting on its medulla with the jaw thrust forward and the eye sockets glowing ochre in the reddish beam of the flashlight.

"Jesus Christ!"

He swept the flashlight beam back and forth on the deck of the compartment below pausing as it fell upon the curves of a rib cage and then the obvious wishbone of an ulna and radius.

"You're right, ladies. There's a human skeleton down there," Kincaid said.

Kincaid sat up and directed the beam of his flashlight upward to avoid blinding his companions.

"Now which one of you wants to tell me who that was?"

Gale Johnston's face was pasty white and skeletal in the diffused glow of the flashlight beams crisscrossing the compartment. Albright scratched her head and studied Johnston with a combination of professional detachment and personal empathy.

"You OK Gale?"

Johnston nodded.

"Do you want to answer, or should I?" Albright asked. Johnston rubbed her face with both hands.

"That's the man who killed me, or one of them anyway." Albright's gasp told Kincaid that wasn't the answer she was expecting.

Johnston sat down cross-legged on the floor and began to keen. She wailed like a coyote calling its mate to a fresh kill. Albright knelt beside her.

"You can handle this," Albright told her. "Compartmentalize. And breathe! Take deep breaths. Remember who you are can't be hurt by who you were unless you let it happen!"

Johnston did not reply, but her breathing slowed and her rocking diminished. Her wails subsided to sniffles and, finally, she was still.

"His name," Johnston said, "was Burt Lancaster."

Her voice and demeanor surprised them. It was as if she was a ventriloquist's dummy. Her jaw movements were mechanical, and her voice had a deep masculine timbre.

"And he shot me. Twice. Once right here." Johnston left hand rose languidly and she stroke a patch of skin on her neck right above the collarbone. "And once right here." She tapped the center of her chest just above the diaphragm. "But I didn't die, at least not right away. That's the horror of it."

Johnston's jaw clenched. And she stared at Albright with a virulence that made Kincaid gulp.

Albright didn't shrink. She leaned forward and grabbed Johnston's wrists in both hands.

"Easy Gale. Remember who you are. Subdue who you were."

Johnston relaxed and Albright let go of her wrists.

"They thought I was dead and they dropped me down there," Johnston said.

She gestured toward the open hatch with her right hand.

"I was unconscious for a while. I don't know how long, and when I woke up. He was lying there on top of me. Dead. With a wire wrapped tightly around his neck. His buddy must have killed him. Don't ask me why."

Kincaid had a thousand questions, but Albright grabbed his wrist and shook her head, silencing him.

Johnston took a deep breath, composing herself. "And now, if you direct your flashlights forward you'll find my last resting place. I crawled up there before I died."

Albright and Kincaid stretched out on their stomach, peered into the compartment below, and did as she instructed, illuminating a scene none of them would ever forget. There, supported by the crisscrossing structures Johnston had called panting struts, was a human skeleton posed like Christ at Calvary.

The skeleton's arms, legs and torso were entwined in the struts between two frames. The frames and struts apparently had supported his weight as he died.

Kincaid switched off his flashlight and climbed to his feet. Albright arose as well. "Come on Gale," she said, offering a hand to Johnston. "We've seen enough."

Johnston stood.

"Oh my God," Kincaid said. "How could he have died in that position?"

"I had no choice," Johnston said. "I didn't want to sit on top of Lancaster's body." Her shoulders shook.

"Easy Gale," Albright said. "You knew what we would find here. Think of this as vindication. You're not crazy. You have lived and died before and there is the proof of it."

Kincaid's skin crawled like maggots on a corpse. "Jesus Christ," he said. "You're crazy, the both of you. I can do without this horror in my life."

He made to leave, but Sharon put a hand on his arm.

"Mike," she said. "You're going to have to trust me on this one, but I'm pretty sure that we've just discovered what happened to your father. You said that your stepfather worked on this ship. Isn't it possible your father did, too?"

Kincaid was stunned. "You're telling me that's the skeleton of John Kincaid?" he asked.

"That's right. And Jacob killed, me," Johnston said.

She fixed Albright in a steely gaze. Kincaid noticed her voice had dropped in register and that her countenance suddenly was consumed with hate.

"Come on John, you know that's not true," Albright said, addressing Johnston. The tonal quality of her voice also had changed and Kincaid was suddenly flattened by a childhood memory. It was the voice of his mother imploring his father not to be stupid, to quit drinking, to behave for the boys' sake if not for her own.

Albright smiled at him. "Disconcerting, isn't it?" she asked in a New Jersey dialect that was unique to the little village of

Fairview. "Welcome to our world. It's liberating if you can handle the memories."

It was obvious that Johnston at that moment wasn't handling the memories very well. "It was so dark and cold, once he welded the hatch in place," Johnston said. Her voice was thick and deep and scratchy with self-pity. "Jacob sealed this compartment with me inside it. Jacob should have helped me. He saw me hanging there. I know he did, but he welded the compartment shut anyway!"

"I killed JFK!" Mike Kincaid said. "My father's full name was John Franklin Kincaid. Amazement and horror were written on his face.

Johnston was pallid and sweat plastered her hair to her forehead. She shivered like a patient fighting off the flu. "Help! Oh please help me. I'm here below. I'm alive. I'm alive. Don't leave me here!"

Gale's voice was a strangled whisper and Albright was torn between sweeping her up in her arms and letting her be. Her instinct as the physician Sharon Albright was to console her. Her predisposition as the woman who had been Kathleen Kincaid Manley was to revel in the suffering of her abuser. Kathleen's compassion won the day. Albright embraced Johnston and pulled her close.

Kincaid felt like a nephew called to the deathbed of an uncle he scarcely knew. He could tell that the women were locked in a nightmare that he could perceive only peripherally, but he felt strangely moved to intercede, to do something, but what?

44

OFF THE COAST OF NEW JERSEY — Marcie McDermott read the weather alert a second time then studied the barometer in the wheelhouse of Daddy's Little Princess. Nope. It was holding steady at 29.9 inches, but the weather report portended heavy weather in another eight hours or so.

Marcie didn't have the watch and there was no reason for her to be in the wheelhouse, but she was there just the same. She would be looking over Kirk Cramer's shoulder, if he were there.

"Where's Cramer?" she asked Fred Taylor, who had the misfortune of standing the helm watch while the relationship between his first mate and captain followed its tempestuous course.

Taylor plucked his pants from his ass crack with one hand and said. "He's in the engine room. The evap boiler's acting up again."

Cramer chose that time to reappear on the bridge. "Hi Marcie."

McDermott weighed in like a welterweight answering the bell. "God damn it Kirk, I told you I saw the flash of binoculars from the forecastle of our tow. There's someone aboard that ship, and now we've got a storm brewing."

She waved the radio dispatch for emphasis and swept an arm at the barometer as if she were introducing the actor portraying the villain in this particular play.

"I'm telling you, we have to go investigate. If someone's stowed away on that ship and they get hurt in the storm . . . our insurance just might not cover it."

"And I'm telling you that I disagree," Cramer replied. "It will take us forever to slow that behemoth down. We'll lose at least a day of transit time and risk a bonus. The crew will mutiny."

"None of us will get a bonus if McDermott Towing gets slapped with a law suit," Marcie said. "Besides if we use the Zodiac, we can just keep chugging."

Cramer shook his head in disbelief. "You're proposing we go bouncing over the ocean in a rubber boat with a storm brewing and climb aboard a ship two stories above the water line, just to check out your intuition that we have a stowaway?"

"It's not an intuition. I saw the flash of binoculars, damn it. Someone aboard that ship was watching us," she rejoined. "Besides, now's the time to do it, before the weather turns rough."

Cramer shook his head stubbornly. "It's a fool's errand, Marcie. This is my command, and I say we keep going."

"It's your command, provisionally," McDermott reminded him. "You don't have your captain's papers, yet."

"Are you threatening me?" Cramer asked.

He puffed out his chest like a male gorilla protecting his territory.

Marcie hesitated, considering her alternatives. She could pull rank on Cramer, but that would be like cutting off his balls in front of the crew. The prospects of that held a certain appeal to her as a jilted lover, but she was also a businesswoman and Kirk Cramer, for all his faults, was a valuable commodity, worthy of nurturing.

"I'm not threatening you," she said.

McDermott imbued her response with the inflection of a subordinate female, although it galled her to do it. "I'm begging you, Kirk. Now please don't make me cry."

She batted her eyelashes like a debutant, and Cramer couldn't help but laugh.

"You haven't cried since you were 12 years old and caught your finger in a winch," he said. "Your dad still loves to tell that story."

He decided not to test her resolve, or his authority. "Let me see that weather report."

She handed him the dispatch, which he scanned quickly. "We do seem to have an eight-hour window," he said. He took off his ball cap, exposing a bald spot on the top of his head. He scratched the fringe of hair on the back of his head and reset his ball cap.

"Let's call it six hours to be safe. Think we can wrap this up in six hours?"

"We can do it in four," Marcie said.

Cramer sighed.

"Start slowing us to four knots, Fred, and tell Bill to relieve you on the helm so you can ready the God damn Zodiac. And Marcie?"

"Yes."

"I'm going with you to make sure I don't have to tell Edmund McDermott I lost his only daughter at sea."

Marcie threw the old seadog a bone. "Aye, aye Captain," she said.

45

SATURDAY, OCTOBER 18, 2003

OFF THE COAST OF NEW JERSEY — Mike Kincaid stepped carefully over Burt Lancaster's bones, which had been strewn about the deck by the pounding of the remorseless sea. As he approached his father's remains his emotions roller-coastered back and forth violently among filial piety, horror and disgust. The guts of the old ship reeked with the redolence of a crypt, ancient, musty and forlorn. The beams of the flashlights directed from above by his two companions crisscrossed the compartment like luminous sword strokes.

John Franklin Kincaid's corpse when captured in the beam of his son's flashlight was clad in khaki work pants and a long-sleeved denim work shirt. Time had desiccated the flesh, but the skeleton, remarkably, was in good shape, given the pounding this compartment had taken over the years as the bow cut through often hostile seas. Kincaid concluded that his father's skeleton, unlike that of Burt Lancaster's, was intact because it was entwined in the panting struts.

"Check around my waist," Johnston called from above. "I was wearing a money belt."

Kincaid shivered.

God, he wished she wouldn't talk like that. It gave him the creeps. Kincaid tucked his flashlight under his arm and stepped forward. Kincaid raised the shirttail and, sure enough, hanging loosely around the stark bones of the pelvis, was a wide canvas belt.

Kincaid held his breath and with thick fingers unfastened the belt buckle, wincing as he pulled it free. He lowered the belt to the deck behind him and forced himself to raise his eyes to the skull. Draped around the neck was a leather thong that disappeared beneath the collar of the work shirt. Johnston had told him to look for the New York Ship medallion all workers were required to wear when they were on the job.

"The badge had a pin, but I didn't like to put holes in my work shirts," she told Kincaid as he was preparing to descend into the tomb. "So I poked the pin through a piece of rawhide and wore the medallion around my neck. I tucked it under my shirt because I couldn't stand it bouncing around while I worked."

Kincaid wondered at the specificity of her recollections. She was experiencing events of fifty years ago with the clarity of yesterday. He almost remarked on that observation, but he bit his tongue, unwilling to dispel the mood of quiet reflection that had descended on his acerbic companion.

"Do you see the medallion?" Johnston asked.

Her voice deepened. Kincaid prayed that she'd be able to forestall the oppressive influence of the man she had been. The man whose corpse he now confronted. His father. God. It was tough to wrap his head around that. He couldn't grieve for the mean son of a bitch who beat his mother. But part of him was grateful. By his absence, John Kincaid had shaped the men his sons had become far more positively than they would have been shaped by his presence.

"I'm working on it," Kincaid said. "This isn't exactly a walk in the park, you know."

With the flashlight still clamped tightly in his armpit, Kincaid pinched the thong on either side of the corpse's neck between the thumb and index fingers of both hands. He pulled the thong wide to gain enough slack and lifted it gently over the skull.

Stepping back, he directed the flashlight on a medallion about the size and color of a tarnished silver dollar emblazoned with black lettering. Along the rim from 9 o'clock to 3 o'clock were the words NEW YORK SHIP BUILDING. In a crescent below, was the word CAMDEN. Along the bottom from 5 o'clock to 8 o'clock was the word CORPORATION, and above that in a crescent outlined in black were the letters N.J. In the center was a five-digit number.

"Got it!" Kincaid called out.

"What's the number on the medallion?" Johnston asked.

"You tell me."

"My New York Ship ID number was 8-1-2-0-7," Johnston called back without hesitation.

Kincaid's vision narrowed. And a voice called to him across the years. "Is this world for real or for pretend. Come see me again, Mike, and I'll answer you that."

The medallion was indented in the center as if a ball pein hammer had struck it, but the number was still clearly legible. "8-1-2-0-7," Kincaid called out, just to be sure.

"That's right," Johnston replied. "Is there any damage to the medallion? Does it look like a bullet struck it? That's why I wasn't killed outright. The bullet deflected off the medallion."

Kincaid had enough.

"You can see for yourself in a minute or two. I'm coming up."

Mustering the last bit of his resolve, Kincaid felt around in the corpse's back pocket and drew out a wallet. He carried the money belt, medallion and wallet with him as he made his way carefully up the ladder to the women who waited for him above.

46

OFF THE COAST OF NEW JERSEY — They stumbled from the bowels of the *Compass Island*, talking and laughing among each other like children dismissed early from school. A brilliant October day greeted them, as first Sharon Albright, then Gale Johnston and finally Mike Kincaid, stepped over the threshold of the watertight door and drew in huge lungs-full of fresh ocean air, which deposited a fishy film reminiscent of boiling shrimp upon their mucus membranes.

The breeze had picked up a bit and they turned their sweaty, grime-encrusted faces gratefully into a refreshingly exfoliating ocean spray. Now, with the horizon serving as a point of reference, the sensation of movement was enhanced as the *Compass Island* wallowed under tow. Gale Johnston began to feel a bit ill . . . again . . . but fought back the sensation. Her lifelong torment had been explained and that realization was more efficacious than a draught of milk of magnesia. She was not crazy and even more importantly, people who recognized that (and were important to her) could affirm her new world view, her new sense of selves, her new sense of . . . belonging.

"So let me get this straight," Kincaid said. "You used to be my mother and Gale was my father. Right?"

"No! Not right!" Albright said. "That kind of gross over simplification relegates past-life exploration to the kooky fringes."

Johnston, shrugged, and smiled at Kincaid.

"I'm new to the kooky fringes, so I'll defer to my wife," she said.

Sharon stomped her foot. "Stop it! Both of you. A better way to think of it is that Gale and I are the psychic descendants of a host of people who happen to include Kathleen Jablonski and John Kincaid . . . respectively."

Blinking in the bright sunlight, Kincaid noticed a figure in his peripheral vision, moving toward them from the port side of the ship. As his pupils adjusted to the light he noticed that Emilio Sanchez was holding a gun out in front of him, elbows locked, like a police officer canvassing a dark alley. He realized with a shock that the gun Sanchez was pointing at him was the .45 caliber Colt automatic that had disappeared from his trunk.

"Skeeter you mother fucker. You killed him didn't you? You killed my stepfather and planted the murder weapon in my trunk. Didn't you?"

"I planted the gun and the letter from the insurance company, too," Sanchez acknowledged, "but I didn't kill your stepfather. My co-conspirator saved me that trouble, didn't you Gale."

Kincaid shifted his gaze to Johnston, whose shoulders slumped.

"I'm so sorry Mike," she said. "He gave me no choice. He fired first and I was just reacting, although I must admit that at the time killing Jacob gave me . . . gave John Kincaid . . . a satisfaction that has haunted me ever since. Now I understand why."

"Why were you in Jacob's house?" Kincaid asked.

Sanchez answered for her: "Gale agreed to help me search your stepfather's house as background for our book. I told her we were looking for a tape of a meeting among three mafia bosses forty years ago at which the assassination of John F. Kennedy was plotted. Jacob somehow stumbled on the old tape and used it to blackmail my employer. You wouldn't happen to know its whereabouts, would you?"

Kincaid thought of Sylvia Hanrahan and her cryptic message at Jacob's funeral all those weeks ago. Struggling to keep that revelation to himself, he said: "So Gale, you've added breaking and entering and murder to your reporters' resume. What were you doing with a gun, anyway?"

Johnston hung her head.

"He gave it to me. He said that if I was going to commit burglary I might as well be equipped for it."

Albright weighed in. "Sanchez has a genius for exploiting the weaknesses of others. He aimed you at Jacob didn't he? He could sense your emotional turmoil and he set you up to do his dirty work."

Gale licked her lips and glared at Sanchez.

"We were searching the kitchen," she said. "We heard a noise. Jacob was home! Sanchez turned off his flashlight and motioned me to do the same. I heard the back door open and close. He snuck out and left me there alone. The bastard. Then Jacob burst into the room, threw on the light."

"And the crazy bitch shot him," Sanchez said. "You think you're smart, don't you DOCTOR Albright."

His emphasis on doctor was caustic.

"Well you don't know shit. I've played you like a cheap fiddle from the very beginning. I gave her the gun, sure, but just for a laugh. I didn't even show her how to turn off the damn safety. I didn't want her to kill Jacob. Scare him, maybe. Hell he was an eighty year old man."

"But tough as nails," Kincaid said.

"Yeah, but I didn't know that, did I? I needed that tape. Still do, although I've got a pretty good idea of where it is now. I was two rows back when you had your little conversation with Sylvia Hanrahan at Jacob's funeral. I deferred paying a call on the little old lady because I didn't want to spook you before I lured you all aboard this ship."

"To murder us," Kincaid said.

"That's a harsh characterization. I prefer to think of it as tidying up the nursery."

"Well, go ahead. Get on with it. You bastard!" Gale Johnston's voice was sneering and deep. She was possessed once again by the essence of John Franklin Kincaid.

Sanchez noticed and stared at her appraisingly. "Taunting your executioner is never good policy, Gale. Besides we've got another hour or so before my ride shows up. Wouldn't you like to savor this moment for a while longer? Wouldn't you like to know why you're about to die?" Sanchez asked.

"I've got a pretty good guess already," Kincaid said. "I'm betting that you never intended to sell your story. This is all about blackmail. You promised to deliver documents that could derail the vice-presidential aspirations of Wiley Patterson and he promised to buy you off."

"Not quite, but close. Wiley Patterson covets deniability. His brother embraced a permanent solution to his public relations problem and has pockets deep enough to pay me off."

"You're calling complicity in the murder of a president, a public relations problem?" Johnston asked. "It's a fucking disaster."

"Not if you have the courage to pull the trigger of a gun registered to Mike Kincaid and kill off the only three people in the world with enough pieces of the puzzle to implicate the senator's family in the murder of a president."

47

SUNDAY, JULY 1, 1990

WALLINGFORD, PENNSYLVANIA — The room smelled of old people, of liniment, lanolin, Lysol and of the pervasive essence of urine and feces that no amount of Lysol could obscure.

A single sheet pulled up to his chin defined the sunken contours of an old man who was collapsing inch by inch into himself. Berto Rinaldi had navigated the peaks and troughs of a mild dementia for five years while enduring the first-class accommodations of an exclusive skilled-care nursing facility. But a fall, a broken hip and a bout with pneumonia had landed him finally in terminal care. A Hospice nurse visited regularly with instructions to summon the family to his bedside at the appropriate time.

Rinaldi stirred and muttered in his sleep at 2 a.m. on a starless night as a ghostly form settled into the visitor's chair positioned near the foot of his bed.

The specter in the chair rocked back and forth and made a buzzing sound through clenched teeth. Rinaldi's dementia dissipated like smoke before an electric fan. His eyes popped open.

"Do I know you?" he croaked.

His voice was suffused with phlegm and carried but a wan vestige of the Harvard erudition that had made him such a formidable defender of the Philadelphia mafia for such a long time.

His visitor buzzed. It was the sort of sound made by the faulty ballast of a fluorescent light. The buzzing carried a meaning only Rinaldi could discern.

"We've never met, but you ordered my murder. You son of a bitch."

Pushing with spindly arms against the mattress, Rinaldi rolled himself onto his right hip so he could better see his visitor.

"Where are my glasses?" he asked.

"You don't really want to see what's coming, do you?"

The old man coughed up a wad of phlegm and swallowed. "You mean to kill me, don't you?" Rinaldi asked. His voice was stronger now and carried a vestige of his old confidence mitigated by what? Resignation?

"Figured that one out all by yourself did you, old man?" The visitor's voice was a deep baritone, or at least Rinaldi perceived it so.

"If you're going to kill me, at least come closer so I can see you," Rinaldi said.

The vinyl of the chair squeaked. The visitor arose and floated wraith-like to the old man's bedside.

"This better?"

"Who are you?" Rinaldi asked.

"My name is John Kincaid. Mean anything to you?"

"But you're a woman."

"No I'm not," Gale Johnston said. She yanked the pillow from beneath the old man and held it tightly over his face.

Berto Rinaldi didn't have much fight left in him. His struggles were feeble and futile. His nurses weren't surprised when they found him dead the next morning. His family was much relieved that Nonno had died peacefully in his sleep.

48

SATURDAY, OCTOBER 18, 2003

OFF THE COAST OF NEW JERSEY — Fred Taylor piloted the 14-foot Zodiac Pro as it danced across two-foot swells stirred by a stiffening wind and an approaching storm. He was amazed that Kirk Cramer had signed off on McDermott's harebrained scheme. He could tell it was a harebrained scheme because Cramer was toting his .38 police special in a button-down holster on his right hip.

Cramer and McDermott had fought about the gun. She didn't think he needed it. He disagreed. "I'm not going to crawl aboard that old tub without some sort of protection," he said. "If you're right, and someone has stowed away, they just might object violently to our hunting them down. It's best to be prepared."

McDermott had given in, grudgingly. Score one for the good guys.

Taylor was predisposed to side with Cramer and to disparage any proposal originating with Marcie. Taylor, a closet chauvinist, was fundamentally opposed to women in HIS workplace. It was a predisposition he had carefully hidden from management at McDermott Towing for obvious reasons. Edmund McDermott was a man's man and Taylor's admiration and loyalty to him knew no bounds. But Marcie was an altogether different subject.

Cramer and McDermott sat port and starboard, respectively, at the bow of the Zodiac as it drove forward, powered by a 65 horsepower Evinrude. The Zodiac was rated for five passengers and could hit 20 knots, more than enough speed for the job at hand.

They closed the distance between the two ships quickly. Taylor spun the wheel and nosed the Zodiac's to a position about twenty feet from the port side of the ship just aft of the superstructure. The *Compass Island* towered above them like an iron behemoth. He maintained his position, using a combination of throttle and rudder. It was a neat piece of seamanship and Taylor was proud of himself.

The plan was for Taylor to hold the Zodiac close to the big ship while Cramer and McDermott clambered aboard, using a rope secured to a grappling hook. Anticipating Taylor's maneuver, both McDermott and Cramer had moved to the centerline to afford greater stability. Cramer picked up the grappling hook and shook out two feet of slack from the coil at his feet. He swung the hook in ever-wider arcs, picking up momentum, and then hurled it up and over the bulwark of the big ship, allowing the rope to play through his gloved left hand. The hook cleared the rail and Cramer hauled back on the rope until he was satisfied of a secure purchase.

Taylor brought the Zodiac right alongside the big ship. He adjusted the throttle to match speeds, maintaining a stable relative position.

McDermott started up the rope first. Taylor was disappointed to see that she climbed like a monkey. She wormed her way upward, alternately locking and unlocking her ankles around the rope, as she pulled with her arms and shoulders.

Once he was assured that McDermott had things under control, Cramer started up the rope behind her. He paused as McDermott, demonstrating remarkable upper body strength, pulled herself up, threw a leg over the rail of the ship and disappeared beyond the bulwark. Cramer, burdened by an extra 100 or so pounds of body weight, struggled a bit more than Marcie when it came his turn to clamber over the bulwark.

"What's the matter fat man," McDermott asked as Cramer gained his feet, huffing and puffing, on the deck of the *Compass Island*.

Cramer ignored the jibe. "Here we are. Got any idea where to start looking for your stowaway?"

"He could be anywhere on deck, or maybe somewhere inside the superstructure. I can't imagine he'd want to wander around down below in the dark. I saw the binoculars flash from the forecastle, so let's start there and work our way back."

They made their way forward with Marcie in the lead, crossing under the overhang of the superstructure. Suddenly she stopped placed a hand on the davit that years ago had secured the captain's gig. She leaned forward, cocking her head.

"What's up?" Cramer said.

"Shh! I hear voices!"

Cramer took off his work gloves, tucked them under his belt and un-holstered his revolver.

49

OFF THE COAST OF NEW JERSEY — The satellite phone clipped to Sanchez's belt twittered, startling them all. Sanchez switched to a one-handed grip on the Colt, but the big gun still was pointed directly at the center of Kincaid's chest. They were bunched together, so shooting them down wouldn't be much of a challenge, even for an average marksman.

"You'll have to excuse me while I take this call," Sanchez said.

He pulled the phone free with his left hand.

"Don't get any brave ideas. I can drop the phone and shoot you before you take two steps."

Sanchez slid his right index finger out of the trigger guard and brought the phone to it to stab the receive button. He wedged the phone between his left shoulder and ear.

"Hello," he said. "Yes, things are in hand. My fellow passengers are comfortable and won't impede my departure. How far out are you?"

Sanchez listened. "Sounds like a plan. See you in an hour." He lipped the phone to his belt. "OK," he said. "Who's first?"

Kincaid studied his old shipmate carefully, looking for any signs of indecision. Finding none he tensed to charge. Gale Johnston laid a hand on his arm.

"Shoot me first you bastard, if you've got the nuts!" she screamed.

Johnston sprinted forward toward the startled Sanchez, who had to slide his finger inside the trigger guard before firing a round that caught Gale in the center of the chest. A .45 is a formidable weapon and this time there was no New York Ship medallion to protect her. Gale Johnston's heart exploded. She was dead by the time she hit the deck.

Sharon Albright experienced the departure of her soul like the flutter of a butterfly's wings on her cheek.

A second explosion shattered the moment.

"Man with the gun!" Kirk Cramer screamed. "Drop it."

Sanchez spun around. Cramer fired a second round. The slug ripped through Sanchez's right elbow. Sanchez dropped the gun and went down on one knee, cursing.

Kincaid was frozen with shock, but Albright sprinted forward and kicked the gun away from Sanchez. It spun across the deck and came to a stop directly in front of Marcie McDermott, who stooped, picked it up and pointed it, for lack of a better target, at Emilio Sanchez, who had turned a pasty white and was cursing weakly under his breath.

"Mother fucker. Mother fucker. Mother fucker."

"Anyone care to tell me what the fuck is going on here." Marcie McDermott said.

Albright ignored her and dropped to one knee beside Johnston's body. She didn't need her medical degree to tell that Johnston was dead. Blood pooled around her and her eyes were empty. No one was home. To be sure, Albright placed the index and middle fingers of her right hand on Johnston's neck. She looked at Kincaid and shook her head.

Albright did what her medical training and Hippocratic Oath demanded. She tended to her other patient, the murderer Emilio Sanchez.

"Anyone have a handkerchief?" she said. "I need to make a tourniquet."

Cramer patted his back pocket. "Got one," he said, fumbling out a blue bandana.

Albright crossed the deck and took the bandana from Cramer. "Perfect," she said. She knelt beside Sanchez who was now sitting down on the deck with his legs splayed before him. She wrapped the bandana around his bicep and tied it as tightly as she could.

"I don't suppose anyone has a pen," she said.

Kincaid patted his back pocket. "No but I have a crescent wrench," he said, holding it out for inspection. He had shoved the wrench in his pocket in case he needed it to loosen the nuts securing the hoses to the acetylene and oxygen bottles.

"That'll do," she said.

Albright tied the loose ends of the bandana around the crescent wrench and twisted the tourniquet tight. Anticipating her need, Kincaid took off his shirt and tied the ends of the sleeves together. "Here," he said. "You can use this as a sling."

He was wearing a T-shirt, but he shivered in the quickening breeze.

Albright adjusted the makeshift sling around Sanchez's neck and damaged arm.

"That's the best I can do for him for now," she announced. "I didn't bring any medical supplies aboard."

"The bastard deserves to bleed to death," McDermott said. "He murdered that woman. Anyone care to tell me why?"

Kincaid looked at his wristwatch.

"I promise you we'll tell you the whole story, eventually. But right now we have a more pressing problem."

"And what's that?" Cramer asked.

Kincaid pointed at Sanchez. "His friends are on their way by helicopter and I'm betting they're armed and dangerous."

"Why's that?" McDermott wanted to know.

"Let's just say that we have something they want and my guess is they won't hesitate to use force to get it," Kincaid said.

"We have two handguns," Cramer said, waggling his .38 special. "And there's a thirty aught six on the tug."

"Yeah, and it wouldn't surprise me if our visitors come equipped with assault rifles and hand grenades," Kincaid said. "But I've got an idea on how we can discourage them. We stumbled upon an old 20 mm cannon inside the forecastle there. And it looks like there were a couple of drums of ammo as well. Anyone know how to load and shoot a 20mm cannon?"

"Kirk was a gunner's mate in the navy," McDermott said.

"Thing's probably rusted solid," Cramer grumbled.

"We've got WD-40," Kincaid said.

"And I think there's some motor oil in the Zodiac," McDermott added.

"OK. Let's go have a look at your cannon," Cramer said.

50

PHILADELPHIA, PA — Skip Skinner was proud of his vintage Super Seasprite helicopter. He had saved it from the scrap heap and lovingly restored the old bird, ostensibly to haul the very rich on jaunts from Philadelphia north as far as New York City and south to metropolitan Washington-Baltimore. The helicopter was missing the antisubmarine electronics and weaponry it had sported in the service of the United States Navy and the lighter weight gave the machine a range of 600 nautical miles.

Built by Kaman Corporation of Connecticut, the Super Seasprite is the U.S. Navy's workhorse intermediate-range helicopter. Powered by two gas turbine engines, it is used in its various incarnations for antisubmarine warfare and in search-and-rescue applications. Skinner had flown the Super Seasprite off and on during his 10-year career in naval aviation, which had crash landed when the Navy decided it didn't need a helicopter pilot whose personal flights of fancy included stopovers at kiddy porn sites on the Internet. He should have never have used his computer at the base.

Searching about for another career, Skinner had picked up the 1980s model Seasprite from a Naval Reserve squadron, which was upgrading its inventory on Uncle Sam's dime. The helicopter was capable of hauling a pilot, co-pilot, antisubmarine warfare officer and eight fully equipped Marines. Skinner had modified it to accommodate 12 civilian passengers and their luggage.

The tourist flights were a necessary part of his business, but he would have starved if he had been forced to survive on them alone. They were window dressing for a far more lucrative vocation. When the moon was new and the cloud cover cooperated, Skinner removed the passenger seats to accommodate a white powdery cargo he collected late at night from ships at sea in international waters.

Burdened with four passengers, carrying rifle bags and canvas ammo satchels, he had taken off from Philadelphia International Airport at 12:30 p.m. and followed a southeasterly course crossing the shoreline between Ocean City and Wildwood, New Jersey, at about 1:30. He then turned due east and headed to his rendezvous with the tug and its tow about 80 miles out to sea.

It was an uneasy trip. Skinner's foreboding about this mission was visceral. His bowels loosened every time he thought of setting his precious helicopter down on the deck of the former USS *Compass Island*. His resolve stiffened when he reminded himself of the one hundred thousand dollars that occupied the gym bag under his seat.

Those crisp new green backs carried yet another worry. He had quadrupled his usual asking price for a four-hour flight and his employer had paid up without batting an eye. What obscene acts would he be forced to live with as a result of his greed? The rifle bags and ammo satchels were proof that this was not a peaceful mission.

Who was he working for? Skinner wasn't sure. Sid Palermo had asked him to take on the job as a personal favor. Sid was his agent for cocaine runs for the Philadelphia mob and keeping Palermo happy was a good hedge against cash flow problems in the future. Palermo had set up a meeting with a man named Luco Pepitone, a short, stout, swarthy caricature of an old-time Mafioso who smelled of Aqua Velva, tomato sauce and Chianti. Pepitone described the job in terse terms.

"I want you to fly me and three other guys out to sea where we'll rendezvous with a tugboat that's towing this old navy ship across the ocean," he said. "You'll be following a GPS beacon so finding the tub won't be any problem. This old Navy ship has a helipad. If it looks safe, you can land on it while we pick up a friend. Or you can just drop a ladder or something down and this guy can climb aboard. You OK with that?"

Skinner had a hundred questions, principal among them: Why would it take four guys to collect one passenger? But he had learned in his dealings with Palermo that it was best not to ask too many questions. Pepitone said that he'd need to make a 400-mile round trip from the Philadelphia airport, well within the range of the Seasprite.

An hour into the flight, Skinner made a quick mental calculation of how much flight time he had left before he had to start to worry. Stronger-than-expected headwinds were a concern. He was using up fuel about five percent quicker than he had anticipated and he had a twenty percent cushion. He prayed the head winds would become tail winds on the way back.

Among his passengers were two muscular men who looked as if they'd been punched out by the same cookie cutter. They were both about an inch under six feet and weighed 210 or so pounds. They wore their hair military style and dark aviator sunglasses obscured their eyes. An olive hue to their skin color suggested Hispanic ancestry.

The third man didn't look like he belonged. He was short, wiry and white-haired and smelled faintly of expensive cologne. He carried himself erectly, with the demeanor of a career military officer. His voice had a patrician air to it and Pepitone and the other two men treated him with deference even though he was improbably clad for the golf course in British tan pants, loafers, a polo shirt and cardigan.

To avoid the appearance that he was eavesdropping, Skinner kept his aviator headset firmly in place and tuned into an I-pod playlist he'd designed to distract him on long flights. It included Barry Manilow, Johnny Mathis, Frank Sinatra and Tony Bennet. Skinner loved his crooners and he tried to lose himself in the music, but his passengers made him as wary as a gazelle at the watering hole with lions nearby.

"Just fly. Don't think," he told himself for the thousandth time.

The tugboat and its attendant tow appeared as small specks on the horizon at 2:25 p.m. There were no other contacts in sight. It was a picture-perfect day, although the weather report suggested a storm would arrive in this area by dusk.

The headwinds subsided as Skinner gradually lost altitude in preparation of landing. He was about 300 yards out and closing fast when something caught his eye just aft of the superstructure on the starboard side of the old naval vessel. "What was that?" he asked himself, his senses tingling as if he'd just stuck a screwdriver in a light socket.

Movement! A gun barrel! Someone was training a gun on them from a station on the aft edge of the helio deck on the starboard side. A fucking 20 mm cannon was tracking his approach! What was its range? Shit!

Skinner slammed the helicopter hard right and put it into a steep climb. Heavy men and heavy gear bounced around in the compartment behind him and expletives rent the air like AA flack.

"What in the fuck are you doing fly boy," Luco Pepitone gasped as he settled himself into the co-pilot's seat after Skinner had leveled off. "Bert just got a lapful of hot coffee and his buddy Ernie wants to come up here and tap dance on your skull. Mr. Cabot just told me it was OK to shoot you."

"We'll you can tell Bert and Ernie and Big Bird or Cabot or whatever the fuck his name is that being scalded with coffee is a lot better than getting a 20 mm cannon shell shoved up your ass at high velocity," Skinner said.

"What!"

"I'm telling you someone on that tub down there was training a 20 mm cannon on us. You told me we were picking up a friend. Looks like you may have a couple of enemies on board as well."

"Take us in closer I want to have a look," Pepitone said.

"No way! That's it! I'm taking this bird back where we came from. I didn't sign up to get shot out of the air. You can keep the 100 Gs."

Skinner felt something hard and cold press into the base of his neck. "If you don't land this bird right now, the new owner will be cleaning pieces of you off the windshield for a month," Pepitone said.

"Yeah, right! Cock sucker. Like you're going to blow my brains out and let this thing crash into the ocean. Piss off. I'm going home."

The gun barrel dug deeper into his neck as Pepitone settled on one knee beside him. "Ernie is qualified to fly one of these things," he said. "Makes no difference to me which one of you lands this bird on that ship!"

Skinner's bowels rumbled. He wouldn't be trusting a fart. Not for a while anyway.

"You're bluffing!" he said, but his voice lacked conviction. 242

Pow! Pow!

The passenger compartment reverberated with the sound of gunshots and Skinner felt a rush of air from behind. Bastards. They'd shot out a window. They intended to fire on whoever was operating that cannon with the assault rifles they'd brought on board.

"Ernie get your ass up here I may need you to fly this thing. Last chance, asshole. I shoot on three."

"No! No! No!" Skinner screamed. Shit leaked out between his clinched ass cheeks. "Don't shoot. I'll do it."

The pressure on his neck disappeared. "Good man," Pepitone said. "But try to keep a tighter asshole. You smell like shit."

Skinner fought to control himself.

"Tell Bert and Ernie to be careful where they shoot," he said. "I don't want them to blast off our tail rotor. I'm going to come around over the top of the tugboat and settle in over the superstructure. Gun mounts have stops on them to prevent them from firing inboard, so they won't be able to get a bead on us."

"I knew there was a reason we paid you so much money," Pepitone said.

He settled himself in the co-pilot's seat.

"Ernie, hand me one of those AK-47s," Pepitone said.

"If you want to get a shot at whoever is manning the gun mount, lower the window, will ya? I don't need any more holes in my aircraft. It's going to get cold enough in here on the flight back."

Skinner overflew the tugboat and approached the *Compass Island* from the bow. Once he cleared the superstructure, he descended and swung the helicopter around so it was parallel to the helio deck on the port side of the ship. His vision was obscured as Pepitone rose up in his seat and loosed a couple of bursts from the AK-47. Bert and Ernie opened up too.

Spent shell casings danced over the floor of the helicopter and spilled out through the shattered windows. The air smelled of cordite. Skinner was about 50 feet above the landing pad approaching it from the port side to stay out of the range of the 20 mm when Pepitone sat down to jam another clip into the rifle.

"I think I got one of the bastards," he said.

Skinner was too horrified to reply. When Pepitone sat down, the pilot got an unobstructed view of the gun mount and realized that the 20 mm cannon had tracked inboard.

A puff of smoke belied his worst fears. But there was no shell whine. "Cannon must have misfired," he screamed at Pepitone. "Shoot the bastards! Shoot the bastards!"

51

OFF THE COAST OF NEW JERSEY — "There's no need for that," Emilio Sanchez said for the fourth time.

But Kirk Cramer didn't falter. Gale Johnston's murder had galvanized his cooperation. McDermott's too. Cramer worked motor oil into the action of the old 20 mm cannon while Kincaid recovered from the task of muscling the heavy gun from the emergency radio room to a mount on the starboard side of the helio pad.

Sanchez leaned against the rail and watched as Fred Taylor sped off in the Zodiac with Marcie McDermott's instructions to warn the rest of the tugboat crew that trouble was brewing.

"Give me the satellite phone. I'll call the helicopter off. I'll tell them you're armed and dangerous. They'll back off. I know they will. They won't want to risk losing the documents."

"Come on Skeeter. You can't be that naive. They aim to kill you. They aim to kill us all and destroy your precious documents," Kincaid said.

Sanchez's wound diminished him. It was as if some essential part of him was already dead. Dead and gone. Somehow he mustered the gumption to sneer.

"The Pattersons are two generations removed from the old Mafioso. Albert Patterson has balls, but he wouldn't authorize a murder. He's already paid me a million dollars. It's in an account in the Cayman Islands and only I have the access code. Think they'd walk away from a cool million?"

"Well if you're so sure of that, you can wait for the helicopter right there in the middle of the helio deck. Maybe they'll drop a hook and pull you up. Me? I'm going to help Cramer with the gun," Kincaid said.

"I need medical attention, thanks to your new friends," San-chez replied. "So yes, I will take my chances on the helio deck."

Sanchez, moving slowly and listing heavily to starboard, made his way to the center of the helio deck. Kincaid watched him for a moment and decided he could do no harm. Sanchez had been relieved of his satellite phone and couldn't communicate with the inbound helicopter. The documents were secured with their supplies on the quarterdeck, along with John Kincaid's money belt, New York Ship medallion and wallet.

Cramer worked the bolt back and forth vigorously, shook his head and spat, for a little extra juice. "If I'm lucky, I'll be able to get off three or four shots," he said. "These cannon are bad to jam if they're not lubricated properly and this thing is as old as dust. Best case scenario, they see it and run."

Cramer sent Kincaid forward for the acetylene torch and, when he returned, went quickly to work shearing the metal stops from the gun mount.

"What are you doing?" McDermott asked.

"Fixing this thing so it will fire inboard. If I don't, the heli-copter can hover beyond my angle of fire."

Just then Kincaid glanced at the horizon and saw what he initially took for a large seabird. Something about its steady determined approach told him that Sanchez's ride had arrived.

"We've got company," he said, pointing to the sky.

Cramer shut off the torch and surveyed his work. "That should do it."

He looked at Albright and McDermott.

"There's no point in us all getting shot. I'll need Kincaid to keep the ammunition from kinking but why don't you two ladies take cover inside the quarterdeck?"

McDermott snorted. "I've got the gun we took off Sanchez," she said. "If they start shooting, I intend to shoot back."

"Me, too," Albright said. She stepped forward and reached for the .38 revolver holstered on Cramer's hip. He made to stop her but then shrugged.

"Seems we have a couple of spitfires here, don't it? OK, it's your funeral. But why don't you crouch behind the armor for the portside gun mount?" Cramer said.

As the helicopter drew near, the sound of its twin turbine engines built to a roar. Cramer rotated the 20 mm cannon on its mount, tracking its approach. Suddenly the pilot broke sharply right and climbed steeply. The pitch of the engines increased dramatically.

"Pilot must have spotted our little pop gun." Cramer shouted.

"Now what?" Marcie asked.

"Now we wait and see how big his stones are," Cramer said. Kincaid ran forward a couple of steps as the helicopter juked and jived. He cupped his mouth with his hands and yelled: "Last chance Skeeter. I think your friends are going to start shooting. I'm pretty sure I saw rifle barrels poking out the rear windows."

"It's no wonder with you assholes waving a gun at them," Sanchez replied.

The roar of the helicopter's engines increased dramatically and the clattering metal raptor appeared overhead. Sanchez was exposed in the center of the helio deck as gunfire erupted from the helicopter.

Bullets danced across the helio deck and ricochets whined all around them. Kincaid gasped as a bullet nicked the calf of his right leg. Glancing to his left, he saw Marcie McDermott rise up and fire his big .45 at the helicopter.

Returning his attention to the helicopter, Kincaid could see the pilot working the controls. Then a gunman rose up in the co-pilot seat and fired what appeared to be an assault rifle at them. Through the back windows of the helicopter at least two men were visible working the actions of similar rifles and directing a steady stream of bullets at the deck of the *Compass Island*.

Emilio Sanchez pitched forward. He landed in an awkward heap with his extremities jutting out at odd angles from his torso. He looked like a doll tossed aside by an inattentive child on her way to another plaything.

The bullets streaming from the helicopter arrived silently their passage masked by the roar of the helicopter turbines. The thrashing rotor churned the air around them. It was as if they had been cast in the drum of a huge industrial drier. With the deck rocking beneath him, and the rotor wash tearing at his clothes, Kincaid was hard-pressed to concentrate on the task at hand.

"Bang! Bang! Bang!

Albright fired off three rounds just to his right and Kincaid shook his head like a man emerging from a nightmare. Cramer swung the barrel of the 20 mm cannon inboard and pulled the trigger. There was a puff of smoke but no explosion.

Cramer screamed: "Damn! Round's a dud! Mike, straighten out the belt there!"

Kincaid pulled the slack from the ammunition belt and Cramer chambered another round. He swung the barrel a degree or two to port, lining up a second shot.

The gunmen in the back of the helicopter had the range now. Bullets danced across the deck in a straight line right toward Marcie McDermott.

Albright screamed a warning and dove toward McDermott, knocking her aside. A bullet took Albright high in the fleshy part of the hip and spun her around like a bumper car at the fair.

In that pristine moment with spent shell casings tumbling from the sky like God's tears, Kincaid recognized his mother's immortal soul in the selfless act of her psychic descendant. He abandoned his post and surged forward to protect her just as Cramer pulled the trigger on the 20 mm a second time.

This round was no dud. It crashed through the cockpit of the helicopter and took the pilot square in the chest. The pilot slumped forward over the controls and the helicopter spun crazily and dove toward the sea. The tail rotor clipped the heavy metal plating of the ship's hull and the helicopter plunged into the ocean nose first at a sharp angle. Within seconds, it had sunk out of sight.

52

OFF THE COAST OF NEW JERSEY — "What in the hell were you thinking?"

Lieutenant Harris Thompson, executive officer of the United States Coast Guard Cutter Dependable, based in Cape May, New Jersey, was eager to be on his way before the storm arrived in earnest. He and two armed enlisted men traversed a steep accommodation ladder that rose and fell at the whim of a quartering sea. They convened a kangaroo court on the main deck of the former USS *Compass Island* alongside the helio pad where Emilio Sanchez's bullet ridden body had fallen.

"What in the hell were you thinking?" Thompson repeated.

Kincaid didn't respond. His mind was racing because he'd just spotted a glint of brass in the starboard scupper. Shit. They'd policed the area carefully for spent shell casings, but they'd missed one. Kincaid caught McDermott's eye and nodded toward the scupper. McDermott wandered casually to the side of the ship and bent as if to tie her shoe. She pocketed the shell casing and Kincaid relaxed.

"I can think of four or five things right off the top of my head, I could charge you two with. So cooperate. Tell me why you stowed away on this ship."

"I heard the cruise director was a real pro and that the chef is out of this world," Kincaid said.

Thompson's neck thickened and his face reddened.

Albright defused an imminent explosion by laying a hand on Thompson's sleeve and leaning close as if she had a secret to share.

"You'll have to forgive my friend, Lieutenant," she said. "He considers himself a wit. Unfortunately, he's only half right."

Encouraged by Thompson's grin, Albright continued:

"We were looking for evidence of a fifty-year-old murder and we found it."

She leaned back to enjoy the look on the officer's face.

Thompson took off his ball cap and scratched the back of his head.m "You're kidding. Right?" He was off his game now but eager to regain control.

Albright shook her head. "I've never been more serious. In late August of 1953, while this ship was under construction in Camden, New Jersey, two men, a shipworker named John Kincaid and a thug named Burt Lancaster were murdered and their bodies were hidden in a void in the bow."

"How could you possibly know that?"

Albright smiled.

"What would you say if I told you I know because I used to be John Kincaid?"

"Jesus Christ. I ought to just arrest you and let the civilian authorities sort all this shit out. I'm due on station in the Caribbean in 36 hours. We were on our way when we got your distress call."

"Drug interdiction?" Kincaid asked the question as a delaying tactic.

"None of your God damn business."

Turning to one of the enlisted men, Thompson said: "Henderson, slap some cuffs on these clowns. We'll haul them aboard the Dependable and let the tugboat crew prepare to ride out this storm."

Kincaid, who had some recent experience with handcuffs, turned around and put his hands behind his back. Over his shoulder, he said:

"It would be much easier to climb aboard your ship if our hands were free."

"What's the matter Lieutenant? Don't you believe in reincarnation?" Albright asked.

Thompson motioned Henderson to stand down and Kincaid dropped his arms to his side.

"No, but I met Elvis the other day," Thompson said.

"Sneer if you will, but I can prove it."

"Prove what?"

"That I've lived before as John Kincaid. Show him, Mike," Albright said.

They'd rehearsed this play with Albright in the role of the late Gale Johnston.

So Kincaid was prepared. He pulled his father's ID medallion and wallet from his jacket pocket and handed them to Thompson.

"We found these on a body hidden in the forward hull of this ship," Kincaid said. "They belonged to my father, the late John Franklin Kincaid, who disappeared in August of 1953."

The lieutenant examined the medallion and flipped open the wallet, which contained, among other things, thirty three dollars, John Kincaid's driver's license and union card, a grocery list and two Trojan condoms.

"Even if that's true, why wouldn't you have just called the police?" Thompson asked.

"Yeah. Right. They'd have had us committed," Kincaid said. Albright smoothed things over.

"I'm a scientist, Lieutenant. I wanted to prove I wasn't crazy. We found the body because I knew where to look," Albright said.

Thompson raised his arms palms up and shrugged his shoulders, like a coach questioning a referee's call.

"Suspend your disbelief for a moment and just listen," Albright said. "Ever since I was a little girl, I've been haunted by a recurring nightmare in which I was welded alive into a tiny compartment. I died screaming for help that never came.

"It was that nightmare that prompted me to become a doctor and then a psychiatrist. But I couldn't cure myself. So I sought the services of a specialist. Under hypnosis I was able to recall details of my murder in another lifetime when my name was John Kincaid," Albright said. "With a little detective work, I located my son, Mike."

She motioned toward Kincaid.

Albright picked up her story before Thompson could interrupt.

"Mike had always wondered what had become of his father," Albright said. "We discovered that this ship had been sold to the U.S. Navy, renamed the *Compass Island* and that it was mothballed in the James River Reserve Fleet at Fort Eustis, Virginia."

Thompson stared at Albright like a man mesmerized by a bon fire.

"You still with me lieutenant?" Albright asked. He nodded.

"Anyway, Mike agreed to help me search for the remains of his father. We persuaded a civilian contractor who was doing some work here to help us board the ship. We were surprised when a tugboat took us under tow. When we found what we were looking for, we alerted the tugboat crew to our presence and they called you. We're glad you showed up. It's a long way to England."

"Whew," Thompson said. "How long did it take you to construct that house of cards?"

"Our story is much more substantial than that," Albright replied. "Come with me and I'll show you my crypt."

53

VILLAGE OF FAIRVIEW, CAMDEN, N.J. — Sylvia Hanrahan found Mike Kincaid before he had a chance to seek her out. She happened upon him at 9:30 a.m. in the produce aisle of the Bi Rite Supermarket as he was trying to find a ripe banana. Kincaid wasn't a fan of bananas, but Marcie McDermott was and that was good enough for him.

Kincaid saw Hanrahan approach out of the corner of his eye and winced. He'd left Marcie in the car while he ran in for a quick provisioning, and he didn't have much time. The real estate agent was going to meet them at 11 to go over the details of listing Jacob Manley's house on Tuckahoe Road.

"I never thought for a minute that you shot Jacob," Sylvia said. "There's no reason for you to sell his house. You'd be welcome back here, you know."

Kincaid smiled. "I'm not so sure of that. I'll be under a cloud until they catch Jacob's murderer. Some people will always think I'm guilty."

Kincaid couldn't tell Hanrahan that the police would never find Jacob's murderer. Gale Johnston was dead and the remorseless sea had consumed her body.

"Some people are assholes," Hanrahan said.

Kincaid's laugh died as Hanrahan's eyes pooled up with tears.

"I loved him you know," Hanrahan said.

"I know. He loved you, too. He told me so," Kincaid replied. Actually, Jacob Manley had never mentioned his relationship with Sylvia Hanrahan, but it seemed kinder to pretend that he had. The first Kincaid knew of the relationship was when the lawyers read Jacob's will and he learned that his stepfather had left $10,000 "to his long-time companion Sylvia Hanrahan. His brother Francis, an inveterate know-it-all, pretended like it was old news, but Kincaid could tell that he was surprised, too.

Hanrahan snapped open her purse and pulled out a small package of Kleenex. She blew her nose, wadded up the Kleenex and buried it inside her purse.

"I told you at your dad's funeral that he had left some papers for you at my place, but you never came by to pick them up. I think you should. They're important."

"How would you know that?"

"I've read them; he told me I should."

Kincaid looked at his watch. He'd hoped to breakfast with Marcie then disappear into the Philadelphia Inquirer for an hour or so before the real estate agent arrived, but what the heck.

"Why don't you finish up your shopping and I'll run you home."

"That would be nice, Mikey. Jacob and Kathleen were good parents. You and your brother Francis are a testimony to that, although there were times I was sure you'd end up in reform school."

Kincaid laughed.

"I ended up in the Navy, which was almost the same thing. I'm almost done here, but take your time. I'll meet you out front. I'm in a Honda Civic. I'll beep the horn."

The murder charge against Kincaid was withdrawn two days before his scheduled court hearing. Sworn affidavits from the President Judge of Perry County Court of Common Pleas and his chief clerk proved to be an ironclad alibi. The issue of the 9 mm Sig found in Kincaid's trunk was resolved, unexpectedly by correspondence from the Central Intelligence Agency. The district attorney received a letter from the deputy chief of covert operations stating that the identity of the person who had planted the gun was known to the CIA but was a matter of national security. So Jacob Manley's murder would remain on the books as unsolved. Kincaid wasn't about to help the police close it.

It was a moot point, anyway, because Gale Johnston and Emilio Sanchez were dead and buried at sea.

It hadn't taken the party of stunned survivors very long to conclude that it would be a colossal mistake to inform authorities of their deaths and of the demise of the men Albert Patterson had sent to kill them. The gunmen's bodies would lie forever in an unmarked grave under a thousand feet of ocean.

Working together as a team, Kincaid, Albright, Cramer and McDermott washed the blood stains from the deck of the *Compass Island* and picked up the spent shell casing that had spilled from the sky as the gunmen banged away at them from the helicopter. Before summoning the Coast Guard to collect the "stowaways," Marcie McDermott organized a funeral service and the bodies of Emilio Sanchez and Gale Johnston were committed to the deep. Kirk Cramer read from a Gideon's Bible Fred Taylor had stolen from a Best Western in Baltimore.

Sharon Albright was able to treat herself and Kincaid with the rudimentary medical supplies on board Daddy's Little Princess.

Kincaid's wound was just a scratch. Albright painted it with Mercurochrome and gave him a tetanus shot, just to be safe. A few sutures and a shot of penicillin took care of Albright's wound as well. The bullet had tiptoed carefully through her flesh without serious injury to arteries, veins, muscles or tendons. She ran a fever for a couple of days, but was able to mask her injury from the Coast Guard.

It was a wild story, but Thompson, was persuaded by the bones of John Franklin Kincaid and Burt Lancaster which on December 10, 2003 were laid to rest in Saint Joseph's Cemetery not too far from the plot shared by Jacob and Kathleen Manley. It was a simple service notable only by the presence of U.S. Senator Wiley Patterson who alighted with another man from a Lincoln Town Car at the last possible minute. Both men stood silently with their heads bowed as Father Flynn conducted a short graveside service. They sped off before Kincaid could ask why they were there.

Upon some reflection, Marcie McDermott signed off on Kirk Cramer's master's ticket. She caught a ride on the Dependable with Kincaid, leaving Cramer in full command of Daddy's Little Princess. Albright, who always traveled with her passport, decided to stay aboard the tugboat with Kirk Cramer.

They delivered the *Compass Island* to Hartlepool, England, six weeks later after a trip notable only by an encounter near the Canary Islands with Portuguese authorities who didn't want a ghost ship in their little patch of ocean and refused to let him refuel at Las Palmas.

Marcie McDermott and Mike Kincaid began a conversation aboard the Coast Guard cutter on their way back to Cape May, New Jersey, that had continued to this day. Kincaid was flattered by Marcie's attention and dumfounded that she would be interested in a man twenty-five years her senior.

Marcie restored his soul. She opened the rooms of his heart to sunshine and fresh air and chased Alice's ghost from them. It was time for Alice to leave. She had outstayed her welcome and she knew it. These days when Kincaid thought of her, he smiled.

Kincaid agreed to sell the newspaper to his longtime editor Jiggs Baughman and was planning to move to Virginia Beach to be close to Marcie McDermott who was taking over management of McDermott Towing, now that Edmund McDermott had retired, finally, to pursue his new interest, Cheryl Miller.

In Kirk Cramer's absence at sea, Miller had acted on a suppressed attraction and consummated a relationship with Edmund McDermott. A candlelight dinner, champagne and Viagra were involved.

That was OK with Miller's erstwhile fiancé. Kirk Cramer's infatuation with Sharon Albright was consummated on the long sea voyage to Hartlepool, England. At the moment, the two were vacationing in London, and Albright was planning to accompany Cramer on the return voyage while she worked on her book.

Kincaid considered these things as Marcie McDermott got a head start on the Philadelphia Enquirer while they waited for Sylvia Hanrahan to finish her grocery shopping. Marcie looked at him as she turned a page.

"Penny for your thoughts," she said.

"Actually, I'm feeling guilty for being so happy," he replied. Kincaid's eyes pooled with moisture.

McDermott leaned forward and kissed him on the lips. "That's a problem I can help you with. I could become a real bitch and make your life miserable."

"That won't be necessary."

Kincaid opened his car door and went to help Sylvia Hanrahan who had emerged from the Bi Rite, struggling with two bags full of groceries.

54

VILLAGE OF FAIRVIEW, CAMDEN, N.J. — Mike Kincaid and McDermott took seats opposite each other across Sylvia Hanrahan's kitchen table while she put away her groceries and busied herself with making coffee and putting out some vanilla wafers "for dunking," as she explained it.

When they were provisioned with coffee, cream and sugar, Sylvia excused herself and returned a few minutes later with a cardboard box, which she put on the table beside Kincaid.

"Before you look in the box, read this," Hanrahan said, handing Kincaid an envelope.

Kincaid pulled his reading glasses from his shirt pocket, perched them on the end of his nose, opened the envelope and extracted three folded sheets of lined yellow legal paper. He unfolded the paper and began to read.

"Don't be rude, Mikey," Hanrahan said. "Read it out loud. You sound just like Jacob, and I like to hear his voice."

Kincaid sniffed and began to read aloud, squinting occasionally to decipher Jacob's idiosyncratic script and phonetic spelling.

"Just before I retired from the Camden Police Department in 1985, I happened upon a record in the Delaware County Courthouse while I was working on another case. It caught my attention because it noted that on August 14, 1937, agents for Berto Luca Rinaldi III of Bryn Mawr, Pennsylvania had petitoned the court to change his name to Hugh Collins Patterson.

"I found this interesting because I knew that Berto Rinaldi Jr. was a lawyer who had represented the interests of organized crime in the Philadelphia area for decades. I also knew that Hugh Patterson was a paraplegic who had risen above his disability to command a publishing empire which was advancing the political career of his son, Wiley Patterson."

"Where's Jacob going with this," Kincaid said, peering over the top of his reading glasses at Sylvia Hanrahan.

"Don't be impatient, Mikey. Keep reading," Hanrahan said. Kincaid cleared his throat and continued:

"In 2002, the Cat, finally closed and as a former employee, I was offered a chance to go through some of its furnishings to see if there was anything I could use. Workers were tearing apart an old table that hadn't been moved for years because it was nailed to the wall outside the men's room.

"I noticed that the paneling behind the old table was loose and that a manila envelope was wedged behind it. The envelope contained four strips of film negatives, two sheets of paper, and a tiny audiotape cassette.

"The contents, which I will describe, made me certain that the envelope had been shoved behind the paneling on the evening of Monday, November 18, 1963 by a Philadelphia police officer named William Berde. I can be specific about the date because that was the night Lenny Davenport visited the Pink Cat and that I was called to Merrimac Road to investigate Bill's murder.

"I never made an arrest in that case because witnesses were too terrified to testify, but I was certain that Bill had been garroted by Jules Tripoli, a mob hit man and associate of Berto Rinaldi, who also was at the Cat that night. In the envelope was a note from Bill identifying the mobsters whose pictures he had taken outside Rinaldi's house on the evening of Nov. 17.

"Bill also described the murder of Rinaldi's maid, Maria Ginoble, whom he had persuaded to record their conversation. Bill had seduced the young girl; said he loved her, which explains why he got so drunk that night at the Cat.

"Ginoble was tortured garroted, and left on Bill's doorstep on the morning of Monday, November 18. The murder of Maria Ginoble was never solved. You'll find a copy of the Philadelphia PD's file on Ginoble among my papers, but I'll warn you that the photos are gruesome.

"You'll want to listen to the tape yourself, of course, but I'll spare you the suspense. It records a conversation among four mafia bosses in Berto Rinaldi's library on the evening of Sunday, November 17, 1963, in which they discuss their plans for the assassination of John F. Kennedy."

"I was perplexed by what to do with this information, but my good friend Sylvia Hanrahan persuaded me that we could use it to save our community. And so I arranged a meeting with Wiley Patterson, New Jersey's junior United States Senator, in which I was able to persuade him to back a multi-million dollar housing rehabilitation program for our little corner of paradise."

"To solidify our deal, I gave Senator Patterson prints of the photographs Bill Berde had taken all those years ago as well as a transcript of the tape recording, which Sylvia typed up for me on the old Royal typewriter she keeps in her spare bedroom. I intimated that the originals would be secured somewhere out of reach in the event of my untimely demise."

Mike paused. As he skimmed over the next passage of Jacob's message from the grave, his shoulders slumped under the burden of a profound sadness. Marcie McDermott could sense the change in his demeanor.

"What's wrong Mike? What is it sweetheart?"

Marcie was an inventive lover and a lively companion, but she had never called him sweetheart. The endearment was a balm to his soul.

Mike wiped his eyes, readjusted his reading glasses and continued reading, out loud:

"If you are reading this, it is likely that I am dead."

Kincaid's voice cracked. He cleared his throat and took a sip of coffee.

"So I might as well get this off my chest, too. It has tormented me for fifty years and tarnished my relationship with my sons, particularly with my stepson. Mike, it pains me to confess this, but I am responsible for the death of your father.

"In August of 1953, shortly before I was laid off at the shipyard and went to work for the Camden PD, I was part of a welding crew that put the finishing touches on a modular forecastle right before it was moved to Way J where the SS Garden State Mariner was under construction. I heard a mewing from below as I was completing the welds for the hatch to an emergency trunk on deck three.

"The trunk led to a void in which the engineers had specified the installation of panting frames and struts because it was to be below the waterline at a point that would take the brunt of the ocean's assault. I shone my flashlight into the compartment and there was Big John Kincaid, all tangled up in the panting struts.

"John was a mean bastard, not at all like his son whose personality was shaped by my gentle Kathleen. Just two nights before, John had come home drunk from the Pink Cat and broke Kathleen's nose.

"I wanted to murder the bastard, but Kathleen talked me out of it. I could tell that John was grievously injured, but I didn't want to take the chance that the son of a bitch would survive. So I sealed that space tight and went on about my business as if nothing had happened. I've been both proud and ashamed of that decision ever since.

"Proud, because there was never a bastard who deserved to die more than Big John Kincaid. Ashamed, because nobody deserves to die that way. Even a rabid dog deserves a bullet to the brain. I denied Big John Kincaid that final kindness and will carry that guilt to my grave."

Kincaid dropped Jacob's letter on Hanrahan's kitchen table and stared at Sylvia for a full minute without saying anything.

Breaking the silence, he said: "Jesus Sylvia, you knew this all along and didn't take it to the police?"

"I wasn't sure what to do with it," she replied. "I didn't want to smear Jacob's name by revealing that he was a murderer, and I was pretty sure that the police would sweep the whole business about JFK under the table. Besides, I was afraid the people who killed Jacob would kill me, too, if they knew I had this."

She waved her hand at Jacob Manley's cardboard box. "And now I just don't care anymore."

Kincaid glanced in the box, which Hanrahan had plopped on the kitchen table beside him. From it he took a group of eight-by-ten black and white prints that William Berde had taken of the visitors arriving at Berto Rinaldi's house. Someone, Jacob Manley or Berde himself, had written names on the back of the pictures. The third picture down was inscribed with the name Martin Pauli.

Kincaid dropped the picture face up on Sylvia Hanrahan's kitchen table.

"Recognize anyone in this picture?"

Marcie and Sylvia bent forward.

"Is that who I think it is?" Marcie said.

"Yep. Emilio Sanchez. And here's a fitting epitaph for a spy: He killed JFK, or might as well have."

DEAR DIARY

Merion Hall
Bryn Mawr College
Friday, November 1, 1935

Dear Diary,

I've met a boy! Not just any boy, mind you. I think he just might be the one!!! He just doesn't know it yet!! He's a freshman at Princeton. My roommate, Abby, lives in Princeton and is dating a Princeton man named Frank Abbernathy. Frank's a halfback on the football team.

I met Jack, that's my fellow's name, outside the stadium right before the football game. He dropped a book on existentialism on my feet practically. I don't know much about philosophy, but Jack, sure is cute, even though I wonder why he brought a book to a football game. Maybe he's just behind in his studies. He's got this delightful Boston accent. The rest of his family all went to Harvard, but not my Jack. He's a rebel. He broke with tradition and settled on Princeton instead. Funny thing. He said that he'd just arrived on campus last week, more than a month late. I wonder why.

Jack has the cutest little dimples up on his cheekbones and he's so tan. He wants to be a lawyer.

I told him I want to get my degree, get married and raise a family. When his eyes started to glaze I embellished a bit and said I also wanted to make love in the surf and fly in a hot air balloon and that made him laugh and throw back his head, which mussed his thick brown hair.

When he stood up to leave at the end of the game, he staggered a bit and grabbed the shoulder of the fellow sitting in front of him. I asked him if he was all right, and he replied that he was merely intoxicated by the presence of such a beauty! What a charmer!!!

Jack lives in Reunion Hall and his roommate Biff is a blue-blooded snob!! When I stopped by Jack's dorm on Sunday before we headed back to the Main Line, he wouldn't even come to the lobby to tell me Jack wasn't there. His other roommate, George, wandered through about that time, and told me in a very patrician manner that Jack was "indisposed." When I asked him what that meant, he snickered and said, "He's at the infirmary you silly muff," and walked off just like that.

Merion Hall
Bryn Mawr College
Monday, November 4, 1935

Dear Diary,

It's cold and rainy. The heat works well enough, but condensation collects on the window above my bed during the night and drips on me sometimes when I sleep. Abby bitches all the time about the draft around the windows and doors in Marion Hall.

But none of that matters because I'm in love!!!! And even better Papa will just love him!!!! Got to go. Have to study some more for English 202 if I want to maintain my genteel C. God I hate Milton. He's so dense!!

Merion Hall
Bryn Mawr College
Sunday, November 10, 1935

Dear Diary,

It's almost midnight but I'm so excited I can hardly sleep!

Princeton's football team is undefeated! We beat Harvard 35-0 yesterday afternoon. Frank Abernathy ran for two touchdowns and Abby's been strutting around like she's the Queen of Sheba or something. But that doesn't matter . . . I got to sit beside Jack again at the football game. I met his Mom and Dad and brother Joseph. I didn't like Jack's Dad so much though. He seemed kind of stuck on himself. Mentioned right away that he's a good friend of President Roosevelt. La-de-da. That doesn't mean a thing to me. Papa has had Roosevelt's ear for decades practically.

Joseph didn't like the game very much because he's a Harvard man and Jack didn't seem well. He shivered so that I offered him my tartan stadium blanket. He grinned at me and said, "Only if you sit with me underneath it." So I did and his folks couldn't tell that he had his hand between my legs the whole time. I was a bit shocked when he touched me, but it made me all warm and wet down there. And when he put my hand on him he was rock hard!!! Oh my, my!! I really and truly am falling in love!!!

————

Merion Hall
Bryn Mawr College
Thursday, November 14, 1935

Dear Diary,

Abby is so mean! She says all I talk about is Jack, which just isn't true. Besides, I listened to her go on about what a wonderful guy her Frank is. She says that Jack is just interested in one thing. That he's leading me on just to get me into bed, not that I'd mind that one little bit because I'm in love and that's what people in love are supposed to do, right? Make love?

————

Merion Hall
Bryn Mawr College
Sunday, Nov. 24, 1935

Dear Diary,

Don't tell anyone, but I'm a woman now. Jack and I made love last night!!! I met him outside the football stadium before the game just like we planned and he looked awful. He was shivering, coughing and I could tell he was running a fever. I said come on you poor boy; you need to go to bed. He grinned and said that was the best offer he had all week but he wanted to see Princeton beat Dartmouth and remain undefeated. Besides his roommates would never let him hear the end of it if he missed the game. But when I took his arm and he came along as meek as a lamb.

When we got to Reunion Hall, Jack had me stand outside while he checked to see if the coast was clear. In a minute or two he came back and reported that there was nobody at the security desk and that the lobby was empty, probably because everyone was at the football game.

After we had sneaked into Jack's room, I noticed that he was so hot and clammy that his face was flushed beet red, well practically. I went down the hall to the bathroom and filled a basin with lukewarm water. Back in Jack's room, I poured a bit of rubbing alcohol in the basin and swirled it around.

Then I stripped off Jack's clothes right down to his underwear. He was burning up!! I wet a washcloth and began to sponge off his face, arms and chest. His skin had a peculiar hue and the area around his nipples was almost purple!!! Isn't that strange? His fever broke and his teeth began to chatter, so I put him to bed and pulled a blue comforter all the way up to his chin. He smiled at me and winked. But his teeth kept chattering and he scrunched around in bed trying to get comfortable. "Why don't you hold me so I can get warm?" he asked, with a cute little leer on his face.

I still don't know why I did it, but I stripped down to my bra and panties and slipped into bed with him. Yikes! He was naked! All that scrunching around was to take off his boxer shorts. His man thingy was stiff and hot and when he pressed it against my stomach right below my belly button I felt a feeling like I've never felt before!! If this is what it feels like to be a woman, I wonder why I waited so long!

————

Merion Hall
Bryn Mawr College
Monday, December 2, 1935

Dear Diary,

I am worried sick. I just learned that Jack has quit school. I had to beg Abby to take me home with her to Princeton for the weekend. She and Frank have had some sort of falling out and aren't seeing each other anymore. I stopped by Reunion Hall to check on Jack. His roommate Biff met me in the lobby after I called for Jack to come down. He handed me a note, smiled sympathetically (the first time he has ever been nice to me) and said "Jack asked me to give you this. He's left school. It couldn't be avoided."

When I tried to ask him more, he waved his hand. "It's all in the note. Read it," he said. He bent over and kissed me on the cheek, then turned and walked away. I sat down in the parlor in one of those scruffy leather wing chairs and unfolded Jack's note. This is what it said:

"Sport (that's what he's taken to calling me for some reason). "Sorry I have to break the news to you this way, but I've left school for reasons of health. Don't be concerned for me. It's nothing serious. Jaundice, the doctors are calling it. I took ill in London and should never have tried to recover in time to join the Class of 1939 at Princeton. It would have been better for me to wait for a year and recuperate.

"Thank you for all the kindness you have shown me. I am forever . . .

Yours Truly, Jack

YOURS TRULY ???!!! Is that the best he could do? Wouldn't "love Jack," have been more appropriate after what we did? Forgive me! I'm being bitchy. My period's overdue and I always get moody this time of month. I should be thinking about Jack, not me. Poor boy!!! I must send him a get-well card. I do love him so!

———

Home with Papa
Monday, Dec. 23, 1935

Dear Diary,

Merry Goddamn Christmas. Well almost any way. To make a long story short, I think I'm pregnant, and Jack is ignoring my letters. When I call him on the phone, it's always the same; a man answers and says, "Young Mr. Kennedy is indisposed. May I take a message?" And I say "have Jack call me right away. This is Sophia, Sophia Rinaldi. It's important!"

But Jack never returns my calls. Maybe Abby was right. Maybe Jack was only after one thing and now that he has got it, he's decided to move on. How I hate to think like that because I still love him so and I can't wait to tell him about our child. I don't know what to do. I can't tell Papa he'd be so hurt. Ever since Mama died he's had me on a pedestal. Calls me "his little princess." Well Papa, I'm not your little princess any more I'm Jack's whore. I'm damned if I'll let him treat me this way.

———

Merion Hall
Bryn Mawr College
Sunday, February 23, 1936

Dear Diary,

There is no hiding it any longer. I'm beginning to show, although the good news is that I haven't thrown up for three weeks. Mrs. Reingold, my adviser, called me into her office the other day and reminded me of Bryn Mawr's policy regarding pregnant undergrads. I'm going to have to withdraw from school. I'll be allowed to return when I'm not pregnant any more. So I'm going to have to tell Papa what has happened to me. He'll be furious. I just hope he doesn't try to take it out on Jack. That would be a disaster for us all.

Home with Papa
Sunday, March 8, 1936

Dear Diary,

Papa didn't rant and rave when I told him the news. I almost wish he had. It would have been easier. He demanded to know who the father was. When I refused to tell him he took on this icy look. I've seen that look before when he is dealing with employees bearing bad news. It's a dangerous look that turns strong men to jelly. It had a similar effect on me but I didn't dare let him know it. So I sat still and shut up and refused to say another word.

"So that's how it is?" he said. "Well I'll tell you young lady, I have a whole lot more patience than you do. You can just sit there until you decide to tell me the truth."

I held out for three hours there in his office while he went about his business, thumbing through piles of paper, and making phone calls with cryptic instructions to employees, pretending all the while that I wasn't even there.

Finally I couldn't stand it anymore. "I need to pee," I said. "Not until you tell me the name of the father."

"I really have to pee."

"So pee. The maid will clean it up."

Further resistance was futile. "Jack Kennedy," I said. "I met him at Princeton. Met his father, too, he's some sort of ambassador or something."

"Joe Kennedy's son?" Papa asked incredulously. "Wonder how that old bootlegger is doing. I haven't seen him for 15 years I bet. I'm going to make some phone calls bambino. Don't worry. Papa can fix this.

Still at Home with Papa
Friday, March 13, 1936

Dear Diary,

I've never seen Papa so mad. Jack's father won't let him marry me. Won't let Jack see me ever again. I'm so mortified I could die. Papa has called a council of war. Jules Tripoli is strutting about the house with his chest all puffed out. He gets that way before Papa sends him out on a job. I know Papa is thinking about doing something dreadful. I must talk him out of it. Jack has disrespected and dishonored me but I'm sure he's a good man at heart. It's his father's influence that's keeping us apart. We're just like Romeo and Juliet.

———

Still at Home with Papa
Tuesday, March 17, 1936

Dear Diary,

Father Jerome, our parish priest, showed up at the house today and conferred with Papa. They met in Papa's office for 45 minutes and when Father Jerome came out, he saw me pacing in the hall. He winked at me and said: "Don't worry bambino, your father will take care of you. You have sinned, but our Heavenly Father will forgive you. I expect you to say 20 Our Fathers and 30 Hail Marys and see me in confessional on Saturday night. God forgives the repentant heart."

———

Still at Home with Papa
Wednesday, August 19, 1936

Dear Diary,

I've given birth to a beautiful baby boy!! I've named him for Papa. He is Berto Luca Rinaldi III. And he's absolutely perfect.

He resembles Jack so much that it's scary. There is no hope for any sort of reconciliation with Jack, but Papa has been magnificent! He's set aside a suite of rooms, including the most delightful nursery, and has hired a nanny to help me with the baby. It was a difficult breech birth and they had to take him by Caesarean section.

I lost a lot of blood and the doctors say I'll never be able to conceive again. Papa dotes on Breto so. I'm his only child and now Berto is his only grandchild. I still miss Jack so, but I have my baby and my books. That will just have to be enough.

———

Still at Home with Papa
Thursday, October 14, 1936

Dear Diary,

I won't do it! Papa insists that I marry a pompous priss named Baird Collins Patterson. He's the son of an influential publishing family and Papa says it's high time for him to diversify, to get away from the stigma of his current business associations, whatever the hell that means.

What's worse, Papa says that he wants to have precious Berto's name changed, legally to Hugh. Hugh Collins Patterson!

Can you imagine that? Papa was so pleased when I named my baby after him. Now he wants to . . . what's the word? Anglicanize? My poor baby boy. He says that Hugh will find it much easier to prosper in the business world with Patterson as his last name.

To shock me into accepting Baird, Papa told me it's probably best that Jack and I never married. Joe Kennedy has grandiose expectations for his boys and I would have been an impediment to Jack seeing as how he aspires to high government office. Jack couldn't run for congress while married to the daughter of an organized crime boss.

I know how Papa thinks. He's struck a deal with the devil. By letting Jack get away with disrespecting me he's acquired some political chips that he'll use later on for some evil purpose. And by marrying me off to Baird Patterson he's creating a financial alliance that will advance his own goals. I'm sure of that.

I'm just a pawn that Papa is willing to sacrifice by marrying me off to a God dam pederast. That's what Abby says anyway. She says that Baird is as queer as a three-dollar bill. I don't think she's just being mean by saying so.

Oh Jack, what harm you have done by not loving me!

A FOND FAREWELL

Lt. Commander Hugh Patterson
USS *Compass Island* EAG 153
FPO 46173, Brooklyn, N.Y.
Sunday, October 15, 1963

Dear Hugh,

By the time you read this I'll be dead by my own hand.

I've been stockpiling the "nerve" pills Dr. Emerson prescribed for me and feel confident that I have enough now to ease my passage from this world to the next. (Please tell your grandfather that it's not Emily's fault. She has doled the pills out to me one at a time just as the doctor ordered, but I've only pretended to take them.)

I have decided to risk purgatory rather than continue as I have been continuing for these many years bereft of the company of the only man I have ever loved (other than you and your grandfather, of course).

The final straw is a letter I received from the great man himself only last week. I had sent him a missive updating him on your accomplishments in the Navy. To which he responded (on White House stationery no less) in this fashion:

"Sophia, I am of course delighted that YOUR son (my emphasis not his) is doing well in the service of our great country. However, I implore you to be more discrete in your correspondence with me. I would hate for anyone to conclude that my genteel affection for you has affected your son's career in the Naval service. As always, I wish you well.

"Fondly, Jack."

The best he could muster for me, the mother of his firstborn child, was a "genteel affection." I need much more than that. I deserve much more than that. So now, stripped at last of all hope that he might have felt something more, I choose not to go on.

Please. Please. Please. Do not blame yourself, or revile me for being weak. I have been strong for far too long. And now it's time for me to go.

But remember this: I will always love you.

Fondly,
Your Mother

55

WEDNESDAY, JANUARY 14, 2004

WASHINGTON, D.C. — "I've read your book and I don't suppose there is anything I can do to dissuade you from publishing it, but there are a couple of changes you're going to have to make . . . unless you want me to sue you."

Mike Kincaid half rose from the overstuffed leather settee opposite U.S. Senator Wiley Patterson's big walnut desk.

Patterson patted the air with his right hand.

"Relax, Mike. I can call you Mike, can't I? Please sit down and hear me out."

Kincaid plopped back on the settee, but he perched on its edge, ready to bolt if he didn't like what Patterson had to say next.

"Good. I've consulted with your editor and he's OK with the changes I'm going to suggest to you. In fact you may find that they are a condition for the publication of your book. You wouldn't want to give back that twenty five thousand dollar advance, would you?"

Kincaid already had used the advance to pay off his fine to the United States Coast Guard. Giving it back wasn't an option.

The intercom on Patterson's desk buzzed before Kincaid could react.

"Yes Jamie what is it?"

"Your father has arrived."

"Good. Show him in."

The heavy, walnut-stained office door whispered as it opened over plush carpeting. Jamie Sheaffer nudged a doorstop into place with her right foot and pushed an older man in a wheelchair into Patterson's office. It was tough going on the thick pile. Sheaffer positioned the wheelchair so the man faced Kincaid with the senator on his right.

Sheaffer left the office without comment, closing the door behind her.

"Forgive me for not standing," the newcomer said. "My name is Hugh Patterson. I have the honor of being the father of the lout sitting behind the big desk. The last time I saw you, you were much younger."

Kincaid's memory of the *Compass Island*'s director of special projects was forty years old. He strained to recognize something of the young naval officer in the wheelchair bound man now sitting before him.

Patterson's legs were withered beneath immaculately pressed charcoal slacks, but his upper body was muscularly fit and clad in a white dress shirt and a tweed sport coat. A blue and grey striped tie bearing the seal of the U.S. Naval Academy was neatly Windsored about his neck. Hugh Patterson's complexion was ruddy and his eyes sparkled.

He offered his hand and Kincaid arose to shake it.

"I remember you as being much taller," Kincaid said.

Hugh Patterson belly laughed. "You've got that right, sailor."

Addressing his son, he added: "Get me up to speed. What have you two been talking about?

"Well I was just explaining to Mike that there are going to have to be a couple of changes to his book if he wants to avoid litigation," Wiley Patterson said.

Hugh Patterson smacked his forehead with the palm of his hand.

"Jesus Wiley I thought I taught you to be a better poker player than that. Mr. Kincaid holds the better cards here and he knows it."

Mike Kincaid eased his body back on the settee and crossed his legs. He wanted to see how the Pattersons would play out this game of good cop-bad cop. They must have some cards up their sleeve. Otherwise his editor, Tom Bradley, wouldn't have asked him to attend this meeting.

"First of all. I'd like to apologize," Hugh Patterson said. "Your book asserts that my grandfather ordered your father's murder. It's probably true. My grandfather was a bastard."

"My father probably deserved it. He was a bastard, too. He beat my mother. Regularly," Kincaid said.

"Yes, but grandpa wasn't trying to protect your mother. He was acting in his own self-interest. Now, regarding your book, you've got a slam-dunk here, Mike. There's no doubt about it.

My grandfather was a conspirator in the murder of John F. Kennedy. It will do us no good to contest that, but his motives were much more Machiavellian than you suspect."

"What do you mean by that?"

"If I understand it, you are going to suggest that Berto Rinaldi plotted to kill the president because Kennedy deflowered my mother and was complicit in her suicide and in my crippling."

Kincaid squirmed uncomfortably on the leather settee. "That's right."

"Unfortunately, your book rests on a false premise."

"How so?"

"I too am a bastard, but John Fitzgerald Kennedy was not my father. I wish I had known that back in November of 1963. I wouldn't have socked the president in the jaw and I wouldn't be in this wheelchair."

Hugh Patterson slapped his useless right thigh and his eyes misted.

Kincaid didn't respond because he didn't know what to say. Patterson collected himself.

"Unfortunately, until recently I've allowed my sons, to believe that John F. Kennedy was their grandfather. It was the silly pretense of an old man who was ashamed of his origins and it had a tragic consequence. My son Albert, thinking he was protecting his brother's political future, became involved in Robert Cabot's plot to silence Emilio Sanchez. He should have left Cabot to bury his own skeletons."

"Who's Robert Cabot?" Kincaid asked.

"I'll get to that in a moment. Wouldn't you like to know how I am so certain that John Kennedy is not my father?"

"Sure."

"Among my grandfather's papers when I settled his estate was a report from a psychiatrist who treated my mother back in 1953," Hugh Patterson said. "Wiley will give you a copy of that report when you leave. But to summarize, in a series of therapy sessions that summer, my mother revealed to her therapist that she had been raped by a member of her father's household in the fall of 1935 when she was home on break from Bryn Mawr College. I was born nine months later. I am the result of that rape." Hugh Patterson pulled a handkerchief from the inside pocketof his sports coat and blew his nose.

"Mother's fantasy is much more appealing than the truth. I would much rather be the son of John Fitzgerald Kennedy. But the fact of the matter is that I am the progeny of a mob enforcer named . . ."

Kincaid finished the sentence for him:

"Burt Lancaster. That explains why your son was at the funeral."

The old man smiled and nodded.

"I told you he was sharp, Wiley. Actually, I was there, too. In the car."

"How could you possibly know that Burt Lancaster raped grandma?" Wiley Patterson asked.

"Two plus two makes four," Kincaid replied. "My father wasn't alone in his grave. Sealed in the same compartment were the remains of a man named Bertram Cody Lancaster. That was the name on the driver's license, anyway. A wire garrote was still wrapped about his neck."

"The garrote is the signature of grandfather's infamous enforcer Jules Tripoli. It's a safe bet that Burt and Jules killed your father and then Jules, on grandfather's order, took care of Burt."

Kincaid nodded.

"Makes sense to me. But there's one thing I don't understand. If Sophia Rinaldi's recollection of an affair with John F. Kennedy is fantasy, why did the president acknowledge you as his son? "

Hugh Patterson scratched his cheek.

"It's been years since I read mother's diary, but as I remember it she relates a tryst in the president's dorm room in November of 1935 when Kennedy was a freshman at Princeton University."

"That's right. I have the diary with me."

Kincaid nudged the briefcase at his feet.

"Tom Bradley suggested that I give it to you. We have a copy certified by a notary."

"Thanks. That's very generous of you. Look, I don't doubt that Mom met with young Jack Kennedy in his dorm room. But if their relationship indeed was . . . Patterson coughed. ". . . Consummated. It did not produce a child. Mother, I suspect, already was pregnant. Hell, for all I know she seduced young Kennedy to hide the evidence of her rape."

"You can't possibly prove that," Kincaid said.

"Oh yes, I can," Hugh Patterson said.

"Show him Wiley."

Senator Patterson slid open a desk drawer and removed a file folder.

"This is a report of a genetic evaluation of bone tissue samples from the corpse of Burt Lancaster," Wiley Patterson said.

"How did you come by the samples?" Kincaid asked.

"For the right price, you can buy the cooperation of just about any funeral director," the senator replied. "The important thing is that the sample proves beyond any doubt that Burt Lancaster, not John Fitzgerald Kennedy, was my grandfather."

"So to summarize, your book cannot suggest that I am the son of John Fitzgerald Kennedy," Hugh Patterson added.

"Fair enough, but I am going to report that at the time of the assassination, the president thought that Hugh Patterson was his son," Kincaid said.

Senator Patterson nodded and said:

"Sure. That's OK, isn't it Dad?"

"Doesn't matter if it's OK or not. It's the truth. We can't sue him for reporting the truth. We're newspaper publishers, remember?"

"Yeah but we sure as hell can sue him if he suggests that we had anything to do with the helicopter that was sent to collect Emilio Sanchez from the deck of the *Compass Island*," Senator Patterson said.

"It was Sanchez who implicated your brother. He said that you didn't have the stones to order a murder," Kincaid said.

"That may be so," Hugh Patterson interjected. "But Emilio Sanchez is dead and I'm going to suggest to you that you have an even better story if you report a truth that you can prove . . . but only with my help."

"What's that?" Kincaid asked.

"That on November 20, 1963, a spy named Emilio Sanchez delivered hard evidence of a plot to murder the president to his handler, Robert Cabot, then the head of the Central Intelligence Agency's Miami field office and that Sanchez and Cabot conspired to suppress that evidence," Hugh Patterson said.

"How could you possibly know that?" Kincaid asked.

"Robert Cabot and I go way back. I was probably his closest friend. Hell, I may have been his only friend. Anyway, Bob was my math tutor at the Naval Academy and a closet homosexual. He made a pass at me, but I decided not to disclose his sexual preference, which would have ruined his career. Bob was grateful and, years later, was able to repay the favor. At some risk to his career, he took the point in obscuring the evidence of my assault on the president all those years ago on the bridge of the *Compass Island*."

Kincaid said: "I have photographs and a tape recording that prove that Emilio Sanchez was among the conspirators at your grandfather's house when the final details of Kennedy's assassination were plotted. He knew that the president was about to be assassinated, but how can you prove he shared that information with Robert Cabot?"

"I am the executor of Robert Cabot's estate. I know for a fact that he was aboard a certain helicopter that crashed into the sea on Saturday, October 18, 2003, with no survivors. So I have exercised my power of attorney. I have seized Robert Cabot's personal papers. Among them is a file he kept on the Kennedy assassination. It details his decision not to warn the president that an attack was imminent. Apparently he was proud of that decision; claims it was an act of patriotism. He wanted it to be part of his epitaph. I'm offering it to you in quid pro quo. Do you understand what I'm saying?"

Kincaid nodded.

"You're offering me Robert Cabot if I give you Albert Patterson."

It was Hugh Patterson's turn to nod. "That's right. I want you to keep Albert's name out of it. Do we have a deal?"

There were a lot of things Mike Kincaid could have said. He settled for:

"OK."

EPILOGUE

THURSDAY, FEBRUARY 12, 2004

HAMPTON ROADS, VIRGINIA — "Gale'sdead?" Wonder was written on Hiram Johnston's face.

"That's nonsense," the old man said. "I saw her just a minute ago. She brought me a Danish."

Mike Kincaid looked at the nurse, Becky Taylor, who shrugged. She had warned him. Dementia was consuming Hiram Johnston whole.

"Peculiar girl Gale," Hiram said. "Thinks she's a man. Used to drive me and Maggie crazy. Always dreamin'. Always screamin'. That's our Gale."

Hiram's attention settled on the television, which was regurgitating a rerun of Gilligan's Island. He watched the TV for a long minute while Kincaid shifted uncomfortably from one foot to the other at the end of the old man's bed.

Suddenly Hiram's eyes leapt back into focus.

"I buried Maggie last year," he said. "Had to. She was dead." He slapped his thigh and cackled. "Car accident or somethin', wasn't it Becky?"

Kincaid tried again.

"I know this must be difficult for you Mr. Johnston, but I assure you Gale is dead," Kincaid said. "I was with her when she died. She was brave. Probably saved my life."

"Is this world for real or for pretend?"

Hiram Johnston's question made Kincaid gasp.

"What did you say?" Kincaid asked.

"Is this world real or for pretend? Gale used to ask us that all the time when she was a little girl. Drove me and Mags crazy. Mags? Where's Mags? That's right. I buried her last year. Had to she was dead."

Hiram Johnston laughed again. This time his dentures fell out on the bedspread. He picked them up and examined them as if they were a cockroach plucked from his soup.

"Where's the PoliGrip Becky? These suckers have come a loost again."

Spittle flew and Kincaid cringed

"I'll ask George to get your PoliGrip, Hiram," Nurse Taylor said. "Now you'll have to excuse me. I need to have a private word with Mr. Kincaid."

Outside in the hall Becky Taylor confided: "He has good days and bad days."

"Must have caught him on a bad day," Kincaid said.

"Unfortunately, this is a good day."

"Poor Hiram."

"Poor Hiram, indeed," Nurse Taylor agreed. "Is there anything else I can do for you Mr. Kincaid?"

"Not that I can think of," Kincaid replied.

Marcie McDermott was waiting for him in the lobby of Fender's Nursing Home where Gale Johnston had abandoned her last living relative.

"Promise you'll shoot me if I ever come down with Alzheimer's," Kincaid said.

Marcie's smile brightened his mood.

"I'll shoot you sooner than that if you keep flirting. I saw how you were ogling Nurse Taylor," she replied.

"Nurse Taylor has three chins and an aggressive nose wart," Kincaid said.

Marcie laughed and said: "Come on big guy. Time to go."

He followed her through the automatic doors, admiring the way her ass moved as she walked.

Marcie punched the button on her keychain, unlocking the doors of her big Silverado.

Kincaid slid into the passenger's side seat next to Marcie. "Where to now?" McDermott asked.

"Home. Something Hiram Johnston just said may have broken the log jam on my writer's block."

"Inspiration from a crazy man?" Marcie asked.

"Any port in a storm," he replied.

"That sort of thinking landed me with you."

"Shut up and drive, Marcie."

As soon as they arrived at the Virginia Beach condo they now shared, he retreated to the second bedroom, which did double duty as his study.

Sharon Albright had told him that Gale Johnston had been pursued by nightmares throughout her early childhood and on into adulthood. They were vivid dreams of her life as the abusive John Franklin Kincaid. Hiram Johnston in his own crazy way had just confirmed that.

Kincaid knew those nightmares. He had lived them himself. He settled in behind his Mac laptop.

When the hard drive was spinning, he opened a word document that contained the long-awaited foreword to his book.

The words leapt from his fingertips to the computer screen, almost of their own volition.

"Is this world for real or for pretend?"

DENIALS AND DISCLAIMERS

Final Voyage is a work of fiction based on an event that scarred the moral psyche of my generation—the assassination of John Fitzgerald Kennedy, the 35th president of the United States, on Nov. 22, 1963 in Dallas, Texas.

Most people of my vintage can remember precisely what they were doing at the time they heard the news that JFK was dead. I was playing football with a group of sixth-grade classmates during recess at Filbert Street Elementary School in Mechanicsburg, Pennsylvania. After delivering the news, the principal wandered off to lower the school flag to half-staff.

John F. Kennedy, his father, Joseph; and his brothers, Joe Jr., Bobby and Teddy, make cameo appearances in Final Voyage, but by design are given little to say. Their roles in these pages are the invention of the author and in no way reflect upon the character of the real Kennedys.

The same is true of the Cubans Fidel and Raul Castro, Enrique Ruiz-Williams, Agustin Cruz and General Juan Almedia. Their roles also are purely fictional creations of the author.

All other characters in the book are fictional. Any similarities with real people, alive or dead, are coincidental and unintentional.

John F. Kennedy matriculated, briefly, at Princeton University in 1935, but his alleged liaison there with Sophia Rinaldi is pure fiction.

President Kennedy did pay a call on a U.S. Navy ship at sea less than one week before his assassination. He spent about 15 minutes aboard the USS *Observation Island* off Cape Canaveral, Florida, on Saturday, Nov. 16, to witness the test firing of a Polaris missile by the submarine *Andrew Jackson.*

In Final Voyage, President Kennedy's visit is moved to the USS *Compass Island*, the true-life sister ship of the true-life *Observation Island*. New York Shipbuilding Corporation of

Camden, New Jersey, built both vessels in the early 1950s under contract with the Maritime Administration as mariner class break-bulk cargo ships (C4-S-1A).

I extend my apologies to the crews of the *Observation Island* and *Andrew Jackson* for rewriting history in the interests of plausible fiction.

I served aboard the *Compass Island* in the early 1970s, while she was home-ported in Brooklyn, New York. And we often crossed paths with the *Observation Island*, which was based at Cape Canaveral, on our way to the Caribbean Sea to conduct navigational research operations.

The *Compass Island* did encounter the schooner Curlew foundering off Bermuda in November of 1962 and rescued her crew in the manner described in Final Voyage. The ownership and crew of the Curlew and their mission, however, are products of the writer's imagination.

The *Compass Island* was towed from the James River Reserve Fleet in October of 2003 to Hartlepool, England, where it languished for a number of years, before being scrapped by Able Ltd.

The *Observation Island* only recently was retired from active service.

There is a historic village called Fairview (or Yorkship) in Camden, New Jersey, which was designed explicitly at the onset of World War I to house employees of New York Shipbuilding Corporation. And for years in that tiny village was an establishment known as The Pink Cat. My descriptions of "The Cat," its owners, employees and patrons are fanciful and I apologize to those who frequented there for reconstructing their neighborhood bar for literary purposes.

Wade Fowler
New Cumberland, PA

ABOUT THE AUTHOR

Wade Fowler is a retired journalist, a graduate of Guilford College in Greensboro, N.C. and veteran of the United States Navy.

Comments on the content and form of Final Voyage may be addressed to the author at fowlrman@aol.com.

www.ingramcontent.com/pod-product-compliance
Lightning Source LLC
Chambersburg PA
CBHW031942010726
47493CB00007B/2033